BLOOD BOND
TEXAS
GUNDOWN

BLOOD BOND
TEXAS GUNDOWN

William W. Johnstone
with J. A. Johnstone

PINNACLE BOOKS
Kensington Publishing Corp.
www.kensingtonbooks.com

PINNACLE BOOKS are published by

Kensington Publishing Corp.
850 Third Avenue
New York, NY 10022

Copyright © 2008 William W. Johnstone

PUBLISHER'S NOTE
Following the death of William W. Johnstone, the Johnstone family is working with a carefully selected writer to organize and complete Mr. Johnstone's outlines and many unfinished manuscripts to create additional novels in all of his series like The Last Gunfighter, Mountain Man, and Eagles, among others. This novel was inspired by Mr. Johnstone's superb storytelling.

All Kensington titles, imprints, and distributed lines are available at special quantity discounts for bulk purchases for sales promotions, premiums, fund-raising, educational, or institutional use. Special book excerpts or customized printings can also be created to fit specific needs. For details, write or phone the office of the Kensington special sales manager: Kensington Publishing Corp., 850 Third Avenue, New York, NY 10022, attn: Special Sales Department; phone 1-800-221-2647.

ISBN-13: 978-0-7860-1872-7
ISBN-10: 0-7860-1872-0

First printing: February 2008

10 9 8 7 6 5 4 3 2 1

Printed in the United States of America

Chapter 1

If not for the big man with the long nose, Matt Bodine and Sam Two Wolves wouldn't have gotten into trouble in Buckskin, a growing settlement on the stagecoach route that angled across the Texas Panhandle toward New Mexico Territory.

Or maybe they would have. Trouble seemed to follow them around, after all.

The two young drifters were in a saloon called the Red Queen, named for the card that had won the place for its current owner when he'd drawn it in a high-stakes poker game in Tascosa. That had filled out the royal flush he'd been trying for, and the deed for this saloon in Buckskin was part of the pot he'd raked in. At that time it had borne the unimaginative name Clancy's. The gambler, Thad Milton, had changed it after riding into Buckskin, taking a look at his newly acquired property, and deciding that it was time for him to settle down and become a saloon keeper.

Milton had improved the place quite a bit during his ownership, and as a result the Red Queen did more business than any of the other two dozen or so saloons in Buckskin. The bar was crowded when Matt and Sam came in that evening, but they found places for themselves at the hardwood and ordered beers from the bald, aproned drink juggler.

Both young men were big enough to attract some attention. Tall, broad-shouldered, lean-hipped, they had the look of natural-born fighting men.

Matt wore a blue bib-front shirt and a black Stetson tipped back casually on his dark brown hair. Twin Colts with smooth walnut grips rode in hand-tooled holsters attached to the gunbelt around his hips. His blue eyes usually had a mild look about them, but they could turn to flinty chips of ice when he was angry.

Sam sported a soft buckskin shirt—without all the fancy fringe that dudes tended to favor—and a flat-crowned brown hat the color of snuff. His hair was black as a raven's wing, and that, along with the faintly reddish hue of his skin and the slightly prominent cheekbones, testified to his Cheyenne heritage. His father had been Medicine Horse, a wise leader of his people who had been sent East as a young man to obtain a white man's education. While at school, Medicine Horse had met, fallen in love with, and married a young white woman, who had become Sam's mother a few years later.

Sam August Webster Two Wolves had followed in his father's educational footsteps, attending an Eastern college. Matt Bodine's education had been more of the frontier sort and had included a great deal of life experience to go along with a certain amount of book learnin'. The two young men had been mostly inseparable friends since childhood. Matt, the son of a rancher who still owned one of the largest spreads in Montana, had been welcomed into the Cheyenne tribe as Sam's blood brother. They were *Onihomahan*— Brothers of the Wolf.

Brothers in their restless nature, too. Each owned a ranch of his own in Montana—smaller than the holdings of the elder Bodine but still sizable and plenty lucrative— and they could have settled down on those spreads any time they wanted to.

For the past several years, though, they had left the ranches in the hands of tough, competent foreman and crews and had indulged their wanderlust, traveling from one end of the West to the other and back several times. They were men who had been to see the elephant . . . but still they wanted to see more.

The fella standing near them at the bar in the Red Queen had a nose almost long enough to qualify as an elephant's trunk, Matt thought. He'd been brought up to be polite so he tried not to stare, but it was difficult. He wasn't sure he had ever seen an hombre with such an enormous snout.

Sam nudged him in the side with an elbow. "Yes, it's a prominent proboscis," he said as he leaned closer to Matt. "But you're being rude, brother."

"Yeah, I know," Matt muttered. He focused his attention on the beer in his mug. Folks couldn't help how they looked, and they hadn't ought to be the object of unwanted attention just because the Good Lord had blessed them with an abundance of whatever the hell it was Sam had called it.

Besides, in addition to the big nose, the man also had long, brawny arms and huge shoulders bulging with muscle. The rest of his face was craggy and weathered by the elements. A thick black mustache drooped over his lips. He wore a slouch hat and a shaggy buffalo coat, and had tossed back several shots of whiskey in the time Matt and Sam had been in the saloon. What Matt had overheard of the man's loud-voiced conversation told Matt that he was a hide hunter. That was a rugged breed of men, to be sure.

And a touchy breed, too. Matt hadn't looked away quite quick enough. The man turned his head and directed a dark, murderous glare in Matt's direction.

"You lookin' at me, mister?" he demanded in a rumbling voice like the sound of a buffalo stampede in the distance. "See somethin' funny, do you?"

"Not at all, friend." Matt could be a mite proddy himself at times, but he wasn't looking for trouble. He remembered something in the Bible about how a soft answer turneth away wrath. He hoped the Good Book would prove to be right in this case.

The buffalo hunter shouldered aside the man next to him and took a stride that put him right in Matt's face, close enough for Matt to smell the reek of the raw whiskey on the man's breath.

Close enough that Matt had a moment's worry about that spear of a nose poking one of his eyes out.

"I think you were starin' at me. I don't like it when folks stare at me. When they do that they start laughin' at me, too."

Matt shook his head. "I got no reason to laugh at you, mister."

"No? What about my nose? Don't you think my nose is funny-lookin'?"

As a matter of fact Matt thought the hombre's nose *was* a mite funny-looking, but he wasn't going to say that. Instead he said, "Listen, I'm not looking for any trouble—"

"Well, then, you shouldn't go around starin' at folks like some sort o' damn half-wit!"

Matt was starting to get annoyed now himself. He ignored the warning look that Sam threw at him and said, "If

I offended you, mister, it wasn't my intention. Now why don't you let my friend and me get back to our beers?"

The man glanced past Matt at Sam, and his face darkened even more with barely suppressed rage. "By God, that fella with you ain't another half-wit! He's a half-*breed*! His sort shouldn't even be in a saloon, let alone drinkin' with white men!"

Matt had started to pick up his mug. Now he set it back on the bar without taking another drink and said in a quiet, dangerous voice, "You'd better move along, mister. Just because I said we weren't lookin' for trouble doesn't mean we'll stand for any bullying."

The buffalo hunter sneered. "Mighty big talk for a man who spends his time with a filthy redskin."

A bearded man in greasy, beaded buckskins came up behind the buffalo hunter and tugged on the sleeve of the shaggy coat. "Better let it go, Buckner," the man warned. "I recognize that hombre. He's Matt Bodine."

Buckner drew in a sharp, deep breath—and with a nose like his that accounted for quite a bit of air. Obviously, he knew the name of Matt Bodine. Most folks on the frontier did. Matt had a reputation for being mighty fast and accurate with those Colts of his. Some said that the only man slicker on the draw than Matt was Smoke Jensen . . . and others claimed that Bodine could even give Smoke a run for his money when it came to gun-handling.

Buckner's dander was up, though, and he was too proud to back down, no matter who he was facing. He scowled and said, "I ain't no gunfighter, Bodine. But if you ain't yellow, you'll step outside in the street with me and we can settle this the way real men do . . . with our fists."

Matt was ready to do just that, but Sam put a hand on his shoulder. "Forget it," Sam advised. "It's not worth the time and trouble. Anyway, you don't want to get your knuckles bruised up on this fellow. His head's probably as hard as a rock."

Matt returned Buckner's glare for a second longer, then shrugged and turned away. "Yeah, you're probably right," he said as he reached for his beer again. "It ain't worth it."

Buckner's eyes widened and bulged out until it seemed like they would pop right out of their sockets. "By God, I'll put up with a lot of things—"

Somehow Matt doubted that.

"—but bein' ignored ain't one of 'em!" Buckner grabbed Matt's shoulder and jerked the younger man around to face him again.

That was it. Buckner had pushed things too far by laying hands on him. Matt's shoulders bunched and his right fist shot forward, burying itself to the wrist in Buckner's ample gut. The punch hadn't traveled very far, but packed an incredible amount of power.

Buckner turned a little pale under his sunburn and bent forward, but he didn't double over or take a step backward. Instead he roared in fury and swung a huge fist. The blow would have knocked Matt's head right off his shoulders if it had connected, but Matt ducked under it and bored in, hooking a left and a right to Buckner's already tender belly.

A wild exhilaration filled Matt and sent a battle song humming through his veins. Instead of the cool, icy-nerved, deadly calm that descended on him during gunfights, fisticuffs brought out the brawler in him. There was nothing like a good slugfest.

And that was what broke out swiftly inside the Red Queen. Bellowing in pain and rage, Buckner shook off the effects of Matt's punches and took some more lumbering swipes of his own. He was slow but massively strong, and

Matt couldn't avoid all the punches. One of them landed on his breastbone and slammed him against the bar. His lips drew away from his teeth in a grimace as the edge of the hardwood dug painfully into his back. Buckner raised a fist high. It was poised to come down in a shattering, skull-crushing, sledgehammer of a blow.

Before that blow could fall, Sam's fist practically exploded in Buckner's face, landing right on the nose that had started this ruckus. Buckner screamed in pain as blood spurted. Sam was prone to trying to avoid trouble, much more so than Matt, but when his blood brother was threatened, that reluctance went out the window. Sam walloped the buffalo hunter on the nose, and then followed it up with a stinging left cross to the man's heavy jaw.

"Hey, they're gangin' up on Buckner!" The outraged shout came from the man who had warned Buckner to back off a few moments earlier. He had been afraid of Matt's guns.

But now all bets were off. The man in the beaded buckskins tackled Sam, driving him backward for several staggering steps before both men lost their balance and came crashing down on one of the tables where a poker game had been going on. The table's legs snapped and it collapsed, sending cards and the money that had been piled in the center of the green felt flying everywhere.

"You son of a bitch!" one of the cardplayers howled. "I was gonna win that hand!" He reached down, grabbed the man who had tackled Sam, hauled him to his feet, and punched him in the face.

Matt had straightened and set himself while that was going on. He ducked under another wild, looping punch from Buckner, and then peppered the buffalo hunter with a couple of jabs to the face. Both blows landed solidly and

bent Buckner's already injured nose even further out of
shape. Buckner staggered back, clapping both hands to
his face.

He had quite a few friends in the saloon. A man yelled,
"Get those bastards!" and the crowd surged forward, surrounding Matt and Sam.

They weren't fighting on their own, however. As fists
flew and furniture broke and bottles shattered, it became
obvious that the Red Queen's battling patrons were split
into two roughly equal factions. On one side were the buffalo hunters, on the other the cowboys who worked on
the spreads that had been established here in the Panhandle in the past few years as the vast herds of buffalo finally
began to dwindle. Their dislike for each other was mutual.

The few townies in the place pretty much stayed out of
it. Some of them slunk toward the doors, hoping to get outside before the violence drew them in.

Matt and Sam were trapped in the middle of that whirl-
wind of fists and feet and flying chairs. As they stood in
front of the bar, they put their backs together and lashed
out with punch after punch, decking everyone who came
at them. A few feet away several cowboys had jumped on
Buckner and tried to bring the massive buffalo hunter to
the floor. Buckner shook them off like a bear shaking off
a pack of curs. He swung his tree-trunk-like arms and
mowed down his opponents. Then he picked up one of the
overturned tables and charged forward with a roar, knocking down men and scattering them like ninepins. Blood
still streamed from his nose.

Matt saw that from the corner of his eye as he continued
to fight, and while he still didn't like Buckner, he couldn't
help but feel a little grudging admiration for the buffalo

hunter. Buckner was one hell of a fighting man. "Pure pizen," as some might put it.

The epic struggle inside the Red Queen might have continued until the saloon was completely reduced to a shambles, but the unexpected roar of a shotgun brought the battle to a screeching halt. Men froze with fists lifted to strike blows that never fell. Heads turned toward the doorway, where a man in a white shirt, black vest, black hat, and string tie had pushed through the batwings to discharge one barrel of a Greener into the ceiling. He lowered the weapon so that it covered the brawlers and shouted, "The next man who throws a punch gets blown in half!"

The light from the chandeliers that hung from the saloon's ceiling glinted on the badge pinned to the newcomer's chest.

Into the silence that had fallen, the lawman barked, "Now, by God, I want an honest answer to this question. *Who started this damned ruckus?*"

Every eye in the place, other than their own, turned to look at Matt Bodine and Sam Two Wolves.

Chapter 2

"Wait just a damned minute!" Matt protested. "We didn't start this. *He* did!" He pointed at Buckner.

"You threw the first punch, Bodine," the buffalo hunter rumbled.

"Only because you grabbed me, you lummox!"

"Bodine!" The sharp exclamation came from the shotgun-toting star-packer. "Not Matt Bodine?"

Matt hesitated, but only for a second. He wasn't going to deny who he was. "That's right," he said in a defiant tone of voice.

The sheriff or marshal or whatever he was swung the Greener so that the twin barrels pointed directly at Matt and Sam. Everybody around them scattered to get out of the line of fire. Nobody wanted anything to do with those charges of double-aught buck.

"Drop your guns," the lawman grated.

Matt glanced over at his blood brother. While they had been known to bend the law from time to time in their adventurous wandering, neither of them made a habit of drawing on badge-toters. They weren't owlhoots. They were just . . . rambunctious.

With a sigh, Matt reached for the buckle of his gunbelt. "All right, Sheriff, but you're makin' a mistake here. Sam and I ain't to blame for this."

"It's Marshal," the lawman snapped as Matt and Sam unbuckled their gun rigs and placed them on the bar. "Marshal Harlan Stryker." With self-confidence bordering on arrogance, he added, "And I don't make mistakes. That's why Buckskin is a peaceable town. At least it was until you two hellions rode in. It will be again with the two of you safely behind bars."

Sam nodded toward Buckner. "The least you could do is arrest him, too. He was involved every bit as much as we were. More, actually, since we tried to convince him that we weren't looking for trouble."

Buckner pressed a hand against his broad chest and looked as innocent as a huge, burly, battle-scarred buffalo hunter could look. "That's a lie, Marshal. Them two come in here and started makin' fun o' my nose. Ain't my fault it's so long. I inherited it from my pa. His nose was even longer."

Matt didn't see how that could be possible, and Buckner's innocent, offended tone got on his nerves. "Hell, break out the violins! Next thing you know, you'll be traipsin' off through the daisies with Little Nell!"

Buckner squinted and balled up his fists. "Why, you—"

"That's enough," Marshal Stryker said, breaking in. "You're not fooling me, Buckner. You've caused plenty of trouble in the past and we both know it. But Bodine and Two Wolves have a reputation as real hell-raisers. You're just an amateur. So I'm going to give you a break this time and not lock you up."

Buckner frowned, as if he didn't like being called an amateur hell-raiser and intended to argue the point. But he must have decided that was better than being thrown in jail, because he shrugged his massive shoulders and said, "I'm much obliged, Marshal. You got my word that I'll be meek as a little lamb the rest o' the time I'm here in town."

Buckner backed toward the batwings and gestured with the shotgun. "Come on, you two. Follow me."

"You're really gonna lock us up?" Matt was astounded.

"Damn right I am."

Sam waved a hand to take in their surroundings. The saloon was somewhat worse for the wear and tear of the past few minutes. "We can pay for the damages if that will make a difference," Sam offered.

That was true. Money wasn't a problem for either of the two drifters. Their ranches in Montana were profitable and Matt and Sam both had sizable bank accounts in Denver and Cheyenne. All it would take to cover the costs of repairing the saloon would be sending a couple of wires.

"Yeah," Matt put in. "Just let us go down to the telegraph office—"

He stopped when he saw Marshal Stryker shaking his head. "There's no telegraph office in Buckskin," the lawman said. "But don't worry, you'll pay for the damages, along with fines for assault and disturbing the peace. The circuit judge will be through in about a week. He'll determine the amount."

"A week!" The words were almost a yelp of dismay as they came out of Matt's mouth. To someone as fiddle-footed as him, the idea of being locked up for a week was tantamount to torture.

"That's right. Now, I'm getting tired of flapping my gums. Move!"

Unarmed and covered by the Greener that way, Matt and Sam had no choice but to follow the marshal's orders. They could try to get close enough to jump Stryker and take the shotgun away from him, Matt thought, or they could try to grab Colts from some of the other men in the saloon and shoot it out . . . but either of those moves was likely to result in innocent folks getting hurt, maybe even killed. That just wasn't something the blood brothers wanted to be responsible for.

"Maybe it won't be too bad," Sam said quietly to Matt as Stryker backed onto the boardwalk and they followed the marshal outside. "They'll have to give us three square meals a day. We'll just get some rest while we're waiting for the judge to arrive."

"Yeah, but what if we don't have enough money to pay for the damages and those fines?" Matt muttered.

Stryker overheard the question. He gave them an ugly grin and said, "In that case you'll work off your debt. I can't speak for the judge, but I reckon about six months of hard labor would be about right."

"Six months!" In his outrage, Matt echoed what Buckner had said a few minutes earlier. "Why, you—"

Sam's hand on his shoulder stopped him from saying anything more improvident. Sam looked at Matt and shook his head solemnly.

Matt glared over at Sam. "Let's cut across the Panhandle, you said. We won't run into any trouble there, you said. What could possibly go wrong, you said . . ."

Things were about to go wrong more than either Matt Bodine or Sam Two Wolves—or anybody else in Buckskin, for that matter—could guess. About a mile north of the settlement, under the light of the stars and the rising moon, a large group of men sat on their horses and listened to their leader speak.

"There's a bank, a freight company, a stagecoach station, and more than a dozen other businesses in Buckskin. The money in the bank is what we're really after, of course, but there should be plenty of other loot in town as well. Take what you want, but remember, don't start any fires until we're ready to ride out." A harsh laugh came from the man. "We don't want the settlement burning down while we're still cleaning it out!"

"What about women, Deuce?" asked one of the men. "Can we grab a few of them to take along?"

Edward "Deuce" Mallory laughed again. "Why, sure! If you see a gal who strikes your fancy, bring her along." Mallory's voice hardened as he added, "But get the money first. We're heading for Mexico, and there'll be plenty of pretty little señoritas there."

Mutters of agreement came from the assembled outlaws. They knew their business, these three dozen hard-faced hombres. They had been riding together as a gang for almost a year. A few members had come and gone during that time, but most of them were experienced desperadoes used to working with each other.

They were used to taking orders from Deuce Mallory, too. Mallory was the one who had put together the original gang, numbering only eight men, who had started their string of robberies and killings back in Missouri. Their depredations had quickly grown to rival those of the James gang, the Youngers, and the other groups of outlaws whose infamy was spreading across the frontier. Mallory was a canny leader. He picked his targets and planned his raids well.

He was an educated man, the son of a Illinois storekeeper who had worked hard to send his boy to college. But Edward had a wild streak in him, and even though he was smart enough to handle his classes with no trouble, he had been expelled for gambling—and for bedding the wife of one of his instructors, although that hadn't been written down on any of the official documents ending his college career. The cuckolded professor had caught up to Edward Mallory before the young man could leave town, intending to give him a thrashing.

Instead, Mallory had beaten the older man to death with his bare hands, insuring that he could never go home again. The shame of being kicked out of school was one thing; a murder charge hanging over his head was something else entirely.

The whole sweep of the frontier awaited him, so Mallory had taken off for the tall and uncut. He found that the life of a fugitive wasn't really that bad. He picked up the nickname "Deuce" in Wichita when he bluffed his way to victory in a high-stakes poker game with only a pair of twos in his hand.

Wichita was where he had killed his second man, too, this time in a gunfight, so Mallory supposed the nickname was appropriate for that reason, too. Since then he'd lost track of the number of men who had fallen to his gun. He didn't care about things like that. Notoriety didn't interest him nearly as much as money, whiskey, women, and cards—not necessarily in that order. It just depended on his mood at the time.

Now he swept his gaze over the men who were gathered in the moonlight and said, "All right. You know what to do. Kill as many as you can when we ride in. That'll shock the townspeople into not fighting back."

One of the outlaws laughed. "Even if they do, they

won't stand a chance against us, Deuce. They won't hardly know what hit 'em."

"No," Mallory agreed, "but they'll sure as hell know they've been hit."

With a thunder of hoofbeats, the killers rode toward Buckskin.

Matt thought the clang of the cell door closing was a damned ugly sound. He glowered through the bars at Marshal Harlan Stryker, who stood outside the cell with the shotgun tucked under his arm and a self-satisfied smirk on his face.

Stryker's deputy, a mild-looking little man he'd called Birdie, asked, "You want me to go over to the café and get these boys somethin' to eat, Marshal?"

Stryker shook his head. "They probably had supper before they went to the Red Queen for their evening of drinking and brawling. And if they didn't, well, it won't hurt them to go hungry until morning."

"I'm gonna tell the judge about the way you're treatin' us, Marshal," Matt threatened.

"Go right ahead," Stryker replied with a chuckle. "I think you'll find that Judge Farnsworth has as little patience for lawbreakers as I do. He's not going to take pity on you because you had to miss a meal."

The cell had two bunks in it, one along each of the stone walls at its sides. The marshal's office was a squat building, solidly built of stone blocks and thick timbers. The timbers must have been freighted in, because one thing the Texas Panhandle had in short supply was big trees. Trees of any size were scarce up here mostly.

With a sigh, Sam sank onto one of the bunks and said,

"You might as well stop arguing with the marshal, Matt. It's not going to do any good."

Stryker nodded. "That's right, Two Wolves. You're the smarter of the pair, aren't you?"

"I wouldn't say that."

"I'd say neither one of you is very smart, or you wouldn't be starting fights in saloons." The marshal turned to his deputy. "Keep an eye on them, Birdie. I'm going to go make my evening rounds."

"Yes, sir, Marshal. I sure will watch 'em." Birdie fixed a beady-eyed, intimidating glare on the prisoners. That's what he seemed to be trying for anyway, but he was so harmless-looking that it didn't really work.

Stryker left the cell block. Matt heard his footsteps crossing the office, then heard the sound of the front door opening and closing.

"The marshal's gone now," Matt said. "Why don't you let us out of here, little fella? We didn't start that fight in the saloon. I swear."

"You can tell your story to the judge. He'll be the one to decide whether or not you're tellin' the truth." Birdie started toward the office, then stopped and turned back to say, "If you fellas would like some coffee, I can put a pot on to boil."

Sam said, "That would be very nice, Deputy. Thank you."

Birdie nodded and left the cell block, too. Matt turned to Sam and asked in a quiet voice, "Why're you bein' so polite to that little weasel?"

"He's just doing his job, brother. I don't see any reason to hold that against him."

Matt sat down on the opposite bunk, folded his arms over his chest, and frowned. "I hold it against anybody who has a hand in lockin' us up."

A few minutes of relative silence went by. Matt heard the small sounds of Birdie moving around out in the marshal's office.

Then he lifted his head as a sharp *"Psst! Bodine!"* sounded from the cell's single barred window, set high in the rear wall.

Matt and Sam looked at each other in surprise. They didn't know anybody in Buckskin. Who would be slipping up to the back of the jail to talk to them through the window?

A large, sturdy bucket sat in the corner of the cell so that prisoners could relieve themselves in it. Since it hadn't been used—or at least hadn't been used recently—Matt stood, picked it up, and upended it beneath the window. He started to step up onto it so that he could look through the window, but Sam stopped him with a quick, "Wait a minute. We don't have any friends in these parts."

"Yeah," Matt agreed. "Could be somebody who wants to slap me in the face with a bullet." Keeping his voice pitched low enough so that he hoped Birdie wouldn't notice it in the office, he called, "Who's out there?"

A rumble like that of a grizzly bear came back. "It's me. Buckner."

Matt and Sam exchanged a glance. The belligerent buffalo hunter was just about the last person they would have expected to come calling on them in jail.

Without stepping up on the bucket, Matt said, "If you're here to gloat about us bein' locked up—"

"Naw," Buckner interrupted. "That ain't it. I got to thinkin', and it ain't right that you and the redskin have to take all the blame for what happened."

Sam had stood up and moved over beside Matt, under the window. He said, "So you're going to find Marshal Stryker and tell him that we shouldn't be locked up?"

"Hell, no! Stryker wouldn't believe me anyway. And if he did, he'd just throw me in jail, too. He ain't gonna let you go. He's a vain son of a bitch. He wants to be known as the lawman who brought Matt Bodine and Sam Two Wolves to heel."

"So what *are* you gonna do?" Matt asked.

"I got me a chain and a mule out here. I'm gonna bust you boys out."

Matt and Sam looked at each other again in the light from the lantern that hung in the hall outside the cells. Despite all the ruckuses they'd been mixed up in over the years, they weren't wanted anywhere. Their slate was clean as far as the law was concerned.

But that wouldn't be the case if Buckner helped them escape from jail. They would be fugitives—and rightfully so, even though the charges that had landed them behind bars to start with were bogus.

"Forget it," Matt said. "You don't have to do that, Buckner."

"But hell, if I don't, you'll be locked up for a week or more!"

"Yeah, but I don't want to spend the rest of my life lookin' over my shoulder for the law."

"You sure about that?"

Sam said, "We're certain. If you really want to help, you can stay and testify at our trial."

"Can't hardly do that. There's buffalo waitin' out there on the plains for me to shoot 'em. Wouldn't take but a minute to yank them bars out—"

Matt was about to tell Buckner again to forget about any escape attempt, when he heard something else that caught his attention. It was a low-pitched rumble, like the sound of distant drums.

Sam heard it, too. "Hoofbeats," he breathed. "A lot of them. And they're coming closer."

"Hear that, Buckner?" Matt called. "A lot of riders are headed toward town. Could be trouble."

A moment later that hunch was confirmed, as the drumming of hoofbeats was suddenly joined by the loud crashing of gunshots, shouted questions and curses, and screams of fear.

From somewhere out of the darkness, hell had come to Buckskin.

Chapter 3

Excitement pounded in Deuce Mallory's chest as he led the charge into the settlement. He lived for these moments when he seized power in both hands and clasped it as tightly as he held the pair of Colts he used to fire left and right as he steered his horse with his knees.

The power of fear. The power of life and death. It was like air to him, something he had to have in order to survive. And when he was without it for too long, he began to feel his control slipping away.

An old man with a white beard down to his chest gaped at the riders from the boardwalk. Without even slowing his horse, Mallory slammed two slugs into the old-timer's chest. The bullets smashed him back against the wall of the building behind him. He crumpled to the planks, nothing more than a broken stick figure now.

An old woman came out of the building and screamed when she saw the body on the boardwalk. Mallory was almost past, but he twisted in the saddle and fired another shot, placing it with deadly accuracy. The old woman jerked and collapsed as the bullet bored through her brain.

A lot younger and prettier woman darted in front of Mallory's horse, trying desperately to reach the other side of the street for some reason. Mallory didn't know why that was so important to her. Nor did he care. He never slowed his mount. The young woman went down under the animal's slashing hooves, her beauty disappearing in a crimson smear.

Earlier in the day a couple of Mallory's men had ridden into Buckskin, bought some supplies at one of the general stores, and memorized the layout of the town well enough so that when they returned to the gang they were able to draw a crude map of it. Because of that Mallory knew where the bank was located. He veered his horse toward that redbrick building now as the slaughter continued up and down the settlement's main street. Some of the outlaws had dismounted and stormed into homes and businesses, looking for loot and killing anyone who got in their way.

Mallory didn't hesitate as he neared the boardwalk in front of the bank. His horse took the steps leading up to it in a bound. Mallory wheeled the mount, ducked his head, and sent the horse right through the front window in a leap that shattered glass and splintered the window frame. The horse's hooves thudded on the floor of the bank lobby as it landed inside the building.

More of the outlaws followed through the opening Mallory had made, although they came on foot rather than horseback. One of them carried a lit lantern that illuminated the darkened bank. Mallory pointed to a door on the far side of the lobby and called, "The vault must be through there!"

Several of the men headed in that direction. They had dynamite with them. Mallory knew they would use it to blow the door off the vault. He had recruited them into the gang for that very purpose. They were experts with the explosive cylinders.

The rest of the man arranged themselves at the shattered window and the double front doors of the bank. They held rifles and were ready to defend the place if the local law or even the citizens attempted to storm the bank while the outlaws were inside. Mallory didn't expect that to happen. According to the spies he'd sent into Buckskin, there were only two badge-toters in town, a popinjay of a marshal and his meek little deputy. And Mallory wasn't worried about the townspeople at all. By now they were too scared of dying—and with good reason!—to put up much of a fight.

"I'll leave it with you boys!" he said to his men in the bank. "Clean out the vault and rendezvous south of town!"

He leaped his horse back through the window, onto the boardwalk. Some of the buildings down the street were on fire now, torched by his men when they'd finished looting the places. Those flames would spread and might even consume the entire town. Mallory didn't care if Buckskin burned to the ground, as long as he got what he wanted first.

Right now he wanted to deal out some more punishment to the settlement's citizens, those boring, lifeless drones who were everything he had always despised. Their mere existence was an affront to him. He wanted to kill all of them.

And he would start with the local law, the representatives of everything he hated worst.

He yanked on the reins and turned his horse toward Buckskin's marshal's office and jail.

Convinced now that Buckner's visit wasn't a trick of some sort, Matt jumped on top of the bucket when the shooting started. That brought him up high enough so he could grasp the iron bars and peer out the window.

There wasn't much to see. The window looked out on the alley that ran behind the jail. Matt saw a massive, looming shape in the alley that had to be Buckner. A few yards away was another, even bigger patch of darkness—the mule Buckner had brought along to pull the bars out of the window.

"What the hell?" The exclamation came from Buckner. "Sounds like a damn war just broke out!"

"Must be outlaws raiding the town," Matt said. He saw the buffalo hunter turn away from the window. "Hey, Buckner! Come back here!"

"Got to find out what that ruckus is!" Buckner flung back over his shoulder. "They can't have a fight without me, damn 'em!"

"Blast it! Buckner! Hey! Maybe you better get us out of here after all!"

Matt's shouts didn't do any good. Buckner lumbered off down the alley, turned a corner, and was gone.

Matt hopped down from the bucket and looked at his blood brother. "He's gone. What do we do now?"

Sam shook his head. "There's nothing we can do. We're trapped in here. Our only choice is to wait it out."

Sam's words made sense, but that didn't do Matt any good. Like Buckner must have, he felt the call of battle. The shooting and the yelling were like physical tugs on him. He wanted to be right in the middle of whatever fracas was going on.

The door between the cell block and the marshal's office was flung open. Stryker stood there, his shotgun clutched in his hands. Birdie was with him. Stryker told the deputy, "Get in the cell block and lock the door!"

"I oughta come with you, Marshal!" Birdie protested.

"We have a duty to protect the prisoners," Stryker snapped. "I'll deal with those raiders."

Matt had to give the lawman credit for being brave—or downright crazy. Stryker was going out to face the killers alone, and from the sound of the attack, there were a lot of them. Stryker would be facing overpowering odds.

Matt grabbed the bars of the cell door and called, "Marshal! Let us out of here and give us guns! We'll help you!"

Stryker glared at him. "Forget it! You're locked up and you'll stay that way. I don't need help from the likes of you two."

Sam said, "It sounds to me like you do, Marshal. There must be a lot of those outlaws."

Birdie ventured, "Marshal, maybe it'd be a good idea—"

"Deputy, follow my orders! Get in there and protect the prisoners!"

Birdie sighed and gave a reluctant nod. He stepped into the cell block and pulled the door closed behind him while Stryker headed for the front door of the office. "There goes a mighty brave man," the deputy said.

"Or a damned foolish one," Matt said. "Deputy, show some sense. What's goin' on out there? Is it an outlaw raid?"

"That's what it looked like," Birdie replied. "I saw a bunch of men on horseback before Marshal Stryker hustled me in here. They came chargin' into town, shootin' at everything that moved. I ain't seen anything like it since Gettysburg."

It was hard to imagine the mousy-looking little deputy taking part in that epic battle during the Civil War. Matt supposed there had been all types in the armies of North and South. He and Sam had been a bit too young to take part in that terrible clash, though they had seen more than their share of fighting since then. They had witnessed, from a distant hilltop, the great battle between the assembled Plains tribes and the Seventh Cavalry under Yellow Hair, George Armstrong Custer himself. Sam's father Medicine Horse had lost his life in that fight. And during their wanderings in recent years, the blood brothers had swapped lead repeatedly with the forces of lawlessness and greed. Both of them held tightly to the bars now, and Sam said, "If you release us, Deputy, we promise to help fight off the attack on the town."

Obviously, Birdie was torn. He let out a moan and said, "You know I can't do that, even if I wanted to. The marshal give me strict orders to keep you boys in here."

"He's gonna get himself killed," Matt pointed out, "if he's not dead already. That means you're in charge, Birdie. Let us out and give us our guns back. You know we can help."

For a second Matt thought Birdie was going to do it, but then the deputy gave a stubborn shake of his head. "Nope. I just can't." He drew the pistol holstered at his waist. "But don't worry. I won't let anything happen to you fellas."

Matt and Sam exchanged a glance. If the raiders wanted to break in here, Birdie wouldn't be able to stop them. The idea that the blood brothers might be gunned down like helpless animals made their skin crawl and their souls cry out in protest. Neither Matt nor Sam was particularly afraid of dying, but they wanted to go out on their feet, guns in their hands, fighting to the last breath.

It was starting to look like they might not get that chance. . . .

Mallory knew where the marshal's office was, too, just as he had known the location of the bank. As he spurred toward the squat stone building, the flames shot higher in the air at the other end of town, throwing a hellish red glare over the street and lighting up practically the whole settlement.

In that glare, Mallory saw the marshal emerge from his office. A couple of owlhoots were closer to him than Mallory was. They yelled and opened fire on the lawman, but they rushed their shots. The marshal was able to swing his shotgun up and fire both barrels. The buckshot slammed into the outlaws and their horses at close range, shredding flesh, knocking the horses down, driving the men out of their saddles. The horses kicked a little before dying, but neither of the raiders moved at all.

The marshal broke his shotgun open, shucked the empty shells, and tried to reload. Mallory was almost on top of him by then. Flame lanced from the barrel of Mallory's revolver. The bullet knocked the marshal halfway around and made him drop the shotgun. He caught himself against one of the poles supporting the awning over the boardwalk and clawed with his other hand at the Colt on his hip.

Smiling, Mallory fired again before the marshal could clear leather. This slug drove the lawman backward, but still he didn't fall. Even with two bullets in his body he managed to stumble forward, haul his pistol out of its holster, and struggle to raise the gun.

Mallory had reined in a few yards away. He grinned at the marshal and said, "You are one stubborn son of a bitch, aren't you, badge-toter?" He extended his gun and aimed it deliberately. "I think I'm going to put this one right between your eyes. . . ."

The marshal's pain-wracked face contorted with the effort he was making, but his muscles just wouldn't work well enough anymore. Before his gun was even halfway up, Mallory fired again. The slug smashed into the bridge of the lawman's nose and on into his brain. The marshal went down at last, flopping on his back in the dusty street. His gun slipped out of nerveless fingers.

Still grinning, Mallory waved some of his men over. "Get in there," he told them as he used his gun to point at the marshal's office and jail. "Kill anybody else you find and take all the guns and ammunition." He spotted one of the dynamite men riding past. They must have finished down at the bank, although with all the commotion going on, Mallory hadn't even heard the blast when the vault door was blown off. "Brody! When they get through cleaning out the marshal's office, toss a couple of sticks of dynamite in there."

"Will do, Boss!" Brody responded with a vicious grin of his own. Like all the members of Mallory's gang, he had plenty of reason to hate all lawmen and everything about them.

Mallory rode on down the street, the flames of Hades rising into the night sky behind him.

The sounds of the shooting outside came closer and closer, and Birdie appeared to grow more and more nervous. Matt was about to try again to convince the deputy to release him and Sam, when the outer door of the office was slammed open. "Through there!" a harsh voice yelled. "See if there's anybody in the cell block!"

Birdie didn't wait for the raiders to come in. He threw open the cell block door. A change had come over him. He stood straighter, and the nervous look had disappeared from his face. Instead his eyes glittered like deadly points of fire, and the gun in his hand was rock-steady.

"Eat lead, you dirty owlhoots!" he yelled as he stepped into the doorway and his gun began to roar.

Matt and Sam both dove to the floor of the cell, knowing the raiders would return that fire.

That was what happened, but Birdie's daring attack had surprised the outlaws so much that he was able to cut down a couple of them before they began shooting back. Birdie was jarred by a bullet, but managed to stay on his feet by leaning against the doorjamb while the revolver in his hand continued to spout flame.

The deputy was hit again, and this time it was too much for him to withstand. He sagged to his knees. Half-a-dozen outlaws had entered the marshal's office. Three of them were down, but the other three closed in on Birdie, ready to blast him to pieces.

A long-nosed mountain of a man appeared behind them and came crashing down on them. Buckner knocked all three of the outlaws off their feet. As he landed on top of them, the buffalo hunter grabbed two men by their necks and slammed their heads together. That made a sound like a watermelon dropping to the floor and busting open. Buckner hammered a fist down on the back of the third man's head.

The air was thick with roiling clouds of powder smoke, but through the open door between the office and the cell block Matt saw several more outlaws charge in from the street. "Buckner, look out!" he yelled.

Buckner pushed himself up and swung around, but not in time to stop the raiders from opening fire. Bullet after bullet tore through his buffalo coat and thudded into his huge frame. That didn't stop him from roaring in defiance as he threw himself toward this fresh batch of enemies. With blood running down his hand like a river, he reached under his coat and yanked an Arkansas Toothpick from its sheath. More blood sprayed into the air as he waded into the men with the knife flashing back and forth. Those who escaped the deadly arcs of the long, heavy blade went down under the bone-shattering blows of Buckner's other fist.

Despite this last ferocious attack, Buckner had suffered too much damage to stay on his feet for long. He fell to his knees, taking the last of the outlaws in the marshal's office down with him. His sausagelike fingers closed around the man's neck and squeezed. The outlaw thrashed wildly, but couldn't get free of Buckner's death grip. He wasn't strangled, though, because with one last convulsive heave, the buffalo hunter snapped his neck like a matchstick.

Silence fell over the smoky, blood-splattered marshal's office, although the sounds of fighting and dying continued outside. After a moment, one of the men who had been wounded by Birdie groaned and forced himself upright. He reached under his coat and brought out a small bundle of some sort. Matt and Sam both watched, their eyes widening with horror as they recognized the bundle as two sticks of dynamite tied together. The outlaw fumbled a match from his pocket, snapped it to life with his thumbnail, and held the flame to the fuse dangling from one of the sticks.

Then with a savage grin at the prisoners, he tossed the dynamite through the open cell block door and staggered out of the marshal's office.

Chapter 4

"Son of a bitch!" Matt shouted as he watched the dynamite sail over Birdie's body, hit the floor, bounce, and then roll a couple of feet. It came to a stop about halfway to the cell and lay there as the fuse continued to sputter and spark.

Sam threw himself at the bars and extended his right arm between them as he sprawled on the floor. His fingers wiggled as they reached desperately for the dynamite. If he could get his hands on it, he might be able to toss it back into the outer office. If he could do that, at least the explosive cylinders would be a little farther away when they detonated.

But Sam's attempt came up a few inches short. "I can't get it!" he said. He lunged ahead, driving his shoulder hard enough against the bars to make him cry out in pain, but he still couldn't reach the dynamite.

"Come on!" Matt told him. "Back against the rear wall. We'll pull those mattresses off the bunks and prop them in front of us!"

Even as he spoke, he knew what he was proposing wasn't likely to do much good. The cell wasn't big enough, and the mattresses were filled with corn shucks or something like that. They wouldn't stop the force of the blast.

And the fuse had already burned down more than half its length.

Sam ignored Matt's warning and made another try for the dynamite. The tips of his fingers barely brushed the red cylinders. Sam roared in frustration.

At that moment, Birdie rolled onto his side and groaned. His shirt and vest were sodden with blood, but he wasn't dead. His eyelids fluttered open. For a second, his eyes didn't seem to want to focus. Then horrified understanding came into them as he saw the dynamite.

Matt and Sam watched in fascination, knowing they might have only seconds to live. There was nothing they could do to help as Birdie reached out with a shaking hand. He pushed himself toward the dynamite with his other hand and his feet. The fuse had about an inch left to burn when the deputy's fingers finally closed around the sticks.

With a choked grunt of effort, Birdie pushed himself up and heaved the dynamite toward the door into the office. If it missed, hit the wall beside the door, and bounced back, they were doomed.

The dynamite sailed through the opening, landed on the floor, and rolled to the side. A sliver of a heartbeat later, a huge blast rocked the building on its foundations. The noise was deafening, mind-numbing. The wall between the office and the cell block bulged and then came apart. Flying chunks of stone and a thick cloud of dust filled the air.

Matt and Sam had scrambled for the rear wall of the cell as Birdie threw the dynamite into the office. They grabbed the mattresses and pulled them over their heads. Debris from the explosion sailed between the bars and pelted them like a hundred fists at once. The mattresses helped a little, but the blood brothers were still battered and shaken. Matt couldn't hear anything except a vast ringing in his ears, and suspected that Sam was experiencing the same thing.

Gradually Matt became aware that debris wasn't slamming into him anymore and the earth had stopped shaking underneath him. That meant he had lived through the explosion. He didn't know how badly he was hurt, but he didn't care about that right now. He just wanted to find out whether or not Sam was still alive.

Coughing and choking on the dust in the air, Matt shoved the mattress away from him. "Sam!" he yelled. "Sam, where are you? Are you all right?"

He felt around, and after a moment his hands fell on the sleeve of a buckskin shirt. He followed the arm in the sleeve up to Sam's head. Sam wasn't moving, but Matt found a pulse beating steadily in his neck. Relief washed through him. His blood brother was alive.

The rear wall of the jail seemed to be intact. Matt lifted Sam and propped him in a sitting position against it. Sam muttered something. The air was beginning to clear. Matt made out Sam's face. It was bruised and scraped, but Sam didn't appear to have any serious injuries.

Matt took stock of his own situation and decided that he was all right. He felt like he'd been in the saloon brawl to end all saloon brawls, but his arms and legs worked and he wasn't bleeding except from some cuts and scratches. He realized that his hearing was coming back, too; otherwise he wouldn't have been able to hear Sam muttering as he struggled to regain consciousness.

Looking around the cell, Matt saw that the force of the explosion had sprung the door open. Some of the bars were bent out of shape. Matt gazed past them and saw that part of the wall between the office and the cell block had been blown down. A hand and part of an arm stuck out from under the pile of rubble.

"Birdie!"

Matt crawled to the door and grabbed the bars to pull himself upright. He stumbled out of the cell. Bending over, he began throwing chunks of rock and wood aside, working as fast as he could until he'd uncovered the deputy's head and shoulders. Matt got his hands under Birdie's arms and hauled him out from under the collapsed wall.

Birdie was covered with blood, but he was alive. He opened his eyes again as Matt pillowed the deputy's head against his leg. "Did . . . did I get that dynamite . . . outta here in time?"

"You sure did," Matt told him. "You saved me and Sam, no doubt about it. Saved our lives."

"G-good. That was . . . what the marshal . . . told me to do."

Matt wondered briefly what had happened to Stryker. He would have bet a hat that the lawman was dead by now. Lots of folks in Buckskin were probably dead. Matt realized that the shooting had stopped outside. That meant the raiders were probably gone. He heard the crackle of flames and shouts of alarm, though.

The town was on fire. The bastards had torched it, Matt thought.

Sam stumbled up beside him. "You made it, brother."

"Yeah."

"Birdie?"

"He's alive. Don't rightly see how, but he is." Matt jerked his head toward what was left of the office. "See about Buckner, if you feel up to it."

Sam nodded and climbed over the rubble to reach the office. He came back a minute later shaking his head.

"Buckner's dead. I have a hunch he was gone before that dynamite ever went off. Those bastards must've put twenty slugs in him. It's a wonder he lived as long as he did."

Matt nodded. "Give me a hand with Birdie here. We need to get him to a doc."

With Sam's help, Matt got to his feet. He cradled Birdie's limp form in his arms. The little deputy didn't weigh much, and under normal circumstances Matt could have carried him without any trouble. These circumstances were hardly normal, though, and Matt stumbled a little as he made his way out of the destroyed marshal's office. Sam's strong hand on his arm steadied him.

They emerged onto the street, where the air was clogged not with dust from the explosion, but rather with smoke from the burning buildings. Most of the places that were ablaze were at the far end of town, but the flames were spreading. Matt saw people with buckets of water running back and forth as they tried frantically to contain the con- flagration. Maybe they would be successful. It was too soon to say.

Limp, lifeless bodies littered the street. Corpses were everywhere. Men, women, and children . . . old-timers . . . horses and mules . . . The slaughter had been indiscrimi- nate. The raiders truly had killed anything that moved.

Including Marshal Harlan Stryker. Sam pointed out the lawman's body to Matt. Stryker lay on his back with a bullet hole between his eyes. Even without seeing it, Matt knew the back of Stryker's head would be a mess where the slug had blown the marshal's brains out.

Sam grabbed the arm of a man running past and shouted, "Where's the doctor? We need a doctor!"

The man turned his wide-eyed gaze toward Sam, pulled free, and stumbled backward, drawing his gun as he did so. "You're one of those prisoners!" he yelped. "You were probably in on the raid with those outlaws! And now you've killed the deputy!" He raised his voice in a howl. "Help! Help me, somebody! I got two of them! I got two of the outlaws! Help!"

Men heard the frantic shouts and began running toward them. Guns came out. Matt and Sam looked at each other, knowing that they had landed right back in danger. If the battle-shocked townies took the blood brothers for members of the gang, they would probably open fire, too eager to strike back at the varmints who had inflicted such damage on the settlement to even think about what they were doing.

Matt and Sam were still unarmed, even if they could have brought themselves to open fire on innocent people.

But a panic-stricken citizen could shoot them just as dead as any owlhoot. . . .

The rendezvous point was about a mile south of town where a dry creek bed cut across the plains. The stream had water in it just often enough to support a few scrubby mesquite trees with deep roots along its banks. Mallory's men paused there to let everyone catch up as they left the devastated settlement of Buckskin.

The flames shooting high in the air from the burning buildings were clearly visible from here. The terrain in this part of the Panhandle was so flat the fire was probably visible for twenty miles or more. Deuce Mallory sat and watched the dancing flames with a satisfied grin on his rawboned face. Once again he had struck a devastating blow against the forces that conspired to hold him down and tell him how to live. He hated rules and authority more than just about anything. Those flames represented his vengeance on everybody who had ever frowned at him in disapproval and tried to mold him into something he wasn't, going all the way back to his stern, straitlaced storekeeper father and his simpering fool of a mother.

The gang had ridden away from Buckskin with a lot of loot, too. That made Mallory's grin even wider.

The men who'd been given the chore of cleaning out the bank vault had carried away several large burlap bags full of greenbacks, along with a heavy canvas pouch stuffed to the gills with gold double eagles. Other men had plundered the cash from the general stores and the settlement's other businesses. They had stolen money and jewelry from the families who resided in Buckskin's finest homes.

They had stolen something else from a few of those homes: the wives and daughters of the families who lived there. Mallory estimated that the gang had half-a-dozen sobbing, terrified female captives ranging from teenage girls up to middle-aged but still attractive married women.

Taking prisoners like that was a double-edged sword. The men liked to have their fun with the gals, of course, but losing their womenfolks sometimes made the survivors of a raid more determined to pursue the gang. That was why Mallory would order that the women be released after a day or two. That was long enough for his men to slake their lust, and once a posse had recovered the women, they were less likely to continue chasing the outlaws. The townies were more interested in getting the women safely home. Mallory had worked it all out in his mind. Killing the prisoners and leaving their bodies behind would just make the pursuers more determined than ever to catch up and try to avenge their loved ones. Mallory didn't want that.

Besides, he enjoyed knowing that from then on those damned storekeepers would never be able to look at their wives and daughters again without thinking about all the men who'd ridden them. Hell, some of them would probably even give birth to outlaw babies! Mallory laughed in delight whenever he thought about how much squirming *that* would cause.

One of his lieutenants, a straw-haired man named Larrabee, moved his horse over next to Mallory's and said, "Everybody's here who's gonna be, Boss."

Mallory nodded. "How many men did we lose?"

"I make it eight." Larrabee named them. "Some of 'em are dead for sure, and the others ain't showed up so I reckon they probably are, too."

It was a hard-and-fast rule—anybody who didn't show up for the rendezvous in a timely manner got left behind. Mallory enforced it without exception.

"All right," he said. "We'll head for the Dutchman's and count up the take there before moving on south."

"Mexico's still where we're headed in the long run?"

Mallory nodded. "It's a good place to spend some time while things cool off up here. Warm weather and warmer señoritas, eh, Larrabee?"

The other outlaw chuckled. "Whatever you say, Boss."

Mallory glanced at the burning settlement as he turned his horse to head south, and again felt that fierce sense of satisfaction at the visible evidence of the destruction he'd caused.

"I say go to hell," he whispered. "Each and every one of you."

Chapter 5

Matt and Sam found themselves staring down the barrels of at least half-a-dozen guns as some of the citizens of Buckskin rushed up in response to the man's cries for help. Angry shouts filled the air, competing with the roar and crackle of the flames down the street.

"Kill the owlhoots!"

"Shoot 'em! Fill 'em full of lead!"

"No! String 'em up!"

"Somebody get a rope!"

"I say we blast the bastards!"

Finally, a voice of reason spoke up. "Hold your fire! If you go to shootin' you might hit Birdie!"

"Yeah, a necktie party'd be better!"

One of the men squinted over his gun barrel at Matt and rasped, "Give us the deputy, mister. You won't get away with holdin' him hostage."

The anger that had been building up inside Matt finally exploded. "You damn fools!" he raged. "We're not holdin' the deputy hostage! We want to get him to a doctor!"

"And we aren't part of the gang that raided the town,"

Sam added. "They tried to kill us, too. They dynamited the marshal's office, for God's sake!"

The stubborn looks remained on the faces of the townsmen. "They probably blew up the place tryin' to break you out because you're in cahoots with them," one of the men said accusingly.

"Hand over the deputy," another ordered, "or we'll shoot anyway. I think Birdie's already dead."

As if the deputy had heard those words, he stirred suddenly. Lifting his head, he peered around. The flames made it plenty light enough in the street to see what was going on.

Although weak and thin, Birdie's voice still held some of the fighting spirit he had unexpectedly displayed inside the jail. "Put those . . . damn guns down," he commanded. "Bodine and Two Wolves are . . . tryin' to help me . . ."

"Birdie!" one of the men said. "You're alive!"

"Thanks to . . . these two men."

The man who had originally yelled for help said, "We thought they were part of the gang—"

"Well, they . . . ain't." Birdie looked up at Matt. "The marshal . . . ?"

"Dead."

Birdie closed his eyes for a second, then opened them and went on. "I reckon . . . I'm in charge . . . then. You men . . . back off . . . The prisoners are still . . . in my custody."

Birdie was in no shape to have anybody in custody, but Matt didn't think it was a good time to point that out. Instead he asked the group of men, who were now looking confused and even a little ashamed of themselves, "Where's the doctor?"

"I saw him a few minutes ago in front of the hardware store," one of the men replied. "Come on. I'll show you."

They formed a grim procession as they went down the street, with Matt and Sam in front along with the man taking them to the doctor and the rest of the townies trailing behind. Most of them had holstered their guns, but a few still held their weapons as if they weren't ready to fully trust the blood brothers.

The doctor was no longer in front of the hardware store, but one of the men spotted him farther down the street and pointed him out to Matt. The sawbones was a gaunt, white-haired man with a harried look on his face. No surprise there, since Buckskin was now full of injured people needing his attention.

The doctor was checking over a line of wounded citizens who had been laid out on the hotel porch. He glanced at Matt, saw the bloody figure in the young man's arms, and grunted. "Put him down somewhere," the doctor ordered. "I'll get to him when I can." Then he looked again and exclaimed, "Birdie?"

The deputy summoned up a faint smile. "Howdy . . . Doc."

"Bring him over here," the doctor ordered. "Set him down carefully. . . . Just like that."

Matt lowered Birdie to the hotel porch. The doctor pulled aside the bloody shirt to reveal the bullet holes in Birdie's torso.

"No telling how much damage those slugs did," the doctor muttered, "but it looks like they went all the way through anyway. He's lost a lot of blood. I'll do what I can for him, but I'm only one man and a lot of people are hurt."

"Perhaps I could help," Sam offered.

"You have medical training, young man?"

"No, but I have a lot of practical experience patching up

bullet holes." Sam waved a hand toward Matt. "My friend here seems to make a habit of getting shot."

"Hey!" Matt protested. "I haven't been ventilated all that many times. And you've stopped a bullet or two yourself."

The doctor ignored him and said to Sam, "Some of the less seriously injured patients are down at the far end of the porch. If you'd go see what you can do for them, I'd appreciate it."

Sam nodded. "Right away, Doctor."

He hurried off to see if there were any of the wounded townspeople he could help. No one tried to stop him, so Matt supposed the angry citizens had decided that he and Sam weren't part of the outlaw gang after all.

"Anybody know who was responsible for this?" he asked the men.

They looked at each other and shook their heads. "We don't have any idea, mister," one man replied.

"Never saw 'em before," another put in. "And I don't know if anybody got a good look at 'em anyway. The way they rode in shootin' and killin' like that, folks were just tryin' to get out of harm's way."

Matt nodded. He understood what the men were talking about. In the middle of a battle like that, people didn't worry about much of anything except survival.

Some terrified wailing made Matt swing around to see what was happening now. A middle-aged man in a dressing gown over a nightshirt came stumbling up to the hotel. He must have already retired for the evening when the marauders charged into Buckskin. His thinning hair was standing up in crazy tufts and his pale face was twisted with horror.

"They took her!" he managed to gasp out. "They took my Lucinda!"

The doctor stepped over to him and grasped his arm. "Are you hurt, Mayor?"

The man shook his head and said, "No, I'm fine. Didn't you hear me? Those bastards carried off my wife!" He put his hands over his face and began to shake with sobs.

Matt looked over at one of the townsmen who stood nearby. "That fella's your mayor?"

"Yeah. Timothy Lowell's his name." The townie wore a sympathetic expression. "From what he's sayin' it sounds like those owlhoots kidnapped his wife. Mrs. Lowell's a fine-lookin' woman."

"Are any other women or girls missing?"

The townsman shook his head. "Mister, I just wouldn't know. I'm a bachelor myself. Reckon maybe that's a good thing tonight."

Matt figured the hombre was probably right about that. The possibility that the outlaws had carried off some of the women of Buckskin came as no real surprise to him. Out here on the frontier, most decent women were safe from assault, even when confronted with the most hardened desperadoes. But there were always exceptions, and a bunch of murdering skunks like the ones who had hit this settlement were capable of just about anything. Matt didn't live here, and after the treatment he and Sam had received from Buckskin's marshal, he didn't have any reason to be overly fond of the town. Even so, he felt outrage rising inside him. Those outlaws were worse than animals. Somebody needed to put a stop to their depredations.

These folks weren't capable of doing it, though. Matt wasn't sure they could even muster a posse to go after the raiders. A lot of men had been killed and others were wounded, and the ones who remained had their hands full trying to get those fires under control and care for the injured.

Anyway, a bunch of storekeepers and clerks wouldn't be any match for a gang of ruthless hardcases who would as soon kill a man as look at him. The job of going after those outlaws required men who were pretty tough and gun-handy themselves.

At the moment, Matt could think of only two hombres in Buckskin who he knew fit that description.

And they were *Onihomahan* . . . Brothers of the Wolf.

Him and Sam.

By morning the fires were out in the settlement. Four buildings had burned to the ground and a dozen others had been heavily damaged by flames, including some residences. Twenty-three people were dead, not counting the outlaws who had been killed in the fighting, and another seven or eight were injured so badly that Dr. Lloyd Fentress didn't expect them to pull through.

One of the survivors was Deputy Birdie Phillips. Fentress sent word to Matt and Sam that Birdie wanted to see them.

They had been up all night, helping with the wounded and fighting the fires. Their faces were grimy with smoke, sweat, and dried blood, and their steps weary with exhaustion as they climbed the stairs to the second floor of the hotel, which had been turned into a makeshift hospital. They had poked around in the rubble of the marshal's office and jail until they found their hats, but they hadn't located their guns yet.

Dr. Fentress met them at the top of the stairs and pointed to a door down the corridor. "Birdie's in Room Eleven. I told him he needed to rest instead of talking to you fellows, but he insisted."

"Is he going to recover from his wounds?" Sam asked.

"I'm a physician, not a Gypsy fortune-teller," Fentress snapped. "But I'll say this . . . Birdie shouldn't have lived this long. I've stopped the bleeding and cleaned and bandaged the wounds. The little varmint's so stubborn, I'd say he's got a chance." The doctor's gruff words didn't completely conceal the admiration and affection he felt for the deputy.

Matt nodded, said, "Thanks, Doc. We'll try not to tire him out too much."

"You boys look like you could use some rest yourselves."

Sam gave him a grim smile. "That'll have to wait."

They went down the hall and through an open door into the room where Birdie waited, halfway propped up in the hotel bed. Thick bandages were wrapped tightly around his body. His face was pale and drawn, but his eyes were open and he seemed alert enough.

"Are you fellas all right?" he asked.

Matt shrugged. "A mite banged up and mighty tired, but other than that I don't reckon we can complain."

Birdie smiled. "Looks like you came through that dynamite blast pretty good."

"Thanks to you," Sam said. "If you hadn't thrown those sticks out into the office, we would've been blown to kingdom come."

"Yeah, me, too," Birdie agreed. "As it is, it feels like the whole world fell on me."

"Not the whole world," Matt said. "Just a wall."

"And it must've been you two who dragged me out of there and got help for me. You saved my life."

"The least we could do," Sam said.

"Not hardly. Not after the way the marshal locked you up when that brawl in the Red Queen wasn't your fault."

"You know that?" Matt asked.

Birdie nodded. "I figured as much. Buckner started a fight every time he came to town. Marshal Stryker knew that. He just wanted to be the one who locked up the famous Bodine and Two Wolves."

Matt frowned. "You knew that but you didn't do anything about it?"

"What could I do? I worked for Marshal Stryker. And he was a good lawman, too, don't you think he wasn't. He was just . . . ambitious."

Sam said, "It's all right. Don't tire yourself out, Birdie. We promised the doctor we wouldn't upset you."

Birdie sighed. "I ain't upset with you boys. I just hate to think about what those no-good outlaws have done to my town. Doc Fentress says they kidnapped some women?"

"Six that we know of," Sam said. "Including Mayor Lowell's wife."

"My God." Birdie shook his head. "Somebody's got to go after 'em."

"You think anybody in this town is capable of tracking down an outlaw gang like that?" Matt asked.

Birdie looked him straight in the eye. "Nobody who lives here. But you two boys could do it."

Matt opened his mouth to say something, but Birdie went on before any words could come out.

"I've heard plenty about you fellas. You've fought owl-hoots and got mixed up in range wars and even helped out the Texas Rangers a time or two."

"Maybe you should call in the Rangers now," Sam suggested.

"That'd mean sendin' a rider to the nearest telegraph

office, and that's more'n forty miles away. By the time any Rangers could get here, those owlhoots will be long gone and their trail will be cold. Now, though, it'd be fresh enough for somebody to follow it."

"Somebody meanin' us?" Matt said. He had already thought the same thing himself, but he was reluctant to agree with what Birdie was asking. The odds against him and Sam would be overwhelming. . . .

Of course, that hadn't stopped them on numerous occasions in the past. They'd ridden right into some dustups where they might as well have been charging Hades with a bucket of water—and they'd made it out alive.

"You can have the best horses in town, and if you need guns and ammunition, take whatever you need from Lowell's Emporium."

"Owned by the mayor, I reckon?"

Birdie nodded. "That's right. I've already talked to him about this. He told me to deputize you and tell you that the town will pay whatever you ask if you can get those prisoners away from the gang. Pay you a bounty for every one of those bastards you kill, too."

"You're the marshal now?" Sam asked.

"That's right." Birdie chuckled. "Assumin' I don't die from gettin' shot full of holes."

Matt didn't think that was going to happen. Birdie might look like a mousy little fella, but he had already demonstrated that he was tough as whang leather and full of piss and vinegar.

"I'd bet a hat you'll pull through," Matt said. "We ain't deputies, though, and we ain't bounty hunters."

A note of desperation entered Birdie's voice. "But there's nobody else who can do it."

Matt and Sam looked at each other. Sam shrugged and

said, "I don't like the idea that they carried those ladies off like that. It's like the rape of the Sabine women from Greek mythology. I read about it in Bulfinch."

Matt didn't know where Bulfinch was and didn't care. He said, "I don't much cotton to varmints who try to blow me up either."

"Then you'll do it?" Birdie asked.

"Keep your badges," Matt said. "We'll go after the bastards, but we don't need any tin stars to do it."

"We'll take you up on the offer of some extra horses and guns and ammunition, though," Sam added. "And enough supplies to keep us going for a while."

"Take whatever you need. I'm sure the mayor will agree."

"Did anybody see what direction those outlaws headed when they rode out of town?" Matt asked.

"I was told that they rode south."

Matt nodded. "South it is then. Give us an hour or so to get ready, and then we'll hit the trail."

Chapter 6

The Dutchman's was a trading post run by a man named Hendrick Van Goort. Situated atop the Cap Rock, the rugged escarpment that meanders through West Texas and separates the Staked Plains from the rest of the Lone Star State, it was a regular stop on the owlhoot trail. Honest folks avoided the place at all costs. The Rangers had tried to raid the trading post more than once and arrest the outlaws they found there, but they'd always come up empty-handed. Van Goort had a network of spies scattered across West Texas, especially in towns such as Sweetwater and Big Spring that were near the Cap Rock. Any time the Rangers rode toward the Dutchman's, Van Goort's agents would signal him by means of mirrors. They could pass along a message for miles in a matter of minutes. Van Goort had a watchtower built in one corner of the adobe compound that housed the trading post, and one of his three Indian wives was always up there, scanning the countryside for a warning flash. At night signal fires were used to accomplish the same end.

Because of that, any wanted men who stopped at the

Dutchman's were long gone by the time any star-packers could ride up to the place. That margin of safety was what drew outlaws to this isolated spot.

That, and the barrels of whiskey, the crates of guns and ammunition, and the fact that Van Goort was nearly always willing to buy wide-looped cattle or other stolen goods. A steady stream of ill-gotten gains flowed through the trading post.

Van Goort was a giant of a man, bald with a bushy blond beard, grossly fat and sloppy at first glance. But underneath the fat were slabs of muscle. The Dutchman could break the back of a strong man with his bare hands, and had been known to do so when he had to establish order at the trading post. Word of his strength and ruthlessness had gotten around: Such information always traveled fast on the lonely trails where hard-bitten men heard the owl hoot at night. So even the most notorious desperadoes were generally on their best behavior when they visited the Dutchman's.

Deuce Mallory and his gang had been there before. The guards who worked for Van Goort recognized Mallory and his men when the outlaws rode up to the compound perched on the edge of the escarpment. Heavy wooden gates swung open. Mallory rode in, trailed by the rest of the bunch.

They still had the women from Buckskin with them. The prisoners were bruised, their clothes were torn, and the dull, vacant-eyed expressions on their faces spoke eloquently of the pain and degradation they had been forced to endure during their captivity.

Mallory had intended to release the women by now, but he was a shrewd leader who adapted to circumstances. He could tell that the men didn't want to let them go just yet.

He was willing to bend a little on his rule. But they would leave the prisoners here at the Dutchman's and let Van Goort handle getting them back to their homes. Van Goort would probably even manage to turn a profit on the deal, claiming that he'd had to ransom them from Mallory's gang when that wasn't the case at all. He would demand to be reimbursed for his expense by the families of the prisoners before he'd turn them over.

That was what Mallory figured anyway, so he was a little surprised when Van Goort stepped out onto the porch of the big main building, looked at the women, and scowled in displeasure. The porch had a sod roof, and vines had been planted in it. They'd grown until they hung down in front of the porch, providing some added shade and coolness. Van Goort pushed past the vines, came down the steps, and waddled over to where Mallory and the others had reined their mounts to a halt.

"Mallory," the Dutchman said. "What are you doing with those women?"

Mallory thumbed his hat back on his thatch of bristly, copper-colored hair. He grinned and said, "They wanted to come with us when we rode through a place called Buckskin, up north of here."

Van Goort's scowl didn't go away. "Yes, I can see how pleased they are to be accompanying you," he said. "I thought you knew better than this, Mallory."

The outlaw leaned forward in the saddle. His left hand rested easily on the horn, but his right didn't stray far from the butt of the holstered Colt. "You got a rule against bringing women to your place, Van Goort?"

"Kidnapped women, yes! Men will tolerate many things—robbery, dealing in stolen goods, even murder—but molesting decent women is not done!"

Mallory lowered his voice and said, "Then you'll be happy to hear that I'm going to leave them with you when we ride out. You can send 'em right back where they came from. Hell, you'll even be a hero for *rescuing* them from us."

He saw the light of avarice flare up in the Dutchman's pale blue eyes. Van Goort just hadn't thought it through before now. Slowly, he nodded. "I suppose I could make this gesture. Out of the goodness of my heart, you understand."

"And the fact that I've got more than two dozen men to your handful of guards," Mallory pointed out with a smirk.

Van Goort's pale face was never tanned or even sunburned, despite the fierce West Texas sun. But it flushed in anger sometimes, as it did now.

"You know the rules now, Mallory. In the future, no more female captives."

"I'll keep that in mind," Mallory drawled. "Now, do I tell my men to dismount so they can go in and partake of your hospitality—or do we turn around and ride out?"

Van Goort hesitated, but only for a second. Then he waved a hamlike hand at the trading post and said, "Enter, my friends, and make yourself at home."

That evening, Mallory sat at a table in the big barroom area of the trading post with Steve Larrabee, Gus Brody, Jacob Pine, and Carl Henderson. The four other men were the only surviving members of Mallory's original gang and the ones he trusted to help him keep the rest of their wild bunch in line. They had put away a considerable amount of tequila already. Upstairs, some of the other outlaws were availing themselves of the services of the whores who worked here at the Dutchman's. Others were bidding a not-so-sweet farewell to the women who had been carried off from Buckskin.

Brody gave voice to the thought that was on all of their minds. "What next, Deuce? I know you said we were headin' for Mexico, but there's a lot of territory between here and there. The boys are liable to want to make another raid before we get there."

Mallory tipped up the bottle and splashed more tequila in his glass. He took a sip of the fiery stuff and said, "I was thinking the same thing. We want to have plenty of money when we hit the Rio Grande. Mexico's a poor country. Might be pretty slim pickings on the other side of the Rio."

The outlaws gathered around the table grinned in satisfaction at Mallory's answer. "That's what we were thinkin', Boss," Larrabee said.

"You got some town in mind already?" Pine asked.

Before Mallory could answer, a commotion broke out at the top of the stairs. Two men lurched into view, swinging brutal punches at each other. Mallory looked up with a frown and recognized them as Dave Ash and Mel Warren, two members of his gang. There was no telling what might have started the fight. Put a bunch of liquored-up outlaws under the same roof and let them cut loose, and there were bound to be ruckuses.

Mallory figured to just let Ash and Warren pound on each other until they got tired of it, but then Warren landed a lucky blow and sent Ash flying head over heels down the stairs. It was a hard, out-of-control tumble, and halfway down a sharp crack sounded. Ash screamed and clutched at his leg as he landed in a sprawled heap at the foot of the stairs.

Mallory came to his feet and muttered, "What the hell's happened now?"

He strode toward Ash, but before he could reach the

injured man, Mel Warren rushed down the stairs, drawing his gun as he came. "I'll kill you, you son of a bitch!" he howled. His face was twisted in furious hate.

Ash was still screaming and unable to defend himself. Mallory saw now that Ash's left leg was bent at an unnatural angle. The white, jagged, bloody end of a broken bone stuck out of his calf.

"Warren!" Mallory snapped. "Drop it!"

Warren was too drunk and angry to pay any attention. He had cleared leather and his gun was swinging in line to blast slugs down into Ash's body.

Mallory's hand flickered. His Colt appeared in his fingers as if by magic. He'd been drinking, but was far from drunk. He tipped the barrel up and fired from the hip. Flame lanced from the revolver's muzzle, bright in the smoky, shadowy gloom of the trading post.

The slug ripped through Warren's left shoulder and flung him backward. He landed on the stairs and slid down several steps before coming to a stop. Rolling onto his side, he curled up in a ball and clutched his wounded shoulder as he groaned in pain. He had dropped his gun without firing a shot. That was how fast Mallory's draw had been.

"Stop your bellyaching," Mallory told the wounded man. "You're lucky I didn't just kill you. What the hell were you thinking, Mel? Fighting among ourselves is fine, but we don't shoot each other."

The other members of Mallory's inner circle had come up behind him. Brody chuckled and said, "That looked like some pretty slick shootin' to me, Deuce."

"Ash is a good man. I couldn't let Mel just kill him." Mallory felt a flash of irritation at having to explain his actions. He had never liked being forced to explain himself, even as a boy. And he wasn't going to do it now. He turned away and barked at the Dutchman, who stood behind the bar, "Have somebody look after those two. They won't be able to ride for a while, so they'll have to stay here while they're healing up."

Van Goort nodded. "Yah. But it will cost you extra, Mallory."

Mallory shrugged. "I'll take it out of their share of the loot." He jerked his head toward the table and said to his lieutenants, "Come on. Let's get back to planning where we're going from here."

The five outlaws sat down and poured fresh drinks while a couple of Van Goort's men came in and carried first Ash and then Warren off through a curtained doorway into a back room somewhere. Mallory was in a foul mood now. Losing men in a raid was one thing, but to lose two men to their own drunken stupidity was infuriating.

He tried to get his mind off what had happened by saying, "I have a place in mind where we can strike next. There's a town right on the Rio Grande, about halfway between the Big Bend and El Paso. We'll hit it and ride out, and practically as soon as we leave town we'll be across the river in Mexico."

"Sounds perfect," Larrabee said. "What's the name of this place, Boss?"

Mallory found himself smiling. "From what I've heard, it's a lot rougher than it sounds. It's called Sweet Apple."

Far to the east of the Dutchman's—far, *far* to the east, in the wilds of Trenton, New Jersey—Seymour Standish said, "Oh, dear. Oh, my heavens." He hoped he wasn't going to pass out, right here in the offices of the company his late father had founded.

Rebecca Jimmerson laughed and said, "For God's sake, Seymour, you act like you've never seen a woman smoking a cigarette before."

"I . . . I haven't," Seymour stammered. He pushed his spectacles up on his nose. "It's shocking. Scandalous!"

Rebecca took another puff on the cigarette and then sidled closer to Seymour. He was all too aware of the way her long, honey-blond hair hung down her back. Of the rosy glow of her cheeks and the sweet red lips that made him think of strawberries. Those lips were curved in a mischievous smile now as she said, "Well, if you think that a girl sneaking a smoke every now and then is so scandalous, I'd better not tell you what *else* I've been known to do. It might be too much for your delicate wittle sensibilities."

Seymour's face felt as hot as if the sun was shining directly on it . . . even though, in point of fact, he didn't see the sun all that much, spending most of his days inside as he did. The only time he got out was when he had to make a sales call on behalf of Standish Dry Goods, Inc. And he hated that because—there was no denying it—he was quite possibly the worst salesman in the history of the company. Perhaps even the worst salesman in the history of dry goods.

Rebecca was standing much too close to him. True, he was fond of her. He had been known to stare at her a bit too intently when she didn't know he was looking, and he was utterly ashamed of himself for some of the thoughts that went through his head at those moments. Thoughts of walking along a shade-dappled path with her on a warm spring day, perhaps even reaching over, if he dared, and slipping his hand into hers for a moment. . . . He was smitten with her, but he told himself it was a pure, chaste affection, the sort best indulged from afar. Certainly not from a distance of a foot or so. Why, he could feel the warmth of her breath on his cheek! Her tobacco-laden breath . . .

She suddenly gave a disgusted shake of her head and moved back, as if she had been waiting for something and was disappointed that it hadn't happened. She asked, "Did you want something, Seymour?"

He took a deep breath. He was on firmer footing now that there was business to discuss. Not by much, but at least a little firmer.

"I got a note that said my uncle wanted to see me."

"Oh, yes, of course. I forgot." Rebecca worked as Cornelius Standish's secretary. That was something else a bit scandalous, having a *woman* as a secretary. Evidently it was becoming more common, but it seemed wrong to Seymour anyway. "I'll let him know that you're here."

She went over to the door leading into the private office of the president of Standish Dry Goods, tapped on it, and disappeared inside for a moment. When she came out, she told Seymour, "You can go on in. He's ready for you."

"Thank you." As Seymour walked past her, he dared to pause and whisper, "I won't say anything to Uncle Cornelius about the, the, you know . . ." He held his fingers to his lips and acted like he was puffing on an imaginary cigarette.

Rebecca just rolled her eyes and turned away.

Seymour squared his shoulders, which wasn't as easy as it sounded since they tended to slump naturally. He stepped into his uncle's office and closed the door behind him. It was a big room with lots of dark wood and was dominated by a large desk. His uncle sat behind that desk, and even though it had been several months since his father's death, Seymour still felt a little jolt when he looked at Cornelius. He felt the same jolt, the same sense of loss, every time he stepped into this office and realized once again that Benjamin Standish was gone.

Seymour pushed his glasses up on his nose and said, "You, ah, wanted to see me, sir?"

Cornelius was sixty years old, beefy rather than slender like Seymour, with close-cropped white hair and a face like an angry hawk. He was the older brother, and Seymour had always suspected that it grated on his uncle to work for the younger, more successful Benjamin. Since Benjamin's wife, Seymour's mother, had passed away some years earlier, upon Benjamin's death the dry goods company had been split between his son Seymour and his brother Cornelius. The will made it clear that Cornelius was to be in charge of the company, however. Benjamin had loved his son, of course, but he hadn't allowed that love to blind him to the fact that Seymour would have run the business into the ground in no time. Some people were cut out to be in charge, and some just weren't. Seymour fell into the latter category.

Cornelius shoved some papers around on his desk—the desk that used to belong to his brother—and said, "Yes, Seymour, I've been thinking. The company's doing well, but we need to expand."

Seymour nodded. "That makes sense. As long as we're not too aggressive about it. Father always said that a company gets in trouble when it tries to grow too fast."

Cornelius scowled. He didn't like having his late brother's words thrown in his face, and Seymour knew that. He told himself that he should be more discreet in his comments.

"You know we have salesmen in the Midwestern states and in most of the Western states and territories."

"Yes, of course."

"But one area in which our sales force is lacking is the western part of Texas."

Seymour frowned in thought. "Do people out there really *need* dry goods, sir?"

Cornelius's bony hand slapped down hard on the desk. "Do they need dry goods? Of course they need dry goods! Everybody needs dry goods!"

Seymour nodded some more and hurried to say, "Yes, of course they do. Of course."

"That's why I'm sending you out there. To establish a foothold in that territory. Virgin territory, so to speak."

Seymour's eyes widened in amazement. "You're . . . you're sending me to . . . to *Texas*?"

"That's right."

Seymour felt sweat breaking out all over his body. "But . . . but Texas is the frontier. The wild frontier."

"Oh, don't worry. I'm sure all those stories about the place are exaggerated. Anyway, the town I'm sending you to is very civilized. How could it be anything else with the name that it has?"

Seymour swallowed hard. "What . . . what is the name, Uncle Cornelius?"

Cornelius leaned back in the big chair and smiled. "It's called Sweet Apple, my boy," he said. "Sweet Apple, Texas. It's going to be the perfect place for you."

Chapter 7

Cornelius Standish waited until after his stammering fool of a nephew was gone before he took a cigar from a humidor on the big desk and lighted it. Seymour always coughed and acted like he was choking whenever he was around cigar smoke. Standish had waited not out of any consideration for Seymour, but simply because he didn't want to put up with the annoyance of listening to him.

The door to the outer office opened and Rebecca stuck her honey-blond head into the room. "I gave Seymour the train tickets you had me purchase for him, Mr. Standish." She paused, then went on. "He wasn't very happy about going to Texas, was he?"

Standish lifted a hand and motioned for Rebecca to come into the office. When she had done so, he said around the cigar, "Shut the door."

She looked like she didn't much want to do that, but she closed it anyway and then stood with her hands behind her back, leaning against the door behind her. Standish admired the way that pose made her breasts push forward against her dress. And she knew perfectly well that he was admiring her, too, the little minx.

Standish took the cigar from his mouth and tapped the ash into a heavy glass ashtray. "What did he say?"

"Oh, not much, really." Rebecca straightened and came toward the desk. "Just that he was worried that he might let you down because he wasn't sure how well suited he was for a trip to Texas. But I could tell that he was really worried about going to such a rugged, dangerous place."

A harsh bark of laughter came from Standish. "The boy doesn't know the half of it. I made inquiries before I decided where to send him." Standish leaned back in his chair and smiled in satisfaction. "Sweet Apple, Texas, is the worst hellhole on the frontier. Someone is shot, stabbed, or beaten to death nearly every day there."

Rebecca's eyes widened. "Then Seymour . . ."

"Is doomed," Standish finished for her. "He can barely take care of himself here in Trenton. He won't stand a chance in a place like Sweet Apple." He stuck the cigar back in his mouth and growled, "It's perfect."

Indeed, he was proud of himself for having arrived at such an easy solution to a problem that had been vexing him for quite a while. Even while his brother Benjamin had still been alive, Cornelius Standish had seen how ineffective, how downright useless, his nephew Seymour was. The boy was a terrible salesman, had no head for business, and was so scared of everything that he practically pissed himself every time anyone spoke to him.

And yet Benjamin had given him a place in the company. Why his brother had done that, Cornelius would never know. Looking out for family was all well and good, but not when it interfered with making money. Benjamin should have been able to see that. Cornelius had hinted often enough that Standish Dry Goods, Inc., would be better off if Seymour was let go. Benjamin had always stubbornly resisted the very idea.

Then Benjamin was dead and Cornelius was in charge, and the first thing he planned to do was to send his worthless nephew packing . . . until the terms of Benjamin's will made it clear that they were to share the company, although Cornelius would remain in charge of its day-to-day operations, with the power to make all necessary business decisions.

With one exception. Seymour would always have a place with Standish Dry Goods, for however long he wanted it.

That thorn in Cornelius's side had irritated him no end. He seemed fated to have to put up with that blithering incompetent from now on, no matter how much money Seymour cost the business . . . until the grand idea occurred to him.

He might not have the power to fire Seymour, but he could send the boy to someplace where he was bound to come to a bad end. Someplace like Sweet Apple, Texas.

And once Seymour was gone, not only would Cornelius be rid of an annoyance, but the company would belong completely to him as well. . . .

Standish became aware that Rebecca was biting at her lower lip as if something bothered her. "What is it?" he snapped.

"Well . . . I was just thinking about Seymour. . . ."

Standish's hand slapped down on the desk like a gunshot. He put the cigar in the ashtray and said, "Good Lord, you're not smitten with the little bastard, are you?"

Rebecca was an ambitious young woman. A female had to be ambitious to work her way into such a respected, important position as a businessman's private secretary, as she had been for Benjamin Standish. After his death, she had started to play up to Seymour, no doubt thinking that if she could worm her way into his affections she could take advantage of his newly inherited wealth and power.

Only Seymour had no real power, and Rebecca had soon realized that. She understood that only one man in Standish Dry Goods, Inc., could do her any good—and that was Cornelius. She would do well to forget any residual fondness she felt for Seymour.

"Of course I'm not smitten with him, Mr. Standish," she said now. "He just seems so innocent. So . . . so harmless. I hate to see anything bad happen to him."

"He's not harmless," Standish said. "He costs this company money with his nervous bumbling. That's why he has to be dealt with."

"Yes, but—"

Standish fixed her with a hard glare. "Are *you* going to cost this company money with your sympathy, Miss Jimmerson? I wouldn't be pleased if something like that happened."

Rebecca swallowed hard. After a moment she said, "Of course not, sir. I would never do anything to harm Standish Dry Goods."

He grunted. "Good." As he reached for his cigar, he added, apparently casually, "You'll be home this evening, I take it?"

Rebecca lived in a small cottage in a quiet neighborhood. Every month, Standish gave her cash to pay for the rent, so there would be no bank drafts or anything else to show his connection to the place.

She nodded without meeting his eyes and said in a quiet voice, "Yes. I'll be there."

"Good. I'll probably be working late here in the office, but I might drop by there for a few minutes on my way home."

He would drop by there, all right. There was no *might* about it, and both of them knew it. Despite being perhaps a bit too softhearted for her own good, Rebecca was a smart girl.

She had chosen the right Standish, and as long as she didn't do anything foolish, Cornelius would see to it that she didn't regret her choice. But if she ever crossed him . . .

Well, he would hate to lose her services as a secretary— and otherwise. But as always, he would do what needed to be done.

For the company's good, of course.

After his father's death, Seymour had moved out of the mansion that had been the family home for as far back as he could remember. The place was just too big and rambling and empty for one man alone, even with servants there. And Seymour, being a humble young man, didn't care to have a lot of servants around anyway.

So he'd closed up the mansion and taken a room in a modest but well-kept boardinghouse, and that was where he was early that evening, packing for his trip to Texas.

He wasn't quite sure what to put in his valise. What did one pack for a trip to an untamed wilderness? He had already put in shirts and underwear and a gray tweed suit. He planned to wear the brown tweed on the train.

His eyes moved to the sample case sitting in a corner of his room. It was fully packed already with examples of every line of merchandise carried by Standish Dry Goods, Inc. Seymour wondered how many stores there might be in Sweet Apple, Texas. Enough to justify the expense of a trip like the one on which his uncle was sending him? That seemed unlikely, but perhaps there were other towns in the vicinity where he could hawk the company's wares. He could use Sweet Apple as his base of operations, he mused, and hire a buggy to travel to all the other settlements in the area.

Or perhaps he could rent a horse.

That thought made a nervous frown appear on his face. He had never been on a horse in his life, but that was how Westerners got around, wasn't it? From time to time he had read articles in *Harper's Illustrated Weekly* about the Wild West and had seen the drawings there of cowboys riding huge stallions. On occasion he had even perused a few dime novels, although they seemed too frivolous to him with their breathless, breakneck tales of gunmen and outlaws and savages and beautiful young women who seemed to be constantly in need of being rescued from one deadly peril or another. For all their luridness, Seymour had no doubt that those stories conveyed an absolutely accurate portrait of what life in the West was really like.

As he thought about that, he closed his eyes and suppressed a groan of dismay. What was he doing, going into that . . . that uncivilized milieu? He would never fit in, and his trip would be an unmitigated failure. He was sure of it.

But he couldn't refuse. Uncle Cornelius, after all, was in charge of the company. The instructions left by Seymour's father had made that clear. Seymour had no choice but to follow Cornelius's orders and make the best of the situation.

He put extra underwear in the valise, thinking that he might need it before his trip west was completed.

The soft knock on the door took him by surprise. He turned away from the bed where his open valise sat and said, "Who is it?"

The voice that answered was even more of a surprise. "Rebecca."

Seymour's eyes widened. What was *she* doing here? She had never visited him before. The very idea that she would show up now at his room was . . . well, unsettling, to say the least.

And yet a small tingle of pleasure went through Seymour at the sound of her voice. That was even *more* unsettling, he realized. He wondered briefly if he should send her away.

But he was too much of a gentleman to do that, and anyway, he didn't want to. Instead he said, "Just a moment," and picked up his coat, which he had taken off earlier. He couldn't receive a caller, especially a female one, in such an informal state. He slipped on the coat, tightened his tie, and went to the door.

Rebecca smiled at him when he opened it. "Hello, Seymour," she said. She looked past him into the room. "Getting ready for your trip, I see."

"Ah . . . yes." Seymour stood in the doorway and didn't budge. He slept in this room, after all. He couldn't very well invite a young woman into it. A young, *unmarried* woman.

"Aren't you going to ask me to come in?"

Why did she have to say that? Now Seymour's chivalry had backed him into a corner. He swallowed, nodded, and said, "Of course. Please come in."

Rebecca waited for a moment, then said, "You'll have to step back before I can, Seymour."

"Oh. Oh, yes, of course." He moved out of the doorway. She walked into the room. She was dressed as she had been at the office, only she had added a jacket and now had a small, stylish hat perched neatly on her honey-blond hair.

As she moved past him, Seymour caught a faint whiff of her perfume, and the delicate scent made his pulse beat faster.

He left the door standing wide open. That was the way his landlady would want it—she didn't really approve of her boarders having callers of the opposite sex—and that was the way Seymour wanted it, too. He believed it was always best in life to remove as many temptations to impropriety as possible.

Rebecca had a package of some sort in her hands. It was wrapped in brown paper, tied up with string, and about a foot long, six or eight inches wide, and three or four inches deep. Seymour had no idea what might be inside it.

"I brought something for you," Rebecca said as she held the package out toward him.

"What is it?" Seymour asked, making no move to take it just yet. Accepting presents from a young lady wasn't really a proper thing to do.

"Something for your trip. Something you might need in Texas."

Seymour frowned and shook his head. "I believe I already have everything I'll need. But I certainly appreciate your thoughtfulness, Miss Jimmerson—"

She shoved the package at him again, thumping it against his chest this time. "For God's sake, take it," she said.

Seymour had no choice but to do so. As he grasped the paper-wrapped package, he found that it was surprisingly heavy. He almost dropped it.

"Don't open it now," Rebecca went on. "But I want you to promise me that you'll take it with you, Seymour. This is very important."

"But . . . but what do I do with it once I get to Texas?"

"You'll know. Believe me, if you need it—and I have a feeling you will—you'll know."

He started to shake his head and press the package, whatever it was, back on her, but the look on her face stopped him. He could tell how important this was to her. Something very near to desperation was visible in her eyes.

"All right," he heard himself saying. "Whatever you wish, Miss Jimmerson."

"What I wish is that you'd call me Rebecca just once. What I wish is—" The words had come out of her quickly, but she stopped short and drew in a deep breath. "I'm sorry, Seymour. I didn't want to place you in an awkward position by coming here this evening. And I have to go. I have to be somewhere else tonight. I have . . . an engagement."

"Oh? For dinner?"

"Something like that." She reached out and touched his hand as it held the package she'd given him. Her fingers were soft and warm and the feel of her touch made his breath hiss between his teeth. She went on. "Promise me you'll take that with you and use it if you have to."

"I . . . I suppose . . ." The nearness of her made Seymour's head spin until he had trouble getting the words out.

"Promise," she said.

"I promise," he managed to say.

A smile that was sad somehow touched Rebecca's lips. "All right. Thank you." She moved closer still, came up on her toes, and brushed those lips against his cheek. "Goodbye, Seymour. And good luck."

The fact that she had kissed him shook Seymour to his core. But even though he was ashamed to admit it even to himself, he liked it. He liked it a lot. So much so that for a moment all he could do was blink his eyes and open and close his mouth. Finally he was able to say, "G-good-bye . . . Rebecca."

She turned away to leave, but paused in the doorway and

looked back at him. "One more thing, Seymour, and this is very important, too. If you see your uncle before you leave Trenton . . . don't tell him that I came here this evening."

"Well, I don't think I'll be seeing him, because the train leaves at eight twenty-seven in the morning, so I won't be going to the office, and I doubt that Uncle Cornelius will come to see me off." He was on firmer ground now. Concrete details like a train schedule always made him feel better. They weren't as nerve-wracking as things like a pounding heartbeat and the delicate scent of perfume and the warmth of a woman's hand. . . .

"You have to promise me that, too." Her tone was insistent.

"Of course. I won't say anything to Uncle Cornelius, if I should happen to see him again before I depart."

"Thank you. Good luck, Seymour."

That was the second time she had wished him luck, he thought as she departed and he closed the door behind her. He was grateful, of course. Headed for the wild frontier as he was, he would take all the luck he could get.

He would also take whatever was in the package she had left with him, since he had given her word that he would. He frowned at it as he carried it over to the bed. She hadn't made him promise that he wouldn't open it until he got to Texas, merely that he would take it along on the trip. So he gave in to his curiosity and began to untie the string holding the wrapping paper on the package.

When he got it loose, he pulled the paper away to reveal a plain wooden box with a hinged lid. The lid had a simple clasp and no lock. Seymour unfastened the clasp and raised the lid.

He gasped in surprise as he stared down at the object resting inside the box on a bed of dark blue velvet that was shaped to hold it. The light from Seymour's lamp reflected from polished, nickel-plated iron and what appeared to be hand-carved ivory plates fastened to the handle. No wonder the box was heavy, Seymour thought as his heart began to pound again, this time with fear.

Inside the box was a gun.

Chapter 8

Matt Bodine and Sam Two Wolves had been three days on the trail of the outlaw gang that had raided Buckskin when they spotted smoke rising on the southern horizon in front of them. That was one of the problems with West Texas—a fella could ride and ride and ride and not get anywhere. Everywhere was a hell of a long way from everywhere else. But now Matt and Sam appeared to be approaching civilization again.

Or at least what passed for civilization out here.

The raiders hadn't attempted to hide their tracks. That would have been impossible anyway with such a large group. With every mile that passed under their horses' hooves, the blood brothers had worried that they would come across the body of one or more of the women who had been taken prisoner back in Buckskin and carried off from the settlement. Those wolves in human form wouldn't hesitate to kill the prisoners and toss them aside like broken dolls if they tired of the women.

So far they hadn't made any such grisly discoveries, and

Matt and Sam were grateful for that. Evidently the outlaws were keeping their captives alive.

"Is that a town up there?" Matt asked as he squinted toward the distant smoke.

"I don't think so. Looks more like a fort of some sort."

Matt glanced over at Sam. "You mean an army fort?"

"No, more like a trading post. There appears to be an adobe wall around several buildings."

"You can see that much without a spyglass?" Matt asked with a frown.

"Indian have eyes like hawk," Sam said in a solemn voice.

"Indian full of shit. You don't see any better than I do, and we both know it."

A smile broke across Sam's face. "I think that's the Dutchman's place. I've never been there, but I remember hearing someone talk about it one time when we were in El Paso."

Matt cast his mind back and dredged up the same memory. "Oh, yeah. Some sort of trading post for owl-hoots, right?"

"That's right. The Rangers have tried to close it down, but they've never been able to get any hard evidence against the man who runs it."

"I think Finch said something about it one time, too." Josiah Finch was a Texas Ranger, small in stature but big in fighting spirit. Matt and Sam had pitched in to help him out on a couple of occasions.

"That's right," Sam agreed. "Honest folks have learned to steer clear of the place and never go there."

"But we're goin', right?"

Sam's smile widened into a grin. "The trail those raiders left leads straight there, looks like."

"That answers my question then." Matt heeled his

mount into a trot. It was possible that the men they were after were still holed up at the Dutchman's, and he was eager to find out.

Of course, the question remained—how could he and Sam by themselves take on two dozen or more vicious outlaws?

They would burn that bridge when they came to it, Matt reckoned.

As they neared the place, he saw that the description Sam had remembered was correct. A thick adobe wall about ten feet tall surrounded a compound containing half-a-dozen buildings. One large building housed the trading post itself, Matt supposed, and scattered around it were smaller structures. A wooden watchtower rose in one corner, next to the wall.

Beyond the trading post, the ground fell away, dropping some fifty or sixty feet to another plain. In some places, the slope was fairly steep but manageable; in others, the drop was almost sheer. It was as if, at some point in the dim, distant past, the land to the south and east of the jagged escarpment had dropped suddenly. Either that, or the land to the north and west had been thrust upward fifty or sixty feet by some geologic upheaval. Whatever the cause, that distinct difference in level had been left behind, and the rugged rim of the escarpment had caused people to call it the Cap Rock. The levelness of the terrain on both sides meant that a person could see for twenty miles or more from up here.

There wasn't much to see, of course. A lot of flat, mostly sandy land dotted with scrub brush, hardy clumps of grass, and the occasional mesquite tree.

Sam waved a hand at the vast sweep of territory before

them and said, "All of that used to be covered with water, you know."

"Yeah?" Matt said. "When was that? I don't recall hearin' anything about it."

"Millions of years ago. The Gulf of Mexico reached all the way up here. It was on this side of the Cap Rock, too, but whatever caused the escarpment to form caused the sea to drain, too. But that's why you can dig down in the ground and find the fossilized remains of fish and other sea creatures the likes of which no human eye has ever seen, at least not in these parts."

"Learned about that in school, did you?"

"That's right. I also learned about the great migratory drifts that took place in those ancient eras, when entire races of people would move from one part of the earth to another, when the whole world shook and mountains rose and fell and continents were formed and broken and then re-formed. When this was an ocean, there may have been races of people who sailed on it that are completely forgotten now, entire civilizations that vanished without a trace. We just don't know."

"Well, that's mighty interestin'," Matt said. "Learned a whole heap in school, didn't you?"

"I took an extensive course of study," Sam said.

Matt nodded toward the trading post, which was now only about fifty yards away. "Anything in those books about what to do when folks start pointin' guns at you?"

Sam frowned as he saw that his blood brother was right. Several men, who were evidently standing on parapets inside the adobe wall of the compound, were pointing rifles at them.

Matt and Sam kept riding toward the heavy wooden gates, leading the two pack animals and the two extra saddle horses behind them. The gates swung open. As Matt and Sam rode in, they were aware of the men on the parapet tracking them with the rifles. More men were waiting for them on the ground inside, also armed with rifles.

The gates swung shut behind them, closing with a ponderous crash. If this was a trap, it wouldn't be easy fighting their way out.

As they reined to a halt in front of the trading post's porch with its vine-covered roof, Matt said in a low voice, "If those outlaws are still here, chances are they won't recognize us. The only ones who got a good look at us are dead."

Sam's head moved in a barely visible nod. "So we'll pretend to be on the dodge ourselves until we get the lay of the land?"

"Yeah."

A big man came out of the building and pushed through the vines that dangled from the edge of the porch roof. He was bald and had a bushy blond beard. He was also the fattest hombre Matt and Sam had seen for quite a while. Rolls of fat bulged the white shirt and brown leather vest he wore.

"Gentlemen," he said in a deep voice that contained a trace of an accent, "welcome to the Dutchman's. I am Hendrick Van Goort."

"Name's Smith," Matt said as he returned Van Goort's nod. He jerked a thumb at Sam. "This here's Jones."

"Ah, I see. Many of your relatives have stopped here, yah? I have only one question before you dismount and avail yourselves of my hospitality."

"What's that?" Sam asked.

"You are not lawmen?"

"Us? Lawmen?" Matt let out a laugh. "Not hardly,

mister." He was glad that he and Sam had refused to take those deputy badges that had been offered to them back in Buckskin. Chances are, they and their gear would be searched for any such telltale tin stars.

"You understand, of course, that I cannot simply take your word for this."

Sam waved a hand in a casual gesture. "Feel free to look through our saddlebags. You won't find any badges or anything else saying that we're lawmen."

"All right then," Van Goort said. "Step down and we shall see."

As Matt and Sam dismounted, the Dutchman motioned to several of his guards. The men came forward and pawed through the saddlebags and the supplies lashed to the pack-horses, while the rest of the guards continued to cover Matt and Sam. Once that search was done, Van Goort's men checked the pockets of the two newcomers, too. Matt's eyes narrowed in anger, but he put up with the irritation.

Finally, one of the men nodded to Van Goort, and the Dutchman broke into a gleaming smile. "Come in, gentlemen, come in. We have food and drink and almost anything else you may desire."

"What about women?" Matt asked.

"Of course. Most of them have Indian blood . . ." Van Goort looked at Sam. "But I would venture to guess that so do you, my young friend."

Sam didn't say anything. As they went inside the cool, shadowy interior of the trading post, Matt said to Van Goort, "I was talkin' more about white women." He thought it was possible the outlaws could have left one or more of the prisoners from Buckskin here.

Van Goort tugged at his beard. Matt saw greed warring with caution in the man's pale blue eyes. Greed won out, and the Dutchman said, "As a matter of fact, I do have several white women staying here at the moment who might be interested in some male companionship. If you'd like to see them . . . ?"

"Later," Sam said, his tone curt. "Right now I want a beer and some grub more than anything else."

"Yeah, me, too," Matt said, following his blood brother's lead. "But maybe we'll take you up on the other later."

"Of course. Have a seat at one of the tables. We have beans and stew and tortillas. Someone will bring the food to you, along with the beers."

"Much obliged," Sam said.

He and Matt sat down at a table in the corner, picking one so that they could both sit with their backs to a wall, as men on the run from trouble would habitually do. They seemed to be the only customers at the moment. Matt had taken a look at the corral as they came in and hadn't seen an abundance of horses there. It was starting to appear that the outlaws who had raided Buckskin were no longer here. They had probably stopped for a night or two and then moved on.

"Don't rush things," Sam said in a low voice as he and Matt waited for their food and beer. "You can't just waltz right into a place like this and start asking suspicious questions."

"If we really were hardcases on the dodge, wouldn't it look more suspicious if we *didn't* want any women?" Matt countered.

"Just don't rush it, that's all I'm saying. Van Goort probably has at least ten or twelve men working for him."

"Better odds than what we thought they might be," Matt pointed out with a smile.

"True. But let's see if we can get out of here *without* a big fight."

"What's the fun in that?" Matt muttered as a couple of Indian women appeared carrying bowls of stew, plates piled high with beans and tortillas, and mugs of beer. They set the food on the table, and the blood brothers dug in with genuinely hearty appetites.

Van Goort came into the trading post, approached the table, and nodded to Matt and Sam. "My men are caring for your animals," he said.

And searching our gear more thoroughly this time, Matt thought.

Sam waved a hand at one of the empty chairs. "Would you care to join us, sir?"

"I believe I will." Van Goort sat down on the chair, which creaked under his weight. He flipped a pudgy hand at the Indian woman behind the bar. She brought a huge mug of beer over to him. Foam overflowed the top and dripped down the sides. The Dutchman took a big swallow and then used the back of his other hand to wipe away the foam that clung to his mustache. He smiled at Matt and Sam and said, "I like to get to know my visitors. So, Mr. Smith, Mr. Jones, what brings you to my trading post?"

Sam scooped some beans with a rolled-up tortilla, took a bite, chewed, swallowed. "We're here for our health. We like the climate."

"Yeah," Matt agreed. "It's not too hot here."

Van Goort laughed. "Most people would say that West Texas is hotter than the hinges of hell itself, yah?"

"Well," Matt allowed, "there's hot . . . and then there's *hot.*"

"I take your meaning, young sir. Are the Rangers after you?"

Sam frowned. "Most folks on the frontier make a habit of not asking such personal questions."

"Ah, yes, but I was not raised here, my friend. And I have a stake in knowing such things. The Rangers would like nothing better than to close my business down and arrest me for giving aid and comfort to fugitives they seek."

Matt shook his head. "The Rangers aren't after us." That much was true at least.

"In that case, you are welcome to avail yourselves of my hospitality for as long as you wish . . . and as long as you can pay." Van Goort beamed at them. "Now, since you appear to be almost finished with your meal, shall I send those women down?"

Matt and Sam glanced at each other, then shrugged and nodded. The Dutchman seemed to have accepted them as being owlhoots. They could risk taking a look at the women now. If they turned out to be the prisoners who'd been taken from Buckskin, Matt thought it would be a good idea to go ahead and pay for a couple of them.

Not that he and Sam would actually bed down with them. But they needed a chance to talk to the captives in private, find out exactly what the situation was here at the trading post, and make some plans to get the women out of the Dutchman's clutches. Matt could tell by looking at Sam that his blood brother had the same thoughts in mind. They had ridden together for so long, been through so much danger together, that their brains tended to work the same way.

Van Goort heaved his bulk out of the chair and waddled over to the bar. He spoke to the woman there, who came out from behind the bar and climbed a narrow set of stairs to the trading post's second floor. She returned a few moments later, and down the stairs behind her trailed several women, followed by a hard-faced guard with a rifle.

The women's clothing was tattered and torn, as if it had been through a lot. But their faces showed that hardship even more. They had the cringing, fearful look of whipped dogs, Matt thought, and furious anger welled up inside him as he saw what had been done to them. No doubt they had been assaulted again and again until their senses—and their souls—were numb with horror.

The women weren't tied or chained in any way that Matt could see. They didn't have to be restrained, because their spirits were broken.

Van Goort stepped away from the bar and held out a hand to indicate the women. "White, as you requested," he said to Matt and Sam. "Take your pick, gentlemen. The price will be a bit higher, but well worth it, I assure you."

Matt managed to put a smile on his face despite the rage he felt. Sam did likewise. They stood up and approached the women. Six in all, the youngest about fifteen or six-teen, the oldest in her thirties. Matt nodded toward a woman with tangled blond hair who appeared to be about twenty-five.

"I'll take her."

The Indian woman grasped the blonde's arm and shoved her toward Matt. He patted her shoulder as she stood in front of him, head bowed. He tried to make the gesture re-assuring, but she flinched. He couldn't blame her for that.

Sam selected the next-to-the-oldest woman, a brunette. Her eyes flashed briefly as the Indian woman pushed her toward Sam, a spark of defiance that was quickly extin-guished by a thump to the head from the heavyset Indian woman. Matt saw the muscle jumping a little in Sam's jaw, and knew that Sam was having trouble controlling his anger. Matt felt the same way himself.

But they had to bide their time. Gunplay now wouldn't solve anything.

"Their rooms are at the top of the stairs, gentlemen," Van Goort said. "Please, enjoy yourselves."

Matt took the blonde's arm. "We intend to," he assured Van Goort.

That was true. One way or another, he and Sam were going to rescue these women and settle the score with the Dutchman. That would likely mean powder smoke, flame, and hot lead.

And when that moment came, the Brothers of the Wolf were going to enjoy the hell out of it.

Chapter 9

"What's your name?" Matt asked when he and the woman were alone in a small room on the second floor of the trading post. The room had nothing in it but a narrow bed with a sagging mattress and one rickety-looking chair. A candle sitting on a shelf cast a wavering glow that was the only illumination.

The blonde didn't answer. She kept her eyes downcast and reached for the buttons of her dress.

Matt stopped her. "No," he said as he touched her hand. "You don't have to do that."

She spoke at last, in a thin voice. "I . . . I'll do anything you want, mister."

"Listen to me." Matt put his hand under her chin and tipped her head up until she had no choice but to look at him. He had to get through the woman underneath those dull, uncaring eyes. "My name is Matt Bodine. The folks back in Buckskin sent me to help you."

For a second, she showed no reaction. Then, suddenly, Matt saw something in her eyes that hadn't been there before.

Hope.

"B-Buckskin?" she whispered. "You're from . . . Buckskin?"

Matt nodded. "Yes, ma'am. I've come to get you out of here."

"Oh, my God . . ."

She sagged against him as if every muscle in her body had gone limp all at once. Matt had no choice but to put his arms around her and hold her up. She buried her face against his chest and began to sob in relief.

"I . . . I prayed that someone would come . . . for such a long time . . . and then . . . I gave up."

Somewhat awkwardly, Matt patted her on the back and tried to comfort her. He wasn't at his best with crying women. He suspected that most hombres weren't. But he knew somehow that the best thing he could do now was to just be patient.

After a while, the blonde seemed to cry herself out. She lifted her head, sniffled, and wiped the back of her hand across her nose in an unself-conscious gesture.

"You said your name is Bodine?"

"Yes, ma'am. Matt Bodine."

"I'm Alice Fletcher." Even though her eyes had lost the dull, uncaring look, they were still filled with worry. "What are you going to do? That awful man . . . that Van Goort . . . he has a lot of gunmen working for him. . . ."

"Gunmen are something my brother and I have experience handlin', ma'am."

"Your brother? There's more than one of you here?"

"Blood brother actually. Name of Sam Two Wolves. He's in another of the rooms up here, talkin' to one of the other women like I'm talkin' to you. Nice-lookin' woman a little older than you, with brown hair."

"That's Cara Wilson. The poor dear. She's married. So are Mrs. Sloan and Mrs. Lowell and Eunice Padgett. At least Billie McKay and I don't have to worry about . . . about going back home and facing husbands after we've been so . . . defiled."

Matt shook his head. "Don't you even think about that right now, ma'am. What happened isn't your fault. Not hardly. You just had some mighty bad luck, that's all. I'm sure folks back in Buckskin will understand that."

Even as he spoke, he knew that wasn't necessarily true. Not for nothing did folks say that a woman who was taken against her will was ruined. That was the way most people saw it. Too often Matt had heard stories about white women who were rescued from being held captive by the Indians, only to be shunned because they'd been forced to lay with their captors. Some of those unfortunates had even been known to take their own lives because of the shame they were made to feel.

The real shame, the way Matt saw it, was that people didn't have more sense.

To maybe get Alice Fletcher's mind off that, and because he needed the information, he asked, "What happened to the men who brought you here? Are they still around?"

She shook her head. "They left a couple of days ago. Van Goort struck some sort of deal with their leader. He was supposed to return us to Buckskin, I think, in exchange for some ransom money. But he . . . he decided to put us to work for a while first. That way he could . . . make the most out of us, he said."

Matt's eyes narrowed. He was looking forward to the showdown with Van Goort.

"Do you know where those outlaws were headed?"

Alice shook her head. "I have no idea."

"What about their leader? You know who he was?"

"I . . . I heard his name mentioned. I think it was Mallory. The first name was odd. Deuce?"

Matt nodded. "Deuce Mallory. That's right. I've heard of him but never crossed trails with him. He's supposed to be as mean as a skunk, and the men who ride with him are just as bad."

A shudder ran through Alice's slender frame. "I can testify to that, Mr. Bodine. They're devils, each and every one of them. Devils." She looked up. "You're not going after them, are you?"

"Sam and I sort of promised the folks back in Buckskin that we'd try to even the score for them."

"But there are too many outlaws! You wouldn't have a chance against them!"

"Sam and I are used to long odds," he told her. "Anyway, that's gonna have to wait until we make sure that you and the other ladies are safe."

"You'll take us back to Buckskin?"

Matt hesitated. Turning around and taking the women all the way back to Buckskin would put him and Sam more than a week behind the outlaws. It might still be possible to pick up the trail after that, but the chore would be more difficult. Still, what else could they do? Even after the women were freed from the Dutchman, they couldn't be left alone to fend for themselves and get back home on their own. This was a problem, but Matt didn't see any other solution to it.

"We'll get you home," he promised Alice Fletcher. What else could he say?

She hugged him. "Thank you, Mr. Bodine."

He thought about telling her to call him Matt, but decided that under the circumstances it probably wouldn't be a very good idea. After everything she had gone through, she probably wouldn't want to have anything to do with any gents for a long time.

Something seemed to occur to Alice. She looked up at him and said, "A couple of the outlaws are still here."

Matt's interest quickened. "They are? How come they didn't go with the others?"

"Because they're both hurt. They got in some sort of fight. One of them was shot in the shoulder, and the other has a broken leg. Mallory left them behind to recuperate."

Matt rubbed his jaw as he frowned in thought. "I wonder if they're supposed to meet up with the rest of the gang later."

"I wouldn't know about that."

"I reckon there's a good chance they'd know where Mallory was headed anyway."

"You and your . . . blood brother . . . are still going to go after them?"

"If we can," Matt said. "Right now, though, the main thing is to make sure all of you ladies are safe. You don't know for sure how many men the Dutchman has around here?"

"I've seen . . . eight or nine of them, I think. And there are half-a-dozen Indian women. Van Goort calls several of them his wives. They're as bad as the men. They . . . they beat us and threaten to torture us."

"I reckon the men are scattered all around the compound, too." Matt mentioned the guards who had been on the walls when he and Sam rode in.

"I don't know. We've been kept inside ever since we got here."

What they needed to do, Matt reflected, was get Van Goort and all of his men in one place. That way maybe he and Sam could get the drop on the whole bunch at once. There had to be a way to do that . . .

An idea flickered to life in his head.

"Are all of you kept in the same room?" he asked.

Alice nodded. "That's right. We're locked in together, and one of Van Goort's men is always right outside the door."

"When you get back in there, tell the others who Sam and I are and why we're here. But make sure they understand that they can't act any different than they've been actin'. When you leave this room, you've got to look like you've given up hope, and you have to stay that way."

"So Van Goort won't get the idea that something's wrong."

"That's right. Can you do that?"

She nodded again. "If it means getting out of here, I can."

"All right. I reckon we've been in here long enough to have—I mean—"

Alice summoned up a smile. "It's all right. I know what you mean. And you're right." She took a deep breath. As she let it out, the light in her eyes died again. Her face took on a look of hopeless despair. Matt had to admit that she was putting on a good act. Alice looked as broken in spirit and defeated as she had when they first came in here.

He figured Sam had had the same talk with the women he'd picked out. Cara Wilson was her name, Matt recalled. What he needed now was a chance to talk privately with Sam and explain his idea.

He went to the door and opened it, made a curt gesture for Alice to come out. She followed him meekly. The hard-faced guard lounged nearby with one shoulder propped against the wall. He straightened as Matt and the blonde emerged from the squalid little room. A leering grin appeared on his face.

"Was she worth it, mister?"

"Every penny," Matt said.

Sam came downstairs a few minutes after Matt did. He was alone, too, and Matt knew that the prisoners had all been sequestered again. As Sam sat down at the table, Matt asked in a voice loud enough to be heard at the bar, "How was it, partner?"

"Just fine," Sam replied. "I got exactly what I needed."

Matt nodded, knowing what Sam meant. The talk Sam had had with Cara Wilson had gone well. Quietly, so that only Sam could hear, Matt asked, "Did you tell her to keep actin' the same for now?"

"Yeah," Sam breathed. "She said the Dutchman's got nine or ten hardcases working for him, and that two of the gang that hit Buckskin are still here."

"Yeah, they're laid up because of a fight. We'll have to deal with them, too. But we need to take at least one of them alive."

"So we can find out where the rest of the gang was headed?" Sam guessed.

Matt nodded. "That's right. You have any ideas about how to handle Van Goort and his men?"

"Not yet."

"Well, it just so happens that I do," Matt said with a smile. He pushed his chair back. "Let's go check on our horses."

"Sure." Sam got to his feet, too, and they started for the front door of the trading post.

Van Goort came in before they reached the entrance. "Leaving already, gentlemen?"

"Not hardly," Matt replied without hesitation. "Just thought we'd go take a look at our horses."

"They are in the corral and have been well cared for, I assure you."

"I don't doubt that for a second. But Mr., uh, Jones and I are right fond of the critters. They've carried us out of some mighty tight spots, if you know what I mean."

"Of course. Feel free to come and go as you please." Van Goort laughed. "You are not prisoners here, after all."

Matt and Sam nodded and went on out as the Dutchman stepped aside. As they strolled toward the barn and the corral next to it, Sam asked, "You reckon he's suspicious?"

"Fella like that, running a place like this . . . I'd bet a hat he's suspicious all the time, of just about everybody."

"What's that idea you had?"

"We set the barn on fire," Matt said. "Van Goort and everybody else goes runnin' to put it out. That's when we get the drop on them, while they're all together and not paying any attention to us."

Sam frowned. "The barn's made out of adobe. I don't think it's going to burn."

"Everything that's inside it will, though, especially any hay stored in there."

Sam thought about it for a moment and then nodded. "That might work, especially if we wait until after dark to make our move. Nothing like a big fire in the night to attract a lot of attention."

"Yeah, that's what I thought."

"Say we manage to disarm Van Goort and his men. What then?"

"Stampede their horses, drive 'em out of here, and finish burnin' the place down like the hellhole it is. Then we take the women back to Buckskin."

"That's going to put us a long way behind the rest of the gang," Sam pointed out.

"Can't be helped."

"No, I suppose not." Sam paused. "You know, Van Goort's probably going to put up a fight."

Matt's face was grim as he nodded. "Yeah, I know. After seeing those women and talkin' to the one who was with me, I almost hope he does. I know right where my first bullet's goin'."

They stopped at the corral and looked at their horses. The animals did indeed appear to have been well cared for, as Van Goort had said. The sun was lowering in the western sky, so they had another couple of hours to wait until full darkness had fallen. After that one of them could slip out to the barn and start the blaze that was calculated to draw the Dutchmen and his guards out of the trading post. Whoever stayed inside would have to deal with the Indian women, then join the other blood brother to corral Van Goort and his bunch of gunnies.

They strolled back to the trading post and went inside, figuring to nurse a couple of beers while they killed the time. Van Goort was nowhere in sight. One of the Indian women was behind the bar, while a man the blood brothers hadn't seen before sat at one of the tables playing solitaire with a deck of greasy cards. The man's lower left leg was splinted and heavily bandaged and propped up on another chair as he laid out the cards and took an occasional pull on a bottle of whiskey.

That would be the man Alice Fletcher had mentioned, Matt thought, the one who had broken his leg in a scuffle. One of Deuce Mallory's gang.

Knowing that he was this close to a man who had taken part in the raid on Buckskin made Matt want to pull one of his Colts and ventilate the son of a bitch. No telling how many innocent people the man with the broken leg had gunned down back in the settlement. It was a safe bet that he had participated in the assaults on the female prisoners, too.

A bullet was too good for that bastard. He deserved to die at the end of a rope.

Unfortunately, out here on the edge of the Cap Rock, the only law was what men packed in their holsters. When the time came, Matt or Sam might have to shoot that fella. Either of them would do it without hesitation, and they wouldn't lose any sleep over it either.

Patience had never been Matt Bodine's strong suit. Whenever he had to wait for something, time seemed to drag. That was certainly the case here.

But eventually the sun went down and night settled over West Texas. The other man who had been left behind by the gang had come downstairs and joined his fellow owl-hoot. This hombre's shoulder was bandaged and his left arm rode in a sling. Both of the outlaws had glanced at Matt and Sam from time to time, but didn't seem to recognize them or pay much attention to them. No other hardcases had ridden in during the afternoon, which was a good thing. Matt and Sam already faced a big enough challenge without the odds against them increasing even more.

Van Goort came in and lit several lamps in the barroom. He called over to Matt and Sam, "You want some supper, my friends, yah?"

"That'd be fine," Matt replied. "Much obliged."

One of the Indian women went upstairs carrying a pot of stew. Matt supposed that would be supper for the prisoners. He and Sam gave each other barely discernible nods. They had waited long enough. It was time to put their plan into action.

Sam stood up and stretched. "Think I'll go check on the horses again before I eat," he announced. Matt nodded, but made no move to get up. It didn't really matter who set the fire and who remained inside. Each would face his own set of dangers.

Van Goort seemed to pay no attention as Sam went out, but Matt figured that wasn't really the case. The Dutchman struck him as a man who didn't miss much. But Van Goort had no reason to suspect them of wanting to cause trouble. The man's business was providing sanctuary for outlaws, and they had given him no reason to think they were anything else.

Time continued to slip by with maddening slowness after Sam left. Matt took a sip of his beer. It had gone flat and hadn't been that good to start with.

Then what he had been waiting for happened. A strident shout of alarm came from outside.

"Fire! The barn's on fire!"

Chapter 10

Sam Two Wolves could see almost as well in the dark as a cat. A few minutes earlier, as he'd ambled across the courtyard inside the compound toward the barn and the corral, he had seen tiny pinpoints of orange light, the glowing ends of quirlies being smoked, that marked the positions of the guards on the parapet near the gates. The parapet ran all the way around inside the wall, and Sam figured the Dutchman had sentries posted on all four sides of the compound. Plus there was a lookout in that watchtower, one of the Indian women. The blood brothers had spotted her earlier when they were outside.

A long, low adobe building to Sam's left was probably the bunkhouse where the men who worked for Van Goort lived. A couple of the hardcases lounged just outside the door, sitting on stools and passing a jug back and forth. Sam counted up in his head. He had most, if not all, of the guards located and accounted for.

He paused at the corral fence and gave a low whistle. His saddle horse came over to him and nuzzled his outstretched hand. Sam scratched the horse's nose and talked to him in a low voice for several minutes. That would be enough to lull any of the guards who might be watching him into ignoring him. When he judged it to be safe, he started edging along the corral fence, knowing that his shape would blend in with the dark bulks of the horses as they milled around inside the enclosure.

When he reached the corner of the barn, he slid along the wall to the double doors, one of which was already partly open. The gap was wide enough for Sam to be able to duck through it. He found himself in near-total darkness, but his eyes adjusted even more and after a few moments, he was able to make his way around, guided by the faint starlight that came through the open door and a window up in the hayloft.

That loft was his destination. He found the ladder and climbed it. When he reached the top he took a match from his pocket, cupped his other hand around it, and snapped it into life with his thumbnail. His hand shielded the glare so that it couldn't be seen from outside. At least he hoped that was the case. He didn't want the Dutchman's guards to notice the fire too soon, so that he was trapped in here before he could get out.

The light from the match showed Sam the pile of hay on one side of the loft. He went over to it, kicked at it until he had a trail of hay that led almost to the ladder. The match burned down almost to his fingers, so he had to shake it out. He climbed down the ladder until only his head and shoulders were above the level of the loft. Then he lit another match and reached over to drop it at the end of the trail of hay. The dry stuff caught instantly and began to burn toward the much bigger pile.

Sam hurried down the ladder. Above him, the glare of flames grew brighter and brighter against the ceiling of the barn as the fire spread. Suddenly, the hay pile caught with a *whoosh!* and the burst of flame lit up the whole barn. Sam let go of the ladder and dropped the remaining few feet. Landing lithely, he ran toward the rear door of the barn, which opened out into the corral. As he passed the stalls, he glanced into each one to make sure it was empty. He didn't want any horses getting trapped in the blaze. The stalls were unoccupied. All the horses were outside in the corral.

Glad of that, Sam ducked through the door into the corral himself. The horses had caught whiffs of the smoke now curling from the hayloft and were spooked by it instinctively. They began milling around even more. The presence of a strange human in their midst didn't help calm them down any.

Sam crouched behind a water trough near the fence as the two men who'd been drinking outside the bunkhouse earlier came over to the corral.

"What the hell's wrong with those horses?" one of the hardcases asked.

"Beats me," the other man replied. "Somethin's sure got 'em spooked. Maybe—" The man stopped short, then exclaimed, "Look up at the hayloft!"

The other man must have looked, because a second later he bellowed, "Fire! The barn's on fire!"

The two men were only a few yards from Sam. He could have gunned them down from his hiding place with no trouble. They would have died without having any idea what was going on.

Cold-blooded murder wasn't in Sam's nature, though, even when his enemies were evil men who didn't really deserve such consideration. But he had a practical reason for holding his fire, too. Shots would warn the other men in the bunkhouse, inside the trading post, and on the parapets that something else was going on besides a mere fire. Sam and Matt wanted all of them together before they sprang the trap.

So Sam Two Wolves waited tensely, crouched behind the water trough in deep shadow as the crackle of flames from the barn grew louder.

As the shout came from outside, Van Goort whirled away from the bar, moving fast for a man of his ungainly bulk. The wounded outlaw shot to his feet, but the one with the broken leg stayed where he was.

Matt figured he'd better get up, too, so the others wouldn't get suspicious of him just yet. He followed Van Goort and the owlhoot to the door of the trading post.

The Dutchman yelled what was probably a curse in his native tongue, then turned his head and called over his shoulder, "Everyone out to the barn! We must put the fire out!"

The Indian woman hurried from behind the bar, and three more women, all of them breeds, came running down the stairs. Those were the soiled doves who regularly worked for Van Goort, Matt supposed. The prisoners were still locked up. The man who had been guarding them ran down the stairs behind the whores. Fire trumped just about every other concern on the frontier.

Matt hesitated just enough to let the others rush out ahead of him without being too obvious about it. They streamed across the courtyard in the Dutchman's wake. As soon as Matt was alone in the trading post with the outlaw whose leg was broken, he turned and strode toward the table where the man sat.

"Hey," the owlhoot said, "ain't you gonna help 'em fight that fire?"

"Nope," Matt said. With the speed that had made him one of the most respected—and feared—gunfighters on the frontier, he drew his right-hand Colt and walloped the outlaw with it, laying the barrel alongside the man's head and driving him out of the chair where he sat. The outlaw sprawled on the floor next to the table, out cold.

Moving quickly, Matt holstered his revolver and plucked a Winchester from a rack on the wall. He took a box of cartridges from a nearby shelf and thumbed the rounds into the rifle's loading gate until the fifteen-shot magazine was full.

Then, carrying the Winchester, he stepped onto the trading post's porch and pushed through the hanging vines. Outside, men were running back and forth from the barn to the well, bringing back buckets of water that they flung on the raging flames. The blaze had spread quickly. Great tongues of fire licked out the barn's doors.

Matt didn't know where Sam was, but he was willing to bet that his blood brother was somewhere close by. For a second, worry tickled the back of Matt's brain. What if Sam hadn't been able to get out of the barn before the flames spread? What if the fire had gotten out of control faster than Sam anticipated? He might be trapped in that inferno.

The worry was short-lived. For one thing, Sam was too smart to let something like that happen, and for another, Sam's voice suddenly rang out from the corral in a powerful shout.

"Everybody freeze and drop your guns! You're covered!"

Just in front of the porch, Matt levered a round into the Winchester's firing chamber and brought the rifle to his shoulder. "Do it!" he called. "I'll ventilate the first man who tries anything!"

The Dutchman dropped the bucket he was holding. Water splashed over his feet, but he didn't seem to notice it. Gaping in shock, he turned first toward the corral and then toward the trading post. Several of the other men were looking back and forth, too, obviously confused.

Van Goort's confusion didn't last long. "Kill them!" he screamed. "Kill them both!"

Some of the guards hesitated, but others instinctively followed Van Goort's orders and clawed for their guns as they dropped the buckets. Coolly, Matt lined his sights on one of the men trying to draw, and fired as the hardcase's gun cleared leather. The slug from the Winchester plowed into the man's chest and drove him backward off his feet.

At the same time, gun flame lanced from the darkness of the corral. That would be Sam, Matt thought as he worked the rifle's lever again and shifted his aim. As Sam's Colt barked twice, another of the Dutchman's guards spun off his feet.

One of the gunmen got his iron out and triggered a shot that whistled past Matt's ear. Matt returned the fire, and in the light of the burning barn saw the man double over and clutch his belly where the bullet had ripped into him. He pitched forward on his face.

The glare from the flames made Van Goort's men good targets. Matt and Sam each dropped another man before heavy fire from the remaining guards forced Matt to dive back onto the porch. He rolled behind some rocking chairs that sat there, and ended up on his belly. Splinters from the chairs rained down around him as bullets chewed into the furniture. Matt slammed three more shots from the Winchester as fast as he could work the lever, and saw two guards go down.

Sam was still firing from the corral. Another of Van

Goort's men stumbled, fell to his knees, and then toppled over on his side. The deadly accuracy of Matt and Sam had accounted for more than half of the Dutchman's guards. Van Goort suddenly thrust his arms in the air and screamed, "Hold your fire! Hold your fire! We surrender!"

"Throw down your guns!" Matt shouted.

Van Goort did so, and the men who worked for him followed suit. The Indian women put their hands in the air as well. The fight appeared to be over.

Matt stood up and stepped off the porch again. Sam came to the corral fence and bent to duck between the rails. Both of the blood brothers still held their guns ready to fire at an instant's notice.

A shot suddenly blasted from the watchtower. Matt's hat flew from his head. Sam pivoted smoothly, angled his Colt up, and fired in less than the blink of an eye. Matt was the faster of the two, but not by much.

Sam's shot was rewarded by a screech of pain. A rifle fell from the watchtower and landed on the ground at the structure's base.

"Blast it!" Sam burst out. "I just shot a woman!"

Matt gestured with the barrel of his rifle, herding the Dutchman and the remaining guards together in a compact knot so he could cover them without any trouble. "Go check it out," he told Sam, "but be careful."

Sam nodded and trotted over to the ladder leading up to the partially enclosed platform atop the tower. He holstered his revolver and began to climb. Matt couldn't watch him, because he had to keep his attention focused on the men and women he had just taken prisoner. One of them might still try something.

A moment later, he heard Sam's startled exclamation;

then Sam went, "Owww!" The meaty thud of a fist against flesh sounded.

"Sam!" Matt called. "Are you all right?"

"Yeah." Relief flooded through Matt as he heard his blood brother's voice. "She was waiting for me with a knife and tried to stab me, but all I got was a little scratch. I had to knock her out, though. I hate hitting a woman."

"Better than letting her carve your gizzard out," Matt replied. To the prisoners, he went on. "Move away from those guns you dropped."

"What about my barn?" Van Goort asked. "It's going to be destroyed!"

"I wouldn't go lookin' for a lot of sympathy, mister," Matt snapped. "Not the way you were holdin' those women captive and makin' 'em whore for you."

Van Goort's round, fleshy face was set in lines of fury. "You lied to me! You are lawmen, yah?"

"No, we're not lawmen. But our names aren't Smith and Jones either. I'm Matt Bodine, and that's my brother Sam Two Wolves."

The names of the blood brothers were well known all across the West. Also known was the fact that they hated outlaws and bad hombres of all stripes. The nervous looks on the faces of several of the guards testified that they knew they were lucky to still be alive. They wouldn't want to push their luck any further than they already had by making enemies of the notorious Bodine and Two Wolves.

Matt herded the prisoners into a small stone building that was used as a smokehouse. The thick walls, heavy door, and lack of windows insured that it wouldn't be easy for them to get out of there, especially with the beam that could be dropped in a couple of brackets across the door to bar it closed. Evidently, the building had been used to lock up prisoners on occasion in the past.

"Go let those women on the second floor loose," Matt suggested to Sam, who had climbed down from the watchtower with the unconscious form of the lookout over his shoulder. "I'll check the bodies of the ones we shot."

Sam nodded agreement and hurried into the trading post. Carefully, Matt made sure the men they had downed earlier were really dead. All of them were, which came as no surprise to Matt. He and Sam had been shooting to kill.

One of the dead men, Matt noted with a grimace, had his arm in a sling. During the fracas, there hadn't been time to shoot to wound. This man was one of the outlaws, one of the leads they had to the gang that had raided Buckskin. Matt hoped he hadn't hit the fella with the broken leg hard enough to bust his skull open.

That didn't prove to be the case, Sam reported when he came outside again, trailed by the former prisoners. The women from Buckskin were all laughing and sobbing with relief at being freed. Likely they still faced a lot of hard times, considering what had happened to them, but at least they were alive and no longer being held captive.

"Let's wet down the other buildings, just to make sure the fire doesn't spread," Sam suggested.

Matt nodded. "Yeah. Then we'll have a little talk with that fella inside."

The tone of his voice indicated that the conversation might not be a pleasant one. That would all depend on just how helpful the hombre wanted to be.

Alice Fletcher, Cara Wilson, and the other women from Buckskin were more than happy to pitch in and help, carrying buckets of water from the well to throw on the other buildings in the compound. They let the fire go ahead and burn in the barn, until the place was gutted inside. Since the adobe walls wouldn't burn, the flames began to die out once most of the wood and straw inside was consumed.

Matt and Sam left the women to keep an eye on the dwindling fire, and went inside the trading post. The owl-hoot with the broken leg was still unconscious, although he had begun to stir around a mite. A groan came from his lips as the blood brothers walked over to where he lay on the floor. Matt saw that Sam had taken the time earlier to use the man's belt and tie his hands together behind his back.

"I didn't think he was going anywhere," Sam commented, "but I wanted to make sure he couldn't use his crutches."

"Smart thinkin'." Matt hunkered on his heels next to the man and lightly slapped his cheeks, back and forth. "Wake up, mister. Time we had a talk."

The outlaw came around under Matt's prodding. He blinked in fear, stared up at Matt and Sam, and asked, "Wh-who are you fellas? What do you want?"

"My friend here is Matt Bodine," Sam said.

Matt jerked a thumb over his shoulder at Sam. "And he's Sam Two Wolves."

The way the owlhoot swallowed hard told them that he had heard of them.

"What's your name?" Matt asked.

"D-Dave. Dave Ash."

"Well, I tell you, Dave," Matt drawled as he slipped one of his guns out of its holster. "We know you were ridin' with Deuce Mallory and his gang when they hit Buckskin, a couple of days north of here. There's no point in you tryin' to deny it. That'd just be a waste of your breath and our time."

Sam knelt on the other side of Dave Ash and drew a

hunting knife from its sheath at his waist. Lamplight gleamed on the razor-sharp blade as he turned it from side to side. "My father was a Cheyenne war chief," he said. "The Cheyenne aren't like the Apaches or the Comanches. We don't torture folks for the fun of it." Sam lowered the knife until the tip rested just under Ash's chin. "We torture folks for a reason."

"I wouldn't give him a reason if I was you," Matt advised.

Ash blinked again and quavered, "Wh-what do you want from me?"

"We want you to tell us where Mallory was headed from here. We know he left you and that other fella behind because you were hurt. I reckon he had some destination in mind and didn't want to wait."

"Tell us where we can find him," Sam said.

Ash gulped, then winced as that action caused his chin to move just enough so that the tip of Sam's blade broke the skin. As a drop of blood welled out, he said, "Sweet Apple! That's where Deuce was goin'! A town called Sweet Apple, down by the Rio Grande!"

The blood brothers glanced at each other. "Heard of it?" Sam asked.

"Yeah," Matt said with a nod. "Supposed to be hell on wheels, despite the name."

"Deuce was gonna clean the place out, just like we did Buckskin!" Ash volunteered. "Then head right straight on across the border into Mexico." He gave a trembling sigh as Sam took the knife away from his throat. "Are you boys gonna go after him?"

"What do you think?" Matt asked in a hard voice.

"If Sweet Apple is where I think it is, that's a week's ride or more away," Sam pointed out. "We might not be able to catch Mallory's gang before they hit the town, even if we didn't have to take those women back to Buckskin first. As it is, they'll probably be well into Mexico before we can get down there."

Matt grunted. "Good thing we're not lawmen or army then. I don't intend to let a little thing like a river stop us."

"I'm glad to hear that," Sam said with a smile. "I feel pretty much the same way."

Ash summoned up the courage to ask, "What're you boys gonna do with me and Warren?"

"That the fella with his arm in a sling?"

Ash managed to nod.

"Well, him we'll plant," Matt said. "He didn't make it through that little fracas outside. As for you—"

Before he could go on and explain that Ash, along with the other prisoners, would be taken back to Buckskin and turned over to the law, the door of the trading post burst open and Alice Fletcher ran inside. The blonde looked scared as she said, "Mr. Bodine! Mr. Two Wolves! Someone's coming! It sounds like a lot of horses!"

Matt and Sam exchanged grim looks. A large group of riders approaching the trading post in the night probably didn't mean anything good.

It appeared that their trip to Sweet Apple was going to be delayed even more.

Chapter 11

Matt and Sam followed Alice back outside. They could hear the horses for themselves now. Matt judged that there were at least a dozen of them, maybe more.

He noticed with grim satisfaction that the women had all picked up guns that had been dropped earlier by the Dutchman's men. The hellish ordeal they had gone through hadn't completely broken their spirits. Even the brief taste of freedom they'd had tonight had been enough to restore their courage. That was the way it was with most folks. Once they'd had their freedom taken away, then gotten it back, they would fight like wildcats to make sure that no one ever took it from them again.

Matt tossed the Winchester to Sam, who caught it easily. "Climb up in that tower. You can cover the whole compound from there."

Sam nodded and set off at a run toward the ladder leading up to the watchtower.

"Onto the parapets there by the gates, ladies," Matt told the women. "We have to protect the gates more than anything else."

They didn't hesitate to follow his orders. Matt joined them, climbing onto the parapets and filling both hands with his six-guns.

As isolated as it was, the Dutchman's trading post had been built for defense. Even so, Matt had his doubts that he and Sam could hold the place against a determined force of attackers with only a handful of inexperienced women.

He sure as hell intended to try, though.

The glow from the burning barn had lit up the night sky and had probably been visible for miles around. It had served as a beacon for whoever those riders were.

A band of renegade Comanche maybe. Most of the Comanche were on the reservation up in Indian Territory now, after U.S. cavalry troops under Colonel Ranald S. Mackenzie had pretty much put an end to the Indian Wars in Texas with their victory in the Battle of Palo Duro Canyon a few years earlier. Even so, from time to time a group of warriors anxious to recapture the glories of the past would slip off the reservation and set off on a bloody raid.

Or it could be another gang of vicious outlaws like the one headed up by Deuce Mallory. That made more sense than any other explanation. The Dutchman's place was known far and wide as a haven for owlhoots and killers.

Whoever the riders were, they would get a hot-lead welcome from the defenders inside the trading post. Matt's hands tightened on his guns as he peered over the top of the wall into the darkness.

The hoofbeats slowed and then stopped. The strangers were being cautious. They weren't going to ride right up to the gates. Instead only a couple of them walked their horses forward. One of the men lifted his voice in a hail as they neared the gates.

"Hello, the fort!"

Matt frowned. There was something familiar about that voice, but he couldn't place it. Crouched down so that the wall would protect him in case the strangers opened fire, Matt called back, "Stay where you are! Who are you, and what's your business here?"

A moment of silence answered him, and then that familiar voice asked, "Bodine? Matt Bodine?"

Matt's frown deepened. How'd that hombre know who he was? Without confirming his own identity, he said again, "Who are you?"

"Timothy Lowell. The mayor of Buckskin."

One of the women on the parapet cried out in a ragged voice, "Timothy! Oh, God, Timothy!"

That would be the mayor's wife Lucinda, Matt thought. A feeling of relief washed through him as he straightened.

"Lucinda!" The mayor spurred forward, not being cautious any longer. "Open the gates, damn it! That's my wife in there!"

"Take it easy, Mayor," Matt called down. He didn't holster his irons just yet. "Are those some of the men from Buckskin with you?"

"Yes, blast it! Birdie shamed us into forming a posse and coming after you to help you. We'd camped for the night when we saw the light from a big fire and thought we ought to find out what it was. Now let us in! Is my wife all right? Lucinda, can you hear me?"

"I'm all right, Timothy," she told him. She was sobbing. All the women were as they realized that rescuers from their hometown were right outside the walls. "I thought I'd never see you again!"

Matt slipped his Colts into leather and called, "Hang on, Mayor. I'll get the gates open."

When he reached the bottom of the steps leading up to

the parapet, he found that Sam had climbed down from the watchtower, too. Together, they lifted the heavy bar from the gates and swung them open. The posse from Buckskin rode into the compound. Several of the men leaped from their saddles and embraced the women. For now, at least, the reunions were happy ones.

Matt and Sam stood back until the joyous greetings were over. Then Mayor Lowell strode over to them with one arm around his wife and said, "I didn't expect to find that you two had caught up to those outlaws and rescued the prisoners already."

"We didn't catch up to the gang," Sam said.

"They left the prisoners here and rode on," Matt explained. "They're still ahead of us. Except for a couple of them who got hurt and were left behind, too."

"Where are they?" Lowell asked with a look of grim savagery. "We'll deal with them."

"One of them is already dealt with," Matt said, waving a hand toward the bodies that still lay where they had fallen earlier. "The other one's inside. And in that smokehouse over yonder is the fella who ran this place, a Dutchman called Van Goort, along with some of his hired guns."

"They didn't have anything to do with the raid on Buckskin?"

"No," Sam said. "This trading post is a refuge for outlaws. The gang that attacked your town was led by a man named Deuce Mallory. As Matt told you, they've moved on."

Lowell still glared. "But this man Van Goort, he was still holding the women prisoner?"

"Yeah," Matt said. "I reckon he planned on ransoming them back to you sooner or later."

The mayor's face was dark with fury. "I think we have enough ropes to deal with this problem. There are no trees out here tall enough to hang a man, but that parapet will serve the purpose nicely."

His wife clutched his arm. "No, Timothy," she said. "You can't just lynch those men."

"Why in blazes not? They've got it coming to them! For God's sake, Lucinda, I'd think that you'd be ready to pull on one of the ropes yourself!"

She shuddered. "There's a part of me that would like to do just that," she admitted. "But . . . I know you, Timothy. I know all these other men. You're all law-abiding men."

"The lady's got a point, Mayor," Sam said. "If you string up those varmints without giving them a trial first, you'll have to live with it for the rest of your lives, even if you don't get into any trouble with the authorities over it. It would be better if you took them back to Buckskin and handled things in a legal, proper manner."

"And then string 'em up," Matt added. When Sam frowned at him, he shrugged and said, "The mayor's right about one thing. They've got it comin'."

Lowell thought about it for a moment and then sighed. "You're right, of course, Lucinda. You always are. And you as well, Mr. Two Wolves. We'll take them back and let the law run its course. You'll help us, won't you?"

Matt shook his head. "I'm afraid we can't do that, Mayor."

"Why not?"

Sam said, "Mallory and the rest of his gang are still on the loose. The fellow we captured told us where they were headed from here. They plan to raid another town. We're going to stop them if we can."

"And if we can't," Matt said, "we'll still try to see to it that Mallory and the rest of his bunch get what's comin' to *them*."

"Just the two of you alone?" Lowell shook his head. "We'd come with you and help you, but—"

"No need," Sam said. "You have to take the ladies back to Buckskin, not to mention Van Goort and the other prisoners."

"Anyway," Matt added with a smile, "the two of us have been enough to handle things so far."

Lowell looked around at the scattered corpses and the burned-out barn. "Yes, that appears to be true." He paused. "Where were this man Mallory and the rest of the outlaws going?"

"A settlement down on the Rio Grande," Matt said. "It's called Sweet Apple."

Magdalena Elena Louisa O'Ryan took a deep breath, gathered her courage, and pushed the batwings aside. She strode into the Black Bull like it was a nice civilized parlor in somebody's house, rather than the bawdiest, hell-roarin'est saloon in all of Sweet Apple, Texas.

Better known, for good reason, as The Lord's Waiting Room by those wags who found something amusing about murder and sudden death.

Maggie O'Ryan didn't think it was funny at all.

Even in the middle of the afternoon like this, the Black Bull was crowded. Hard-faced, roughly dressed men lined the bar and threw back shots of whiskey so vile that to call it panther piss or rattlesnake juice was being generous. Other men slapped cards on green felt and eyed their opponents with squinty malevolence, as if they were about to accuse each other of cheating and get their guns to blazing at any second.

Booze and games of chance weren't the only attractions at the Black Bull. Some of the patrons were more interested in the women in low-cut, gaudy dresses who delivered drinks and made their way among the tables, allowing the men to paw them almost at will. Sometimes, one of those hombres would grab a woman's hand and lead her up the stairs to the little rooms on the second floor where the saloon's other main business transactions were conducted. The faces of the soiled doves were just about as hard and flinty as those of the men, although the paint daubed on them concealed that to a certain extent.

Maggie felt her face glowing warmly as she took in all the indecent carousing going on in front of her. The curses, the lewd, raucous laughter, the tinny banging of a piano being pounded on by a drunken man in a soiled, dented derby, the smells of cheap tobacco smoke, spilled liquor, unwashed flesh, and the waste products of untold individuals . . . all of it combined to make Maggie's head spin so furiously she was afraid she was going be sick, pass out, or both.

Her presence hadn't gone unnoticed. Eyes started to turn toward her as she stood just inside the saloon's entrance. People went silent at the unexpected sight of her. That silence gradually spread across the barroom until it reached the piano player. The professor stopped butchering whatever song he was attempting to play and swung around on his stool to join everyone else in staring at her.

Maggie felt a wave of irritation go through her. They were all looking at her like she had two heads or something. She was a perfectly normal twenty-two-year-old woman. A little short maybe, and not as pretty as some of the saloon women. But her long, thick, dark hair was clean and shone from brushing, her skin had a faint olive hue she had inherited from her Mexican mother, and her eyes were a startling shade of green, a legacy from her Irish father. What really set her apart from the other women in the room was her demure gray dress, which had long sleeves and was buttoned up modestly to the throat rather than letting half of her bosoms hang out.

Not that she wouldn't look good in the kind of shameless getup those hussies sported, she thought suddenly, without warning. She would look just fine—if that was the sort of woman she wanted to be. Which she didn't. She was respectable.

Which made her something of an oddity in Sweet Apple, Texas.

Maggie cleared her throat. It sounded louder than she expected. She looked at the man in the dark suit and fancy vest standing at the end of the bar and said, "Mr. Delacroix, you said you were going to send Oliver to school today."

Pierre Delacroix, the owner of the Black Bull Saloon, was from New Orleans, and the soft mixture of accents that characterized those from the Crescent City was in his voice as he spread his hands and said, "A thousand pardons, Señorita O'Ryan. The promise slipped my mind." He smiled at her as he came closer. "And no man should ever be allowed to forget a promise made to a lady, especially one as lovely as you, mam'selle."

Delacroix was tall and slender and handsome. No doubt the sporting women who worked for him thought he was just about the best-looking fella to ever come down the pike. Maggie had no doubt that Delacroix could have any of those girls any time he wanted them. That would have been true even if they didn't work for him.

But she was immune to his charms. All she cared about were the children of Sweet Apple. She had taken upon herself the task of educating those youngsters, and she didn't intend to allow anything to sway her from that goal. Not even the trepidation she felt at entering a place like the Black Bull—and certainly not the easy smile and charm of the saloon's owner.

"Oliver is already behind the other children in his schooling," she told Delacroix. "It's important that he not miss any more time in class."

Delacroix's shoulders rose and fell in a graceful shrug. "We have moved around a lot, Oliver and I."

That's because you probably got run out of town everywhere you went, you tinhorn gambler. Maggie couldn't stop the thought from going through her mind. *Until you landed here in Sweet Apple and couldn't get any lower.*

"But I know that a boy needs to learn," Delacroix continued, "more than the things he can learn in a place such as this, eh, shall we say?" He chuckled. "I will see to it that Oliver comes to school tomorrow, Señorita O'Ryan. You have my word on that."

Maggie didn't point out that he had given her his word before. More than once, in fact. And Oliver still missed more days of school than he attended.

But she forced herself to nod and say, "Thank you." All she wanted now was to get out of here. She had a feeling that Delacroix was laughing at her behind that smooth, handsome façade. She had a feeling that *most* of the people in the Black Bull were laughing at her. The frumpy little schoolteacher, trying to be more than she was. Trying to forget that she was a border breed, her father a drunken Irish soldier of fortune, her mother a . . . Well, the less said about that, the better. At least her parents, a pair of lapsed Catholics if there ever was one, had had the decency to get married before she was born. Maggie was grateful for that even though she couldn't summon up any other good memories of either of them.

She turned away and started toward the batwings. The piano player resumed his ham-handed thumping on the keys.

Behind Maggie, Delacroix called, "Señorita O'Ryan."

She looked back. "Yes?"

"Come back any time, *ma cherie.*"

She flushed again. He *was* making fun of her. She hurried out, slapping the batwings aside. They swung back the other way a little faster than she expected them to and slapped at her. She stalked away along the boardwalk in front of the saloon. Down the street at the depot, a locomotive rumbled and then sounded its shrill whistle as the train stopped there got ready to pull out, but Maggie was so upset that she barely heard the sounds.

She knew she shouldn't let things like the encounter with Pierre Delacroix bother her. By now she should have been used to the mocking smiles and the barely suppressed laughter. She had always been the misfit, the ugly child who had bettered herself by sheer stubbornness, fierce determination, and a surprisingly keen intellect. She had worked hard at whatever honest, respectable job she could find—and they weren't easy to come by in a hellhole like Sweet Apple. She had saved her money and gotten out, had paid for her own education at a school for teachers in Waco. But something had drawn her back to the squalid border settlement where she had grown up. The railroad had arrived in Sweet Apple a few years earlier, and the town was growing. As its population increased, there would be more and more children there, too.

Children who needed an education. Maggie had realized after a while that providing that education was her calling.

She hadn't realized, though, that she would have to spend more time trying to get parents to send their children to class than she would spend actually teaching those children. As she looked around the settlement's wide, dusty main street, she spotted a freight wagon rolling along it being driven by Fred Blevins. He had *five* children of school age who seldom showed up at the one-room adobe school on the edge of town.

"Mr. Blevins!" Maggie called as she started after him, waving a hand over her head. "Mr. Blevins, if I could talk to you for a minute?"

Blevins turned his head and looked back over his shoulder at her, then faced forward again and whipped up his team of mules in an attempt to get them to go faster. Maggie stopped and heaved a sigh. She wasn't going to do anything as undignified as chase him down the street. At least he had seen her, and knew she hadn't forgotten about his children and their need for an education.

She would *never* forget about the children. No matter what the people of Sweet Apple thought about her.

She turned around, and had started looking for some other parents of wayward students, when she jumped and let out a little scream as a gun blasted somewhere nearby and a bullet whistled past her ear.

Chapter 12

"Sweet Apple!" the conductor called as he made his way down the aisle of the swaying coach. The rhythmic clicking of the joints in the steel rails under the railroad car's wheels provided a counterpoint to his words. "Comin' into Sweet Apple, Texas!"

Seymour Standish suppressed the groan of relief that tried to well up his throat. At last, after long days and longer nights, he was reaching the end of his hellish journey.

Uncle Cornelius had bought the train tickets for Seymour, and naturally it hadn't occurred to him to waste the company's money on extravagances like a sleeping compartment. Seymour had been forced to sleep sitting up on the same hard bench seat where he rode during the day. From New Jersey to Chicago, down to St. Louis, through Little Rock and Texarkana and Fort Worth and San Antonio, and then on west to Del Rio and still farther west, following the valley of the Rio Grande toward El Paso . . . Seymour had lost track of the days he had spent in one rocking, swaying railroad car after another, breathing air choked by cinders and smoke that swirled in through windows that were open in an attempt to relieve the stifling heat. All he knew for certain was that he was exhausted and miserable and that every muscle in his body was stiff and sore.

But now his destination was at hand, and no matter how bad Sweet Apple was, it had to be better than all the damned trains!

He pushed his spectacles up on his nose, reached under his seat for his carpetbag, and pushed his spectacles up again since bending over made them slip down. He picked up his hat from where it sat on the bench seat next to him. For part of the trip a large, gaudily dressed salesman had sat there, and when the fellow dozed off, his head had wound up resting against Seymour's shoulder. Seymour had been sickened by the smell of bay rum and stale sweat that wafted from the man, but there was nothing he could do about it. He wasn't going to risk a confrontation by asking the man to move.

Thankfully, Seymour hadn't had a seatmate since the train left San Antonio. He had been able to doze a little himself during that respite.

The train jolted and slowed. Its whistle blew. With a hiss of steam and squeal of brakes, the Baldwin locomotive with its diamond-shaped smokestack rolled into the station at Sweet Apple, pulling the long string of cars behind it. The locomotive came to a stop beyond the station, so that its boiler lined up with the water tank raised on stout wooden legs. This was a water stop, so the train would be here for a while.

That positioning brought the passenger cars even with the long platform attached to the depot. Seymour looked out the window at the low adobe building with its red tile roof. Architecture was certainly different down here in

Texas than what he was accustomed to back East. Brick buildings were rare, and there were no buildings taller than two stories. In fact, as he looked along Sweet Apple's main street, which stretched out behind the depot, he saw that some of the buildings were constructed to appear to have two stories when there really wasn't anything behind the upper part of the façade. He supposed that was what was meant by a building having a "false front." He had heard that term before, but he couldn't remember where.

Well, pondering frontier architecture was interesting, he supposed, but it didn't get him any closer to accomplishing his goal, which was to establish as many new accounts for Standish Dry Goods, Inc., as he could in Sweet Apple and the surrounding area. He settled his hat on his head, grasped the handle of his carpetbag, and stood up to leave the train. He would have to have a porter recover his sample case from the baggage car.

The porter had already placed steps by the platform at the rear of the car, so Seymour went down them to the station platform, clutching his carpetbag to him as he did so, as if afraid that someone might try to take it from him. He had no idea what to expect from these Westerners. If they were all like the rowdies and hell-raisers who populated the yellow-backed dime novels, he would have to be cautious indeed.

Nobody seemed to be paying much attention to him, though. In fact, nobody was paying any attention to him. The other passengers who were disembarking had their own places to go and things to do. Those boarding the train were no doubt thinking of the destinations where they were bound, or the people they were leaving behind here in Sweet Apple. None of them even spared Seymour a glance. He wasn't sure whether to be relieved or somewhat irritated that he was such a nonentity in their eyes.

The smell in the air was even more disturbing. Mixed with the smoke and oil from the train was a haze of dust that made Seymour's shoes crunch grittily on the platform as he walked, and underlying that was the potent stench of manure. He looked behind him, through a gap between cars, and saw the source of that less-than-fragrant aroma. On the other side of the tracks stretched a long line of cattle pens occupied by hundreds, if not thousands, of the mooing, jostling beasts. Several large ranches were located in the area, and they shipped their stock from Sweet Apple.

The cattle weren't the only producers of manure. The street was dotted with piles of droppings from the dozens of horses moving here and there. Some of the animals were saddle mounts; others were hitched to buggies and wagons of various sorts. But all of them shared in common the trait of relieving themselves wherever they happened to be.

The same was true back East, of course. Horses weren't any different there. And New Jersey had its share of trains and factories that produced plenty of thick, choking smoke. Trenton was no bed of roses, Seymour told himself. He just thought that it smelled worse here because everything else was so different. The buildings, the people, the way they dressed and spoke, the fact that men openly carried guns in public . . .

"Watch where the hell you're goin', mister."

The harsh, angry voice sounded in Seymour's ear about half a second after a hard collision against his shoulder jolted him and nearly made him drop his carpetbag. He looked around and saw a man in a big black hat glaring at him. The man wore a black vest over a red shirt, and around his waist was buckled a black gunbelt with the ivory-handled butt of a revolver sticking up from the attached holster. Seymour's heart began to pound harder as he realized that he was looking at that most dangerous of frontier species, the gunfighter.

"I'm sorry, sir," he said. Then some demon prompted him to add, "But I believe that you ran into me."

The man's glare turned into a dark frown of disbelief. "I *what*?" he demanded.

Seymour swallowed and took a step backward. "Perhaps I was mistaken. I'm sure my own carelessness was to blame—"

"Damn right it was. Now get the hell out of my way."

"But . . . I'm not in your way." Seymour groaned inwardly. What was prompting him toward this foolish behavior? He went on. "I was just going down to the baggage car to retrieve my sample case."

The angry Texan squinted at him. "Salesman, eh? I might'a knowed you was one o' them drummers. Bunch o' pansy-faced dudes. Why in blazes don't y'all go back where you come from and leave folks alone?"

"I don't want to bother anyone—" Seymour began.

"Well, you're botherin' me just by bein' here! Get back on that damned train!" The man leveled an arm at the car from which Seymour had just disembarked.

"But . . . but I can't do that," Seymour tried to explain. "My uncle sent me here—"

"Oh, so you're just a flunky, is that it? I should'a knowed by lookin' at you that you couldn't never do nothin' except follow somebody else's orders. You ain't got one damn bit of backbone!"

Seymour's irritation warred with his nervousness. He

said, "I assure you, sir, I'm just as much a vertebrate as you are."

That was a mistake. The Texan's eyes widened with rage. "I don't know what the hell you're talkin' about," he bellowed, "but it sure sounded like you just called me a liar!"

From his limited reading of dime novels, Seymour recalled that Westerners hated being called a liar more than almost anything. He set his carpetbag down at his feet and held up both hands, palms out, in what he hoped was a peaceful gesture. "I assure you, sir, I meant no such—"

"Take a swing at me, will you!"

The world seemed to explode in Seymour's face. He felt himself going backward, and it felt to him as if he were traveling faster than the train had ever managed at its top speed.

Then he crashed down onto his back, landing on the station platform. The impact knocked the breath out of him, so that all he could do for a long moment was to lie there and gasp for air, unmoving.

His stunned brain became aware that people were stepping around and over him, as if they saw him but at the same time didn't see him. They didn't care that he had just been knocked down by a madman.

That was what had happened, Seymour realized. The gunfighter in the black hat had struck him in the face. Now the man loomed over him, fists still clenched threateningly, and said, "You want some more, you little son of a bitch? Get up, damn you!" He kicked Seymour's foot. "Or maybe you'd rather go get a gun and settle this like men!"

The last thing Seymour wanted to do was to tell this lunatic that he already *had* a gun. The revolver that had been given to him by Rebecca Jimmerson during that strange, last-minute visit to his rooming house was packed away securely in his carpetbag. Taking it out would require only a few moments.

But that would be the worst thing Seymour could do, and he knew it. This man wanted to kill him.

He pushed himself onto an elbow and gasped, "Please, sir . . . no more. I . . . I apologize for offending you. It was . . . entirely my fault."

The gunfighter's mouth twisted in a grimace of distaste as he looked down at Seymour. "You're so scared you're about to piss your pants, ain't you, boy?"

Seymour didn't deny the accusation, although he never would have phrased it in such a crude manner.

"What's your name?"

"S-Seymour. Seymour Standish."

"Seymour?" The gunfighter threw back his head and laughed. "Seymour. I reckon it suits you. I never *seen* a *more* cowardly little worm than you are. Seymour the Lily-Livered. That's what I'm gonna call you from now on." The man reached down and grabbed the front of Seymour's coat. He hauled the young Easterner to his feet and then gave him a shove toward the train. "Get your damn sample case and get out o' my sight, Seymour the Lily-Livered. You make me so sick I think I'm gonna puke."

Trembling violently, Seymour looked around for his hat, which had come off when the gunfighter knocked him down. He spotted it lying nearby on the platform and reached for it.

At that moment, the gunfighter drew his weapon with what seemed like blinding speed to Seymour. The revolver roared. The sound was so loud it was like twin fists punching Seymour's ears. He let out a little shriek of terror as the man's shot struck his hat and knocked it farther along the platform.

The gunfighter laughed again. "What's the matter, Seymour? Can't even pick up your hat?"

Seymour looked around wildly. The man had just *fired a gun*. Wasn't somebody going to *do* something? Shouldn't someone summon the authorities?

But the people on the platform just ignored the whole thing, as if there were nothing unusual about someone discharging a firearm in a public place.

"Get your hat," the gunfighter ordered in a low, dangerous tone, forcing the words between clenched teeth. "Go on, Seymour. Pick it up."

Seymour swallowed and reached for his hat again. The gun roared for a second time, and again the hat went spinning away as a bullet tore through it. Seymour lunged after it. Maybe if he could get the hat, the man would stop tormenting him.

Instead, more shots blasted and Seymour had to stop in his tracks, screaming as he clapped his hands over his ears. In front of his horrified eyes, the hat leaped with every shot. It was ruined now, full of holes from the bullets. As the gun fell silent, Seymour swung around and discovered that the weapon was aimed right at him. The opening at the end of the barrel seemed as big around as the bore of a cannon as he stared into it. The gunfighter grinned over the sights at him and pulled back the hammer for another shot.

"All it'd take is one bullet," the man said. "Just one and you'd be out o' your misery, Seymour. And I wouldn't have to look at that scared face o' yours no more neither." He laughed and lowered the hammer, then tilted up the gun barrel. "But you ain't worth it. I've already wasted enough bullets on you. I ain't a-gonna waste even one more." He laughed again and holstered the weapon.

Seymour was so paralyzed by fear that all he could do was stand there and wait for death to claim him. It took a moment for the realization to sink in that the man wasn't going to kill him. In fact, the man appeared to be leaving. He strode past Seymour, deliberately ramming him again with a shoulder as he went by. Seymour staggered, but stayed on his feet. The gunman stalked away without looking back.

Seymour's pulse pounded like a trip-hammer in his head. He couldn't seem to get enough air in his lungs. He felt sick to his stomach.

"Here's yo' sample case, mister."

Seymour jumped and let out a terrified yelp as the voice spoke behind him. His head jerked around as he searched for some new threat. All he saw was a middle-aged black man in the uniform of a railroad porter. The man held Seymour's sample case.

"I . . . I . . ." Seymour couldn't force any more words out.

"I seen that little run-in you had with that fella," the porter went on. "You lucky he didn't kill you, 'stead o' just shootin' up yo' hat. He been known to shoot fellas before just 'cause he felt like it."

"Wh-who . . ."

"He calls hisself Cole Halliday. Don't know if that his real name or not. Prob'ly ain't. He's a bad man, though, ain't no doubt about that." The porter shook his head. "Thing is, he ain't even the worst man in these parts. Not by a long shot."

"Th-the sheriff . . ."

"Sheriff's in the county seat, forty miles from here. And he can't get no deputy to stay down here."

Seymour ran his fingers through his hair. He was calming down some now, but he was still trembling a little. "What about the local constable, or a marshal . . . ?"

"Ain't none. Ain't nobody in these parts damn fool enough to take the job." The porter set Seymour's sample case on the platform and pushed it toward him with a foot as the train's whistle blew. "Here you go. That the only bag you got 'cept'n that carpetbag, ain't it?"

Seymour managed to nod.

The porter said, "You take care now, hear?" and turned toward the train.

"Seymour the Lily-Livered! Seymour the Lily-Livered!"

The jeering taunts came from behind Seymour. He twisted around and saw several children standing there, grinning and pointing at him. Obviously they had heard what Cole Halliday called him, and now they were taking cruel pleasure in repeating it.

"Stop it," he told them, but they ignored him and continued their chanting. Seymour clapped his hands over his ears again, as he had when Halliday was shooting, and cried, "What sort of town is this I've come to?"

The porter paused at the steps leading up to one of the passenger cars and shook his head. With a sad smile, he said, "It's Sweet Apple, mister. Better get used to it."

Chapter 13

A few minutes later, Seymour found himself stumbling down the boardwalk along one side of Sweet Apple's main street. He had his carpetbag in one hand, his sample case in the other. His ruined hat now resided at the bottom of a trash barrel he'd found in the railroad station as he made his way through the lobby. He supposed he would have to buy another hat. He had a little cash with him to take care of incidental expenses.

Like replacing a hat that had been shot to pieces by a gun-toting lunatic.

A couple of the little boys who had taunted him in the depot still trailed behind him, saying in singsong voices, "Seymour the Lily-Livered, Seymour the Lily-Livered." The other children had grown bored with that brutal sport and gone on to something else, but these two were being stubborn about it. They ignored the discouraging looks that Seymour sent back over his shoulder at them, until finally he couldn't stand their gibes anymore.

He turned sharply and glared at them. "Stop that!" he commanded. "Didn't your parents ever teach you to respect your elders? Stop that right now, or I'll . . . I'll . . ." He couldn't think of a suitable threat, not being accustomed to threatening anyone about anything.

"You'll what, Seymour?" one of the boys asked with a maddening smirk.

"We ain't afraid of you," the other boy said. "You're too lily-livered to do anything about it. Seymour the Lily-Livered!"

The first one joined in. "Seymour the Lily-Livered!"

Several people on the street looked at the youths, but no one offered to step in and put a stop to their taunting. A couple of men shook their heads and rolled their eyes, but Seymour wasn't sure if their disdain was directed at the boys—or at him.

He thought he had a pretty good idea, though.

"If you don't stop, I'll tell your fathers!" That would shut them up, he told himself.

He saw right away how wrong he was. The feeble threat just provoked them to gales of laughter. "You just try it, mister," one of the boys said as he wiped away tears of hilarity. "My pa's down at the Black Bull boozin' it up. He'll whip your scrawny ass up one side o' the street and down t'other if you interrupt his drinkin'."

Seymour fumed helplessly as the youngsters continued to laugh. Finally, one of the men on the boardwalk stepped forward and came toward them. "Here, now, you little jackanapes!" he said as he aimed a swat at the head of one of the boys, who dodged it easily and ducked away. "Run along and stop bothering this gentleman."

For a second Seymour thought the little devils were going to ignore the man's scolding, but then they turned away and started across the street, dodging around several piles of horse dung. They were still laughing, but at least they were going away now.

Seymour heaved a sigh of relief and turned to his rescuer. "Thank you, sir," he said. "I was at my wit's end trying to deal with those two imps."

The man was taller than Seymour and considerably heavier. An ample belly bulged the vest he wore under a brown tweed suit. He wore a bowler hat, and a waxed mustache spread its wings under a prominent red nose. That nose, and the network of veins in his cheeks, marked him as a drinking man, but Seymour didn't care about that right now, even though he didn't approve of imbibing alcohol. At the moment he was just grateful for the assistance.

"Better be glad you didn't go down to the Black Bull looking for Andy's pa," the man said. "He gets belligerent whenever anything interrupts his drinking, just like the little bastard said."

"You sound like an educated man," Seymour said. "I was beginning to think that there weren't any in this town."

"Oh, I'm educated, but that doesn't necessarily make me intelligent. I'm still here, aren't I?" The man chuckled and then held out his hand. "J. Emerson Heathcote is the name. I'm the editor and publisher of the local newspaper."

Seymour was about to shake hands with the journalist when something struck his arm. Something warm and wet splattered across his cheek. He jumped and yelled, thinking that he had been shot and that blood had splashed into his face. He gazed down in horror to see how badly he was hurt.

Instead, he saw a large clump of particularly runny horse dung clinging to his coat sleeve, just below his shoulder. Howls of laughter made him look up again. His two tormentors had returned. One of them had flung the manure at him. Now they both turned and ran, staggering and almost falling because they were laughing so hard as they fled.

"You, uh, might want to take your handkerchief and wipe your face," J. Emerson Heathcote suggested.

Stonily, Seymour cleaned the filth from his face. Then he started to put the handkerchief back in his pocket, stopped and looked at it in disgust instead, and then flung the ruined cloth down. He didn't see a rubbish barrel, but he didn't care. No one seemed to care about anything good and decent in Sweet Apple, so why should he be any different?

"The newspaper office is right here," Heathcote said as he waved toward a nearby doorway. "Why don't you come in and sit down for a minute? You look like you need to catch your breath and get your wits about you."

"Thank you," Seymour choked out. "Thank you, Mr. Heathcote. I think you must be the only man with any decency left in this town."

"I try, I try. Maybe you should get that handkerchief and clean your coat sleeve before we go in, too."

Seymour retrieved the handkerchief from the ground and wiped away as much of the dung as he could from his sleeve. Then he threw the handkerchief into the street this time. Let the hooves of passing horses grind it into the dust. He didn't care.

Inside the newspaper office, with its pervasive smell of ink that Seymour found preferable to the stench outside, Heathcote sat him down in a ladder-back chair and brought him a cup of coffee from a pot that was simmering on a stove in the corner. Seymour would have rather had a cup of tea, but he doubted that anyone in Sweet Apple knew how to brew one. He took a grateful sip of the coffee, and sputtered as he realized how strong it was.

"Got a little too much bite to it?" Heathcote asked.

"No . . . No, it's fine," Seymour managed to say. "Thank you." He heaved a sigh. "Is this newspaper office the lone bastion of civilization in Sweet Apple?"

"Well, I don't know about that. We have a school, when poor Maggie O'Ryan can convince enough of the parents to send their young'uns. And there are two churches, one Catholic and one foot-washin' Baptist."

Seymour had no idea what a foot-washing Baptist was, but at the moment he wasn't curious enough to ask. He took another sip of the coffee. Now that he was more accustomed to it, he could feel the bracing effect it was having on him.

Heathcote took off his bowler hat, hung it on a peg, and sat down at a paper-littered desk. "What brings you to Sweet Apple, Mr. . . ."

"Standish," Seymour supplied. "Seymour Standish."

"Yes, I heard what those rapscallions were calling you. What was that about?"

Seymour hated to confess to the humiliation he had suffered at the train station, but there had been plenty of witnesses on hand. If J. Emerson Heathcote was any sort of a newspaperman, he would have heard the story by nightfall anyway. So Seymour told him what had happened, trying not to paint himself in too unflattering a light.

That wasn't easy to do, though, considering the circumstances. The story made him sound like a craven coward.

Which, he supposed, he was . . .

Since Heathcote had asked what brought him to Sweet Apple, Seymour moved on to that subject in short order, telling him all about Standish Dry Goods, Inc., of Trenton, New Jersey, and how his Uncle Cornelius had sent him here to establish the company in West Texas. Heathcote listened with rapt interest, asking a question every now and then to keep Seymour talking.

Finally, Seymour said, "When I first heard the name of the place where my uncle was sending me, I thought it would be a nice, refined town."

"Well, you were way off about *that,* weren't you? Some folks call Sweet Apple The Lord's Waiting Room, because hardly a day goes by here that we don't have at least one killing. Sometimes there's more than that."

"Has, ah, today's killing already taken place?"

"Yes. A couple of greasers stabbed each other to death in a cantina early this morning. But don't let that put you off your guard. Like I said, sometimes we'll have five or six men cross the divide in a day's time."

"Die, you mean?" Seymour asked with a frown.

"That's right."

Seymour remembered what the porter had told him at the depot. "And there's no law here? No law at all?"

"None to speak of. The last couple of deputies the sheriff sent down here to establish law and order got killed, and now nobody else will try it. It would take a team of wild horses to drag the sheriff himself down here, and I'm not sure even they could accomplish it. He's a politician, you know," Heathcote added, as if that explained everything. And Seymour supposed it did. The newspaperman went on. "A while back the respectable folks in town—and there *are* some, you know—got together and decided to hire a marshal. The damn fool who took the job lasted a week before he was gunned down. The next one was dead in four days. Since then . . ." Heathcote spread his hands. "Well, nobody wants *that* job anymore either, and I don't suppose you can blame them."

Seymour shook his head as he muttered, "Incredible.

It's just incredible that such a place could exist in this day and age. I know that Texas is still the . . . the Wild West, so to speak, but surely there's some way to establish law and order here."

"If you figure it out, you tell me, Mr. Standish, and I'll print it in the paper. In the meantime, have you got a place to stay while you're in town?"

"No, not yet. I thought perhaps I'd rent a room in a local boardinghouse—"

Heathcote shook his head. "There aren't any. We've got a hotel, though, and there are usually some vacant rooms there." He stood up, took his coat off and hung it over the back of his chair, and began rolling up his shirt sleeves. "I'd show you, but I've got a paper to get out . . ."

"Oh, don't let me interfere with your work. I've already taken up enough of your time and imposed on your hospitality." Seymour got to his feet. "If you could just tell me where to find the hotel . . ."

"Go on down the street past the Black Bull. That's the biggest saloon in town. You can't miss it. The hotel's in the next block, on the same side of the street."

"Thank you." Seymour started to lift his hand as if he were about to tip his hat politely, before he remembered that he no longer had a hat. Trying not to let that fluster him, he started toward the door. As he stepped out into the late afternoon heat, he caught a whiff of the stink coming from his dung-smeared sleeve. He hoped there was a laundry somewhere in town. He didn't know if it would be possible to get his coat clean, but he intended to try. He started to turn back into the newspaper office to ask Heathcote about a laundry, then decided that they could probably tell him at the hotel where to find one. Carrying his carpetbag and sample case, he started in that direction.

The train was still at the station, Seymour noted as he looked in that direction. It had been about to pull out earlier, so he assumed that some mechanical malfunction must have cropped up to delay its departure.

He could go back down there, he told himself, climb aboard the train, and keep riding until it reached the end of the line. He would have to purchase another ticket, but he could do that. He didn't really care where he went, as long as it was away from this terrible place called Sweet Apple.

But if he did that, he would be abandoning his job and letting down his Uncle Cornelius. Worse than that, he would be letting down the company and his father's memory. Seymour heaved a sigh. He was here, and he was just going to have to make the best of a bad situation.

Besides, the locomotive blew its whistle just then, and the train lurched into motion, pulling out of the station at last. With it went Seymour's only chance to escape.

At least until the next train came through.

He had turned back toward the hotel when a sudden rattle of pounding hoofbeats made him look up. Two riders were racing their mounts along the street toward him. Their gaudy clothing told Seymour they were cowboys. He had seen similar outfits in illustrations in *Harper's Illustrated Weekly*. The men were drunk, or naturally exuberant, or both. They whooped at the top of their lungs, and one of them pulled a gun from its holster at his waist and fired the weapon as the riders thundered along. Seymour jumped at the sound.

Then his eyes widened as he realized that there was a young woman standing on the boardwalk in front of him. Those lunatics on horseback were about to sweep past her, and if the one waving the gun around fired again, the bullet might strike her. The first shot must have already come too close to her for comfort.

And she seemed rooted to the spot with terror, unable to move.

Without stopping to think about what he was doing, Seymour dropped his carpetbag and sample case and threw himself forward.

Chapter 14

Maggie O'Ryan barely had time to realize what was happening. Two crazy cowboys, out on a toot, galloped along the street toward her. One of them had his gun out and had fired the shot that had almost hit her—not aiming at her necessarily, just shooting out of sheer drunken exuberance.

Then someone crashed into her and knocked her off her feet. Less than a heartbeat later, as she landed hard on the planks of the boardwalk, the window of the Black Bull shattered where a bullet struck it. That bullet would have hit Maggie if someone hadn't tackled her and knocked her out of the way.

At the moment she didn't fully understand how close she had come to dying. That was because the fall had knocked the wind out of her and her brain didn't really comprehend anything except that she had to have air. She tried to drag some into her lungs, but the weight pressing down on her chest made that difficult. Her head swam. She finally grasped the idea that whoever had grabbed her was now lying on top of her. She put her hands against his shoulders, pushed, and gasped, "Can't . . . breathe!"

Maggie found herself looking up into the face of a young man with slender, delicate features and brown eyes. His hair was brown, too, and slightly mussed. As she pushed at him, understanding dawned in his eyes and he rolled off her, a bright red flush appearing on his face as he did so. It appeared that he had just realized he was sprawled on top of a young woman with his knee wedged somewhat intimately between her thighs. Maggie's face grew warm, too, but she was too busy trying to catch her breath to worry a great deal about it.

She pushed herself upright. The celebrating cowboys were gone, having galloped on down the street, probably without any idea of how close one of them had come to killing her. Maggie looked up at the broken window. She had been standing right in front of it.

A crowd of people surged out of the Black Bull, led by Pierre Delacroix, who looked angry that someone had just shot out one of his front windows. His expression changed to one of concern when he saw Maggie sitting on the boardwalk. He hurried over to her, saying, "Mam'selle O'Ryan! You are hurt?"

Maggie shook her head. "I'm all right," she told Delacroix. She looked over at the young man who had tackled her. "Thanks to this gentleman here."

He was still blushing furiously. "I just . . . uh . . . I apologize for any, uh, impropriety, ma'am . . ."

"Nonsense," Maggie said. "You saved my life, sir." She extended her hand to him. "You have my gratitude."

He hesitated, but then clasped her hand. His movements were awkward and nervous. It was an inauspicious meeting, Maggie thought as they shook hands. They were both sitting on a dusty boardwalk surrounded by drunken louts from the saloon. At least the crowd began to diminish as the Black Bull's patrons began to file back inside, anxious to return to their drinks and cards.

Delacroix said, "Allow me to help you up, Señorita." He grasped Maggie's arm and lifted her to her feet.

The young man scrambled upright, too, and began brushing dirt and dust off his brown suit. Maggie sniffed. A distinctive odor came from the stranger, and she saw a darker brown blotch on his coat sleeve that could be only one thing.

He noticed and said, "I'm sorry. Some young hooligans threw some . . . well, pelted me with . . ."

"That's all right," Maggie assured him. "You still saved my life, and I'm grateful to you, sir."

"Seymour Standish," he said, and it took Maggie a second to realize that he had just introduced himself.

"I'm Maggie O'Ryan," she said. "Magdalena Elena Louisa O'Ryan, to be precise."

"Precision is good," Seymour Standish said, then flushed again. "I mean, one should always be precise in one's speech, at least to the extent possible."

"Oh, I agree."

Delacroix said, "Did you see who was responsible for this atrocity, Señorita O'Ryan?"

Maggie shook her head. "Not really. It was just a couple of cowboys. Inebriated, no doubt. I'm sorry I can't tell you who they were. I know you'd like to make the man who fired the shots pay for your window."

"The cost of a pane of glass, dear though it may be, worries me less than your health, mam'selle."

Seymour Standish frowned a little and asked, "Are you French or Spanish, sir?"

Delacroix smiled and shrugged. "Cajun by birth, *mon ami,* but this close to the Mexican border, one becomes

Spanish, too." He turned back to Maggie. "Would you like to come back inside and sit down for a moment to catch your breath? Perhaps a small glass of sherry to brace you?"

She shook her head. "No, I'm fine." Despite the fact that Delacroix had been making fun of her earlier, she sensed now that he was genuinely concerned. "If you want to do something for me, make sure that Oliver attends school tomorrow."

"He will be there, Señorita. On that you have my word."

Seymour Standish said, "I could, ah, walk you home, Miss O'Ryan. Just to make sure no other incidents occur."

"That's not necessary." Despite the gratitude she felt, Maggie couldn't help but remember how it had felt to have this young man lying on top of her. She didn't want to compound that embarrassment for either of them. Seymour's face still glowed, and her ears were warm. She went on. "I'm sure you have business of your own to attend to."

He shrugged. "I was just on my way down to the hotel to rent a room. I *am* here in Sweet Apple on business. I represent Standish Dry Goods, Incorporated, of Trenton, New Jersey."

"Really? I've never been farther east than Waco. I can't imagine traveling all the way to Texas from someplace like New Jersey."

"It *was* a long, arduous journey," Seymour admitted.

"Well, I have to get back to the school and prepare tomorrow's lessons."

Seymour lifted a hand toward his head, which was hatless, then stopped. "Yes, of course. Good day to you, Miss O'Ryan."

"Good day, Mr. Standish."

Maggie turned and started along the boardwalk. She

brushed dust off her dress. A part of her wanted to look back, but she didn't do it. A lady always maintained a proper air of decorum, and that didn't include turning to stare at a handsome young man.

She felt her face growing warmer again. Seymour Standish *was* handsome, no doubt about that, but he had nothing to do with her. He'd just happened to be there at the right time and place to save her life. That was all. What she felt was nothing more than simple gratitude.

She told herself that several times, and by the time she reached the small adobe school building on the edge of town, she believed it.

"You are a drummer, no?" the Cajun said.

"No. I mean yes. I mean, I'm a salesman," Seymour said. "For Standish Dry Goods, as I told Miss O'Ryan. My father established the company."

Even as he spoke, his eyes were still on Maggie O'Ryan as she walked along the street. He told himself that he was watching her only to make certain that no other untoward incidents befell her. The fact that she was an attractive young woman had nothing to do with it.

The Cajun chuckled. "Your father owns the company, yet you are a traveling salesman? Sent to this border hellhole, no less?"

Seymour felt a flash of irritation. "My father passed away. My uncle runs the company now, although I own an equal share of it. He's the one who sent me here, and I'm sure he had no idea what sort of place Sweet Apple really is. I think he chose it simply by the name."

"Ah." The man snapped his fingers as if he had just realized something. "You are the one from the railroad station.

Some of my customers were talking about your encounter with Cole Halliday. Now I know why the name was familiar. You are Seymour the—"

Even though the man stopped short without uttering the offensive nickname, Seymour closed his eyes and sighed. Did everyone in town already know about his humiliation? How could he possibly hope to establish any new accounts with the local merchants when he was nothing but an object of derision and ridicule?

"I am Pierre Delacroix, the owner of this establishment," the man went on as he inclined his head toward the batwinged entrance of the saloon. "Would you care to come in and have a drink? On the house, of course."

Seymour shook his head. "I don't imbibe."

"No? I would like to repay the debt that I owe you for saving the life of the charming Señorita O'Ryan."

Seymour frowned as he caught the tone in Delacroix's voice. "You and Miss O'Ryan . . ."

The saloon keeper smiled and lifted his shoulders in an eloquent shrug.

Seymour wouldn't have thought there would be any sort of romantic relationship between Maggie O'Ryan and this suave Cajun saloon keeper. Miss O'Ryan had struck him as the prim and proper type. Of course, that was the way he regarded all women unless and until they gave him reason to revise his opinion of them.

But none of this was any concern of his, he reminded himself.

"Not only that," Delacroix went on, "Señorita O'Ryan and her school represent one of the last vestiges of culture in this misbegotten settlement. Though my own son is a, shall we say, less than enthusiastic student, I would not like to see the school close."

"Well, we agree on that," Seymour said. "Education is important."

Delacroix clapped a hand on his shoulder. "Come. Have a drink."

Seymour stood firm, saying, "No, thank you. I've had a tiring day. I just want to rent a hotel room, find a laundry, have something to eat, and get some sleep."

"Ah, yes, the laundry." Delacroix looked at the stain on Seymour's sleeve and wrinkled his nose. "There is a Chinese gentleman named Wing who operates such an establishment. The hotel can send your garment down to him. I fear that M'sieu Wing will have a formidable task awaiting him, however."

Seymour picked up his carpetbag and sample case. "Thank you for the information." He started down the block toward the hotel.

"Come back anytime," Delacroix called after him. "Except, perhaps, when M'sieu Halliday is in attendance."

Seymour understood what the Cajun meant. Delacroix didn't want any incidents such as the one at the train station to occur in his saloon. The sight of Seymour might provoke Cole Halliday to gunplay again.

The clerk in the hotel lobby sneered at Seymour's soiled coat sleeve, but rented him a room anyway. When Seymour asked about the laundry, the clerk said, "Put anything you want cleaned outside the door of your room. I'll have a boy get it and take it down to Wing."

"Thank you." Seymour took the key to Room Eleven from the man, picked up his bags, and trudged up the stairs to the hotel's second floor.

The room was small and rather spartanly furnished with a bed, a chair, a tiny table with a basin on it, and a chamber pot. Several nails driven into the wall evidently served as a wardrobe. There was one window with a thin, thread-bare curtain hanging over it. The air inside the room was stifling. Seymour put his bags on the bed and went over to the window to open it. As he pushed the curtain aside and raised the glass, he found himself looking out at Sweet Apple's main street.

Roughly clad men strolled up and down the boardwalks. Others galloped heedlessly along the street. A dog squatted to relieve itself, adding to the already abundant feces in the street. In the next block, two women leaned out an open window in what had to be a house of ill repute, judging by their indecent attire, and called lewd invitations down to the men below. A man staggered along, weaving back and forth unsteadily, no doubt from the enormous quantity of rotgut he had taken on, until he tripped and fell as he was passing a water trough. He toppled over into the water, which was covered with bright green scum, and stayed there with his head submerged until Seymour felt horrified and alarmed. Before the man could drown, though, a man passing by reached down to grasp the back of his shirt and haul him out of the trough. The drunk sprawled on his back in the muck and mire, gasping for air, as his rescuer walked on.

"Oh, Uncle Cornelius," Seymour whispered. "What sort of hell on earth have you sent me to?"

By the time Seymour crawled out of the lumpy, uncomfortable bed the next morning, he was ready to flee Sweet Apple by train, stagecoach, or any other means of conveyance. He would even consider leaving on horseback, even though he had never ridden a horse, he thought as he scratched at the numerous welts left behind by the bugs that had shared the bed with him.

The meal he'd had in the hotel dining room the night before had been barely edible, and he held out no hope that breakfast would be any better. He doubted that he would have slept much anyway, between the rocks that apparently filled his mattress and the ravenous insects that called it home, but the constant uproar that came in through the open window all night insured that lack of slumber. Angry shouts, raucous laughter, pounding hoofbeats, tinny piano music, the occasional gunshot or scream of pain or rage . . . it all blended into an aria sung by demons from the depths of hell, at least to Seymour's ears.

He splashed water from the basin on his face and then dressed in his spare suit. He had sent everything he was wearing the day before out to be cleaned, and he had no idea when he would get the clothes back. As lawless as Sweet Apple was, it was possible someone might steal the garments and he would never see them again. Rubbing eyes grown gritty from lack of sleep, he stumbled down the stairs to the lobby, wondering what sort of evil concoction the cook had come up with for breakfast.

The same clerk was still on duty at the desk, and the same sneer was on his narrow, pockmarked face. "Sleep well?" he inquired in a tone that made it clear he didn't give a damn whether Seymour had slept well or not.

Seymour muttered something meaningless, and was about to go past the desk when he saw the newspaper lying on it. One of the headlines caught his eye. He started to snatch up the paper, but then his natural politeness made him stop and ask the clerk, "Do you mind if I have a look at this?"

The man snickered. "Help yourself, Mr. Standish. You're the big story, after all."

Seymour swallowed hard as he picked up the newspaper. It was the Sweet Apple *Gazette,* according to the masthead. The headline emblazoned below that read:

THE MOST COWARDLY MAN IN THE WEST?

The subhead below that was *New Arrival Encounters Local Man, Disgraces Self; Easterner Dubbed "Seymour the Lily-Livered."* The byline was *J. Emerson Heathcote, Editor and Publisher.*

"That son of a bitch," Seymour breathed as he read the story, hardly able to believe what his eyes were seeing. He was so upset that he didn't even notice he had just cursed, which was completely uncharacteristic behavior for him.

After pretending to befriend him and be sympathetic to his plight, the newspaperman had taken everything Seymour had told him and written a story about it, exaggerating the facts so that Seymour came across as even more of a bumbling, terror-stricken oaf than he actually had been. Anyone who read this couldn't help but see him as a ludicrous figure, worthy only of scorn and ridicule. His reputation in Sweet Apple was ruined for all time.

And Seymour was shaken to his core as he realized that Miss Maggie O'Ryan would probably read this newspaper story, too. Without him thinking about what he was doing, his hands clenched, crumpling the newspaper.

"Hey!" the clerk objected. "I wasn't through with that!"

"Here then," Seymour snarled. He threw the crumpled sheet onto the desk and then wheeled around to stalk toward the front door of the hotel.

"Where you going, Seymour?" the clerk called after

him in a mocking tone. "Better be careful. Somebody might say 'boo!' to you!"

Seymour ignored the grinning jackanapes. He had finally been pushed too far. He flung the door open and went outside, ready for a showdown.

J. Emerson Heathcote was going to rue the day he'd made sport of Seymour Standish!

Chapter 15

Seymour hadn't gone half a block toward the newspaper office before someone called out, "Hey, it's Seymour the Lily-Livered!"

"Don't look at him crossways," another man said with a laugh. "He's liable to faint dead away!"

"I hear tell he's the scaredest man west o' the Mississippi," put in a third man.

"Hell, he's the biggest coward in the whole damned country!"

The laughter swelled and grew until it threatened to overwhelm Seymour as he came to a stop and just stood there with his head down. He was still angry, but there was nothing he could do in the face of the whole town's mirth at his expense. And there was nothing he could do about Heathcote's newspaper story either, he realized. The damage was already done. Everyone in town knew who he was. Knew *what* he was. And even though he had stormed out of the hotel with the idea of giving Heathcote a well-deserved thrashing, Seymour knew that was never going to happen. The journalist was larger than him, and anyway, Seymour was no fighter.

He turned to slink back toward the hotel. He would stay in his room until the next eastbound train arrived, he decided, and then he would leave Sweet Apple and go home. Uncle Cornelius would be disappointed in him, and he would be letting his father's memory down, but there was nothing Seymour could do about that. He just wasn't cut out for life on the frontier.

Then he thought again about Maggie O'Ryan, and to his great surprise, he felt his backbone stiffening. The trio of loafers who had first started poking fun at him still lounged nearby on the boardwalk, laughing at him. He turned toward them and snapped, "That'll be quite enough out of you three."

The men fell silent and stared at him in obvious surprise. They were in their thirties, roughly dressed, with beard stubble on their faces and guns on their hips. Not the sort of men who Seymour should be confronting at all. He knew that, but he couldn't help himself. He supposed he had lost his mind.

But even so, it felt good to put them in their place.

Unfortunately, their surprise didn't last long. One by one they scowled, and then the ugliest of the three, a dark-complected man with an eye that tended to wander, stepped forward and growled, "What'd you say, dude?"

Seymour's instincts told him to apologize, to grovel if necessary, and then to get back into the hotel as quickly as possible.

But instead of doing that, he glared right back at the man and declared, "I said that'll be enough out of you three." He didn't even have the sense to leave it at that. He added, "I won't put up with any more childish behavior from ruffians and louts!"

The laughter in the street had died away as Seymour confronted the three men. Obviously, they weren't the only ones who were shocked that he hadn't turned tail and run. Everyone within earshot was staring now.

"I think Seymour the Lily-Livered just called you a name, Jack," one of the men gibed.

A hideous grin appeared on the face of the man with the wandering eye. "Yeah, and he's gonna be damned sorry about it, too." He hooked his thumbs in his gunbelt and sauntered closer to Seymour. "You got a gun, dude?"

Seymour could have lied, but instead he swallowed and said, "As a matter of fact, I do own a firearm. I don't have it with me, but—"

"Go get it," the man called Jack said. "Right now. You and me are gonna settle this like men—even if you *are* a worm!"

Hoping against hope, Seymour said, "Are you suggesting that we have some sort of shooting competition—"

"Haw!" Jack broke in. "That's exactly what I'm suggestin', you spineless little son of a bitch! And the prize is, the winner gets to live!"

Seymour remembered the dime novels he'd read. "You . . . you're saying that you want to have . . . a shoot-out . . . with me?"

"Damn right! Now go get your gun!"

Seymour began to tremble inside. His rage evaporated. This madman was going to kill him if he didn't do something right now to stop it.

"Listen, perhaps I spoke too hastily—"

"Forget it!" Jack roared. "It's too late for that now! I ain't interested in no damn apology. Get your gun and face me out there in the street like a man!"

Seymour's mind cast about frantically for any reasonable excuse. "But I don't . . . I don't have a gunbelt and a holster, like the one you're wearing."

That brought more laughter from Jack's friends. They slapped their thighs and roared. Jack just sneered and said, "Tell you what, dude. I'll let you hold your gun while we do this. I don't mind givin' you a little advantage."

Except it wasn't really an advantage, Seymour thought. By the time he could lift the revolver Rebecca had given him, pull back the hammer, aim the weapon, and press the trigger, Jack would have had time to shoot him three or four times at least.

"Isn't there anything I can do?" he asked miserably.

"You mean you want to back down like a whipped dog?" Jack laughed, and it was one of the most evil sounds Seymour had ever heard. "Sure, but you got to act like a dog, mister. Get down on all fours and bark for me."

Seymour swallowed. This was going to be the worst humiliation of his life. But he could do it. He had to do it. Otherwise his life wouldn't continue much longer.

"But that ain't all," Jack went on, perhaps sensing that Seymour was about to give in. "When you're done barkin', you're gonna crawl over here on your belly like the cur you are and lick my boots." He pointed down at his feet.

Seymour couldn't help but look. Jack wore his denim trousers tucked into high-topped black boots. The boots were filthy, covered with dung both dried and recent and God knows what else.

"You . . . you're speaking metaphorically, of course. You can't expect me to . . . to actually *lick*—"

"Either that or go get that gun o' yours, Seymour."

By now Seymour was shaking all over. The street had fallen silent again as the bystanders waited to see what he would do. He lowered himself into a crouch, preparing to get down on all fours as Jack had ordered. He heard mutters of surprise from some of the townspeople, as if they couldn't believe he would go along with such horrible humiliation.

He could barely believe it himself, but he had no choice. He put a hand on the boardwalk . . .

Then glanced along the street toward the far end of the settlement. He saw a building there with a couple of cottonwood trees next to it. The door was open, and children were going inside. Seymour realized that had to be the school where Maggie taught.

She was nowhere in sight, but that didn't mean anything. She didn't have to *see* what was about to happen. She would hear all about it, probably before the day was over. And no matter what she had already heard about him, or no doubt already read in the newspaper, this would be worse. This would be so bad that she would never be able to see or talk to him again without thinking about how he'd crawled like a dog and licked this man's filthy boots.

He would rather be dead than suffer through that, he realized.

He took a deep breath and pushed himself upright. "All right," he said. "I'll fetch my firearm."

Jack's bushy eyebrows went up in surprise. "You're serious, dude?"

Seymour made himself nod. "That's right. The gun is up in my hotel room. You'll wait here for me?"

Jack's face darkened with anger. "I never run out on a gunfight yet, blast you! Damn right I'll wait for you. Fact is, I'll be waitin' right out yonder in the street! Waitin' to kill you!"

Seymour jerked his head in a nod and turned toward the door of the hotel. As he pulled it open and went inside, a tiny voice in the back of his head told him to get his bags from the room, head out the rear door of the hotel, and keep going.

The clerk didn't know what had been going on outside. "Back already?" he asked with a smirk.

"That's right," Seymour heard himself saying. "I have to get my gun. I'm going to have a shoot-out."

The clerk stared at him as he climbed the stairs.

As Seymour reached his room, he asked himself again if he truly knew what he was doing. If he went through with this, it would be tantamount to committing suicide. Was his pride worth losing his life? Was it worth it to keep a woman he hadn't even met until less than twelve hours earlier from thinking badly of him?

Despite the obvious answers to those questions, he found himself opening his carpetbag and taking out the wooden case that contained the revolver Rebecca had given him. There were bullets in the case as well. With trembling fingers Seymour opened the gate on the side of the weapon and began thumbing the cartridges into the empty chambers of the cylinder.

He loaded it full, then held the gun down at his side. It was heavy. He tried to pull it up quickly, just to see if he could do it. His fingers slipped on the walnut grips and he almost dropped it. Perhaps when he fired, he should grip his right wrist with his left hand, just to steady it, he thought.

Then he told himself how ridiculous that was. He would be dead before he ever got to that point.

By the time he reached the lobby again, the clerk had heard what was about to happen. "Listen, Mr. Standish," the man said. "Jack Keller's pretty good with a gun. If you throw down on him, he'll kill you."

"He insulted me," Seymour said.

"He insults a lot of people." The clerk lowered his voice. "If you tell anybody I said this I'll deny it, but Keller's a jackass, just like a lot of folks in this town. He'll gun you down and won't blink an eye."

"If you're worried that I already paid you for a week in advance," Seymour said, "don't be. You can keep the money."

The clerk shook his head. "That ain't it. I know I gave you a hard time, Mr. Standish, and I wasn't the only one. But I'd hate to see anybody get killed over a little hoorawing."

"I don't know what that is, but I assume you mean being laughed at and humiliated." Seymour hefted the gun. "This is supposed to settle everything, isn't it? This will make everything right. We'll see."

He turned toward the door.

"Damn it, Mr. Standish—"

Seymour walked out before the clerk could say anything else—and before he could lose his nerve. If he suddenly regained his sanity, he would probably turn and run screaming back up to his room. He could crawl into the bed and pull the covers up over his head . . .

Jack Keller was standing in the middle of the street, as promised. The morning sun cast a dark shadow behind him.

The news of the impending gunfight had traveled swiftly. The boardwalks were crowded with people who had come out to watch. Seymour saw the avid expressions on their faces and felt a little sickened. They were eager to see his blood spilled in the street. Eager to see him die.

"Well, dude," Keller drawled. "You came back out. I didn't figure you would. And you really do have a gun."

Seymour forced himself to nod. His voice sounded strange in his ears as he said, "I told you I did."

Keller lifted his left hand and made a lazy gesture. "Come on then. Let's get this over with."

Seymour took a step out into the street. His legs began to shake so bad he wasn't sure if he could walk all the way out there. He willed his muscles to work and took one step, then two.

Pierre Delacroix came hurrying from the direction of the Black Bull. The saloon probably never closed. He caught up to Seymour when Seymour was only a few steps from the boardwalk and gripped his arm.

"Are you sure you want to do this, *mon ami*?"

"Hey, let him alone, Frenchy!" Keller called. "He's a full-growed man. He can make up his own mind when he wants to die. Haw!"

"M'sieu Standish, no one will think less of you if you abandon this mad idea," Delacroix went on.

Seymour looked over at him and said, "We both know that's not true, Mr. Delacroix. It . . . it's too late to back out now."

"But look at yourself! You are shaking so much you can barely hold that pistol. How in the world are you going to shoot it out with an experienced gunman like Keller?"

"I'll manage somehow," Seymour said.

"Or die," Delacroix said.

Seymour managed to smile slightly and raise his shoulders in a little shrug.

"Get out of the street, Frenchy, or you'll be next," Keller warned.

Delacroix could only sigh, shake his head, and step back. "God be with you, *mon ami*," he murmured.

Seymour resumed his unsteady march toward the center of the street. The gun seemed to weigh more with every step, so that by the time he reached the place where he was going and turned to face Keller, the weapon pulled him to the side. His knees shook and his mouth was dry and his pulse hammered in his ears like the pounding of distant drums. Bitterness filled his throat. He worried that he would be sick, right here in front of everyone who had come out to watch the gunfight.

Not that he would have to endure the embarrassment of that for long if it did happen, he reminded himself. Once he was dead, he would be past any shame.

"Seymour, you're shakin' so hard you look like a little breeze'd knock you right over," Keller said with that ugly, confident grin. "You sure you want to go through with this? You can still lick my boots instead, if you want."

"I'm here," Seymour choked out. "Let's get on with it."

Keller laced his fingers together, cracked his knuckles, and stretched. His stance was full of contempt. "Well, if you're sure."

Suddenly, one of his friends called out to him from the boardwalk. "Hey, Jack, wait a minute."

Keller glanced over at him, clearly annoyed. "What the hell is it, Dugan?"

"I was just thinkin' . . . you can see how scared this fella is."

"So?"

"There's a story about him in the paper this mornin'. I seen the headline. It says he's the most cowardly man in the West."

That headline had been a question, not a statement, Seymour thought wildly.

"Yeah, what about it?" Keller said.

"You've faced down some hombres who were pretty good with their guns."

"Damn right I have! Killed six men, ever' one of 'em in a fair fight!"

"What do you think it's gonna do to your rep when folks hear that you gunned down—" The man called Dugan pointed at Seymour and said with utter contempt, *"This."*

Keller frowned as he considered what his friend had just said. After a moment, he replied, "You might have a point there, Dugan."

"You heard what Cole Halliday said about him yesterday. The likes o' him ain't worth wastin' a bullet on. It really would be just like shootin' a dog."

Keller lifted his left hand and rasped his fingers over his beard-stubbled jaw. "Yeah. Folks might start callin' me the man who shot Seymour the Lily-Livered. I ain't sure I'd want that."

Dugan shook his head. "I know I wouldn't."

Seymour had watched and listened to the exchange with a mixture of fear, amazement, and growing anger. Now he burst out, "Are you saying that now you *don't* want to fight me?"

Keller grinned and said, "Yeah, I reckon that's right. I'm gonna let you live, Seymour."

"But . . . but . . ."

"Get out o' here while you got the chance," Keller advised.

"You mean you're backing down?"

Keller's face hardened again, and for a second Seymour thought he had just made the worst mistake of his life. But then the man said, "No, I mean that no self-respectin' gunfighter wants to get tarred with the brush o' killin' the biggest coward in the West. Hell, if I shot you, I'd be a laughin'stock from one end o' Texas to the other!"

Shaking his head, Keller turned away with a dismissive

wave. He rejoined his friends and headed away down the street. The crowds along the boardwalk broke up and dispersed in a hurry.

Seymour was left standing alone in the middle of the street, gun in hand. No one was laughing at him now. No one even paid any attention to him.

Because he was no longer even worthy of scorn.

Chapter 16

Seymour didn't think things could possibly get any worse than they were at that moment.

Unfortunately, he was wrong.

As he looked around, the people who had gathered to watch him die turned their heads. They didn't want to look at him, didn't want to even acknowledge his existence. But despite that, he felt eyes watching him, and as he slowly turned his gaze toward the school at the end of the street, his blood turned cold and sluggish in his veins.

Maggie O'Ryan stood there just outside the door of the school, staring at him. She had witnessed his shame. She had seen the gunman called Keller turn and walk away, totally dismissing Seymour from consideration.

At that moment, Seymour wished he could just melt away into the nothingness that was all he deserved. He would have rather died under Keller's gun than have Maggie see what had happened. He wasn't sure why that was so important to him, but it was.

He turned and stumbled toward the boardwalk, unsure of where he was going or what he was doing, knowing only that he couldn't stay there. Even at this distance he could feel Maggie's pity, and that wasn't what he wanted. He didn't know what he wanted, but that wasn't it.

Pierre Delacroix was suddenly there in front of him. The saloon keeper grasped his arm. "Come with me, *mon ami*," Delacroix said. "You look like you need a drink."

"I told you, I . . . I don't indulge in spirits."

"This is a special occasion. You are still alive."

Seymour gave a bitter laugh. "Only because I'm not worth killing."

"The drawing of another breath is always a reason to celebrate." Delacroix urged him toward the Black Bull, and Seymour was too stunned to put up a fight. He didn't even think about the fact that it was still early in the morning.

"Are you sure you want a pariah like me in your establishment?"

Delacroix shrugged. "No one will care."

Again the bitter laughter from Seymour. "That's the problem. No one cares. Least of all me."

But he allowed Delacroix to lead him into the saloon, and at the Cajun's urging he tucked the pistol behind his belt rather than carrying it. Delacroix took him to a table in a rear corner of the big room and sat him down. At this hour, not many customers were in the Black Bull. No one was sitting close to the table where Seymour slumped into one of the empty chairs.

Delacroix signaled to the bartender. The man brought over a bottle and two glasses. Delacroix sat down across the table from Seymour and poured the drinks. He pushed one of the glasses toward Seymour and said, "I know it does not seem like it now, but everyone will forget about this in a day or two."

Seymour looked at the glass, which had a couple of inches

of whiskey in it, as if he had never seen such a thing before. Then he took a deep breath, reached out, and picked it up.

"That's right," Delacroix said. "It will do you good."

Moving as if his brain had no conscious control over his muscles, Seymour brought the glass to his lips, tilted his head back, and swallowed all the whiskey in one gulp.

No matter how upset and depressed he was, the fiery stuff jolted him as it went down. His throat burst into flame and his belly exploded. His eyes opened so wide they looked like they were about to leap from their sockets. His already pale skin turned the color and texture of thin paper. A second after he had swallowed the whiskey, a spasm wracked him, making him lean forward over the table. His fingers scrabbled feebly against the wood.

Surely not even being shot out there in the street would have hurt this much.

Seymour rested his head on the table and moaned. Delacroix laughed, not unkindly, and said, "You will become accustomed to it, *mon ami*. And you will find that you have no finer friend in this world."

Seymour doubted that. After a few moments, though, the inferno inside him subsided somewhat, leaving behind a warmth that was somehow comforting, even on a summer morning where the West Texas heat was already building to a simmer. Seymour was able to lift his head. He blinked a few times and then forced out, "It's not so bad."

"As I told you." Delacroix picked up the bottle and re-filled Seymour's glass. "Sip this one, instead of taking it all at once."

Seymour did like the saloon keeper said, sipping the whiskey instead of bolting it down. That increased the warmth in his belly without setting him on fire again. He drew strength from that warmth.

Delacroix hadn't taken his own drink yet, but Seymour didn't care about that. He didn't particularly want company at this moment either, but he couldn't very well ask Delacroix to leave. The Black Bull belonged to the Cajun after all.

Seymour sat there in sullen silence, sipping the whiskey. He lost track of time. All he knew was that after a while Delacroix got up to do something else, but the saloon keeper left the bottle on the table. Whenever Seymour's glass was empty, he reached out and snagged the bottle by the neck. His hand shook a little, so that the bottle rattled against the glass as he poured, but overall he thought he was steadier now than he had been earlier. He'd been trembling so bad in the street that it was a wonder he'd been able to stand up.

The *chink-chink-chink* of spurs made Seymour raise his gaze from the table. A man came to a stop a few feet from the table and stared at him. Seymour blinked eyes grown bleary from drink and looked back at him.

The man was stocky, with a dark, squarish face. He wore a black-and-white cowhide vest and a flat-crowned black hat. The butt of a gun with checkered grips stuck up from the holster on his hip.

"You're him," the man said in a gravelly voice. "Seymour the Lily-Livered."

Seymour made no response. There was nothing to say.

"You know who I am?" the man asked.

Seymour managed to shake his head. The motion made the saloon seem to tilt first one way and then the other, but he thought that was just because of the whiskey he had imbibed. The building wasn't actually moving.

"I'm Ned Akin. I'm fast with a gun, and I've killed four men. Folks around here think I'm a pretty bad hombre."

Akin was hardly the first. In less than twenty-four hours, Seymour had encountered Cole Halliday, Jack Keller, and now this man Akin. What was it about him that drew these gunfighters to him like moths to a flame? Did he give off some sort of scent that was undetectable except to those who were prone to bullying and brutalizing those who were weaker than them?

"They say you're the most cowardly man in the West," Akin went on. "I reckon I got to see that to believe it. On your feet, dude. I see you got a gun. But you won't use it, will you? You're too lily-livered for that."

Seymour looked past Akin and saw Pierre Delacroix standing at the bar with a worried expression on his face. The Cajun didn't want this confrontation happening inside his saloon. But he wasn't going to interfere either, Seymour sensed. Probably because Ned Akin was every bit as dangerous as he claimed to be.

"Well, how about it, Seymour?" Akin prodded. "You gonna show me just how cowardly you are, or are you gonna just sit there starin' at me like some sort o' half-wit?"

Seymour laughed. "Go ahead and shoot me," he said. "Get it over with."

Akin frowned. "You *want* me to kill you? You ain't gonna beg for your life?"

Seymour put his hands on the table. "I'm not afraid of you," he said as he pushed himself to his feet, and to his enormous surprise he realized that he meant it. Nothing Akin could do to him would be any worse than the things he had already endured.

Nothing could be worse than making a fool of himself in front of Maggie O'Ryan.

Akin's face flushed in anger. "Damn you, dude, I could kill you right now."

Seymour smiled. "You wouldn't dare." He belched and swayed. "Then you'd be known as . . . the man who wasted a bullet—" Another belch. "—on Seymour the Lily-Livered."

He suddenly doubled over, and all the whiskey he'd guzzled down since coming into the Black Bull raged back up his throat and spewed from his mouth, splattering all over Ned Akin's boots. The gunfighter jumped back with a curse as Seymour emptied his belly. "You son of a bitch!" he howled. His hand stabbed toward his gun.

But he stopped the motion before he drew the revolver. His hand was clenched around the gun butt, but after a second he let go of the weapon and allowed it to slide back down into the holster.

"You're right, you scrawny little bastard," Akin snarled. "Killin' you would just hurt my rep." He turned and stalked out of the saloon, his spurs going *ka-chink, ka-chink* again.

Seymour half-sat, half-fell into his chair again. Now that he had thrown up all the whiskey, he wanted another drink. He reached for the bottle.

Delacroix stopped him with a hand on his wrist. "Perhaps you have had enough, Seymour."

Seymour shook off the Cajun's hand and grabbed the bottle. "I'll decide when I've had enough." He didn't bother with the glass this time, just lifted the bottle and drank straight from the neck. The whiskey didn't burn near as much going down now. With his free hand, Seymour dug around in his pocket until he found a coin. He dropped it on the table and added, "I can pay for my own drinks."

Delacroix looked at him for a moment, then shrugged and swept the coin from the table. "As you wish, *mon ami*."

"And stop calling me your friend," Seymour said. "I'm not your friend. I have no friends."

"That is as you wish, too." Delacroix motioned for the swamper to come over and mop up the whiskey that Seymour had vomited onto the floor. Luckily, the sawdust scattered thickly on the planks had soaked up some of the mess.

The whiskey in the bottle gurgled as Seymour took another drink. It was a nice sound, he thought. He asked himself why he had wasted so many years disapproving of drinking.

That was the last coherent thought he had for a while.

He woke up with the sound of piano music in his ears. The tinny strains were accompanied by a considerable amount of loud talking and laughter. Tobacco smoke tickled his nose. Seymour lifted his head and shook it to try to get rid of the annoyances.

That was a mistake.

His head thudded against the table. He left it there for what seemed like an hour, until all the crazy spinning stopped. When he finally pushed himself upright again and opened his eyes, he was more careful about it.

The Black Bull was crowded now, with most of the spaces at the bar filled and poker games going on at several of the tables. Seymour glanced toward the big front windows. One of them was boarded up, and he recalled the drunken cowboy's bullet that had nearly hit Miss Maggie O'Ryan the day before. Through the other window, he saw the fading golden light of dusk.

He had been sitting there passed out in the saloon all day, Seymour realized.

His mouth tasted awful, and he was parched. A drink of cool water sounded better than anything in the world. But the thought of it made his stomach clench. He hadn't eaten anything in almost twenty-four hours. He needed food and drink.

But not whiskey. A shudder went through him at the very idea.

He had to get out of here. His mind reeled at the idea that he had allowed himself to get so thoroughly inebriated. That wasn't like him at all. He flattened his hands on the table and tried to push himself to his feet.

That made the world lurch to a halt around him and then immediately begin revolving in the wrong direction. As Seymour's brain spun, he would have fallen if not for the hand that suddenly grasped his arm.

"Let me help you, Seymour," Pierre Delacroix said.

Seymour recoiled and tried to pull away from the saloon keeper. "You . . . you've helped me quite enough!" he said. "You . . . ohhhh . . . you were the one who . . . got me drunk in the first place."

Delacroix's face hardened. "No one put a gun to your head and made you drink, Seymour. I provided the whiskey, that is all."

Seymour wanted to argue with the Cajun, but it just wasn't worth the effort. He muttered, "Let me out of here. I want to go."

"Go where?"

That simple question stopped Seymour in his tracks. Sweet Apple wasn't his home. He had no place here except a dingy hotel room.

But that was better than the saloon. He shook off Delacroix's hand and stumbled toward the batwings. Some of the saloon's customers watched him and grinned. Others laughed out loud. Seymour wanted to lash out at them. He didn't, of course. He didn't do things like that. He was too civilized and respectable to get in a shouting match with a bunch of half-drunk louts in a frontier saloon.

He almost fell again when he reached the batwings. He caught hold of them, swung them aside, and lurched out onto the boardwalk. He didn't think he was still drunk, but he was so unsteady on his feet that he had to consider the possibility that he might be. He wondered if a pot of strong, black coffee would help. That thought made his stomach lurch, too.

But he didn't throw up, and by focusing his will on what he was doing, he was able to walk down the street toward the hotel in a fairly straightforward fashion. He might have weaved a little, but he didn't think it was too bad.

When he reached the hotel, he fumbled for a second with the doorknob before he was able to get it open. The same clerk was behind the desk. Seymour blinked owlishly at him and said, "Don't you ever get a break?"

The man ignored the question and said, "You've got some visitors, Mr. Standish."

Seymour had no idea who in Sweet Apple would want to be visiting him. He was a laughingstock, after all, someone to be pointed out and mocked. But then he saw several men stand up from chairs on the other side of the lobby and come toward him. The one who was slightly in the lead said, "Mr. Standish? We've been waiting to talk to you."

The man was portly and well dressed, with muttonchop whiskers and a waxed mustache. The men with him were all similar, with a well-fed, successful air about them. Seymour realized with a shock that he recognized one of them. J. Emerson Heathcote, the newspaper editor and publisher who had done so much to spread that humiliating nickname—Seymour the Lily-Livered—all over town.

"You," Seymour practically snarled at him.

Heathcote raised his hands, palms out. "I don't blame you for being upset with me, Seymour, but you have to admit, it made for a good story."

"You made me look like a cowardly idiot!"

"Silver linings, my boy, silver linings."

Seymour stared at him in confusion for a second before saying, "What are you talking about?"

The first man who had spoken replied, "You're already famous, Mr. Standish. Mr. Heathcote put copies of today's paper on the trains bound for San Antonio and El Paso. He has associates in both places who will pick up the story and run it."

Heathcote nodded, beaming in satisfaction.

"You mean everyone in Texas is going to read about the most cowardly man in the West?" Seymour asked in a choked voice.

"Yes, and if the story is picked up by the Eastern papers, it won't be long until the entire country knows about you, my boy," Heathcote said. "*Harper's* might even send a reporter out here to get the full story."

Seymour closed his eyes and ran a shaky hand over his face. "My God," he muttered. "My God." That meant Uncle Cornelius would find out what an abject failure he was.

Strangely enough, that thought didn't bother him as much he expected it to. He was a lot more worried that the increased notoriety would make him fall even lower in the eyes of Maggie O'Ryan, if that was even possible.

"I'm the mayor of Sweet Apple," the first man said. "Abner Mitchell. You already know J. Emerson here, of course, and these gentlemen are the other members of Sweet Apple's town council. You're going to put us on the map, Mr. Standish."

Seymour had to laugh. It was a bitter, humorless sound. "All because you were visited by a craven coward like me?"

"No, sir. Because you're the man who's going to tame the hell-roaring'est town in the West." Abner Mitchell reached inside his coat and then held out his hand toward Seymour. The lamplight in the hotel lobby gleamed on the star-shaped badge that lay in his palm. "You see, Mr. Standish, we're here to ask you to accept the job of marshal of Sweet Apple."

Chapter 17

Seymour could not have been more surprised if the man had asked him to flap his arms and fly to the moon. He was so shocked that for a long moment all he could do was stand there with his mouth open, unable to say anything.

Then he gasped, "Marshal? You want me to be your marshal?"

The members of Sweet Apple's town council all nodded. "That's right," Heathcote said. "Isn't it a wonderful idea?" He hooked his thumbs in his vest and preened. "I thought of it, you know."

"You're insane!" Seymour said.

The newspaperman blinked and looked a little surprised, not to mention crestfallen.

Mayor Mitchell insisted, "Not at all, Mr. Standish. We think you're the perfect candidate for the job."

Seymour wondered if this conversation was real, or just a figment of his whiskey-addled imagination. Deciding that it was real—but unfathomable—he asked, "Why in the world would you think that? Everyone else who pinned on a lawman's badge in your town has been killed! Gunned down ruthlessly!" Seymour looked at Heathcote. "Isn't that what you told me?"

The newspaperman shrugged. "Yes. But you're different, Seymour."

"How am I different, except that I'm even less of a threat to the lawless element than those other men were?"

Mitchell said, "But you see, that's what makes you perfect." When Seymour just stared at him in incomprehension, the mayor went on. "Cole Halliday, Jack Keller, and Ned Akin—three of the most notorious gunfighters and killers west of the Pecos—have already confronted you . . . and yet you're still alive."

"Because they all said that I'm not worth killing!"

"Be that as it may." Mitchell stepped closer and prodded Seymour's narrow chest with a finger. "You're still *alive*. You faced down those gunmen and survived to tell the tale."

Heathcote put in, "That part of the story will spread rapidly, too."

Seymour shook his head. "I . . . I still don't understand."

"No self-respecting gunfighter wants to be known as the man who shot Seymour the Lily-Livered," Heathcote said. "If someone killed you, that moniker would follow him for the rest of his days. He would become the object of ridicule, not you."

"Of course I wouldn't be the object of ridicule anymore," Seymour muttered. "I'd be dead."

Heathcote didn't pay any attention to that. He went on. "There might as well be a bulletproof wall around you, Seymour. Your lack of bravery actually makes you the safest man in the West."

Based on the evidence of everything that had happened since his arrival in Sweet Apple, Seymour had to concede that Heathcote might be right about that. But he still didn't see how that would make him an effective lawman.

He said as much. "No one's going to pay any attention to what I say if they're not afraid of me. I can't keep order."

"No?" Heathcote arched his eyebrows. "If not for you, there would have been at least one more killing in Sweet Apple. If any other dude had come to town and bumped into Cole Halliday, Cole would have shot him dead. No doubt about it."

The other men murmured agreement with him.

"And we can't forget Miss O'Ryan either," the journalist went on.

"What about her?" Seymour snapped. He didn't want Maggie getting dragged into this ridiculous farce.

"Chances are she would've been killed yesterday afternoon if you hadn't acted when you did," Heathcote said. "Your quick action really did save her life, Seymour."

For a second, Seymour stared at him and thought about that. Heathcote was right, he realized with a shock. Knocking Maggie out of the way of that bullet had been entirely an instinctive reaction, but even so, he *had* saved her.

"So you see," Mitchell said, "you've been of service to the community already, Mr. Standish. If Miss O'Ryan had been killed, Lord knows if we ever would have found another teacher. And a town *has* to have a school if it's going to grow and prosper."

Seymour couldn't argue with that. But these men had forgotten about one important thing.

"I'm a dry-goods salesman," he said. "I have no experience or training as a law officer. I wouldn't have any idea what to do!"

"Just keep the peace," Heathcote said. "Arrest anyone who gets too obstreperous. They'll cooperate with you.

They'll probably think it's all a grand joke, being arrested by Seymour the Lily-Livered."

Seymour winced. He hated that name.

"I came to Sweet Apple to sell dry goods."

"We thought of that," Mitchell said. "It just so happens that I own the largest general mercantile store between Del Rio and El Paso. Mr. Manning and Mr. Lesser here also own emporiums in Sweet Apple. We're all prepared to open accounts with Standish Dry Goods and purchase a considerable amount of merchandise from your company, Seymour . . . if I may call you Seymour."

He nodded as he tried to take in the offer. Being able to deliver three big new accounts might elevate his standing in his uncle's eyes.

"And with that leg up, so to speak," Mitchell went on, "you'd be free to devote more of your time to your duties as marshal."

Seymour wished his head wasn't pounding so bad. The aftereffects of his drunken binge were brutal. He found that it was difficult to think clearly. The idea of him being a lawman was crazy, of course. Absolutely insane.

But these men seemed determined that he take the job, and they believed that his reputation for cowardice would keep him safe and even make him a more effective law officer. On the face of it, the idea made no sense at all.

And yet Seymour knew that in real life, things that seemed to have no chance of working out sometimes did. If they didn't, then phrases such as "against all odds" and "the exception that proves the rule" never would have been coined. Lightning had to strike *somewhere*.

Why not in Sweet Apple, Texas?

And there was one more consideration that began to loom larger and larger in Seymour's mind. Right now, despite the gratitude that she probably felt toward him, Maggie O'Ryan had to hold him in contempt. She knew that he had been humiliated again and again. She had heard the chants of "Seymour the Lily-Livered" and had no doubt read that horrible headline and story in J. Emerson Heathcote's Sweet Apple *Gazette*. No matter what he did now, he told himself, chances are he could only go up in Maggie's estimation.

"All right," he heard himself croaking in a strained voice. He reached out with a shaky hand to take the badge from Mayor Mitchell. "I'll do it." He pinned the tin star to his coat, although it took him two tries to do it.

Heathcote grinned, raised a clenched fist, and said, "Huzzah!"

He was probably thinking about what a fine story it would make for the *Gazette* when the foolish new marshal was murdered, Seymour thought.

The three merchants insisted that he fetch his sample case so that they could conclude their business arrangements. Seymour was still hungry and thirsty, but he knew that a salesman had to take his opportunities where and when he found them. A deal postponed was often a deal lost. So he went upstairs, got his samples, and within half an hour had written three sizable orders to send back to Uncle Cornelius in Trenton.

The other members of the town council, with the exception of Heathcote, had left the hotel. Now the newspaperman took Seymour's arm and said, "I'll show you the marshal's office. We do have one here in Sweet Apple, you know. It's just unoccupied at the moment."

"But no longer," Mitchell said, obviously pleased with

the afternoon's developments. "It won't take long for people to hear that Sweet Apple has a marshal again."

In fact, the word had already spread through the settlement, Seymour judged from the way people looked at him and the buzz of conversation got louder as he and Heathcote and Mitchell walked down the street. The citizens seemed to know what was going on. In fact, some of them started trailing along behind the three men, as if they wanted to see what was going to happen.

They came to a small adobe building with a padlocked door. There were hooks in the wooden awning over the boardwalk where a sign of some sort had once hung, but they were empty. Mitchell took a key from his pocket and used it to unfasten the padlock. He swung the door back, reached inside, and picked up something that was leaning against the wall.

It was the sign that was supposed to hang from those hooks, Seymour realized. Painted on it was the legend MARSHAL—*Sweet Apple, Texas*. The words were still readable despite the fact that half a dozen or more bullet holes were punched through the sign.

"Some of our rowdier citizens had a tendency to take potshots at the sign, especially when they were drunk," Mitchell explained. "That's why we put it away."

"And we didn't have a marshal anymore anyway," Heathcote added. He smiled. "But now we do."

He and Mitchell each took one end of the sign and raised up on their toes to hang it from the hooks. It swung back and forth a little as they let go of it.

Seymour gazed up at the sign and thought that he ought to feel a little pride at the sight of it. He was the marshal now after all.

But instead he just felt a little dizzy and confused and

disoriented, as if he were trapped in a dreamworld where things were happening that had no business happening.

Heathcote and Mitchell ushered him inside. Heathcote lit a lamp that sat on a desk with a scarred top. The desk, like everything else in the room, was covered with a fine layer of dust. Seymour turned to a rack on the wall that held several rifles and shotguns. He brushed his fingers over the smooth, polished stock of a Winchester, leaving marks in the dust that coated the wood.

"We tried to provide the marshal with the tools he needed to do the job," Mitchell said. "You'll find plenty of guns and ammunition here. There's a file drawer in the desk for reward posters and other important papers. A couple of cells in the back where you can lock up prisoners. Also, there's a little room with a cot where you can sleep if you want to."

"We'll have some wood for the stove brought in," Heathcote said. He looked Seymour up and down with a critical eye. "Also, you'll need some clothes that are more suitable. And a hat." He chuckled. "I know you don't have a hat."

Seymour flushed at the memory of how Cole Halliday had shredded his hat with bullets.

"Don't worry about any of that," Mitchell said. "Anything you need, my store can supply, and the town will pay for it. I'll bring over some clothes and a hat. Do you have a gunbelt and holster for that pistol?"

Seymour shook his head.

"I'll get that for you, too. And some coffee, a pot, and a few other supplies. How about a saddle?"

"I don't have one," Seymour said. "I don't have a horse."

"Frank Thomas down at the livery stable can provide a

mount any time you need one," Heathcote said. "The same goes for a saddle."

"What else do you need?" Mitchell asked.

"Something to eat. And perhaps some cool buttermilk." Seymour hoped that would settle his stomach.

"Sit down," Heathcote said. "I'll have Agnes from the café bring a tray over right away."

"I could go over there to eat—" Seymour began.

Heathcote and Mitchell both shook their heads.

"It's taken us a long time to get someone back in this office," Mitchell said. "You just sit down and stay right here, and we'll be back."

"Well . . . all right." Seymour lowered himself into the swivel chair behind the desk. It was covered with worn leather upholstery, but was more comfortable than it looked.

The other two men hurried out, leaving him there alone. They were showing a lot of faith in him, Seymour thought with a wry smile as he took the gun from behind his belt and placed it on top of the desk. He felt a strong urge to run as far and as fast as he could while they were gone, leaving that marshal's badge behind for them to find when they got back.

But instead he looked down at the badge pinned to his coat and stayed where he was. He was trying to remember the last time when anyone had actually had any faith in him. . . .

A few minutes later, a middle-aged woman with graying blond hair and bright blue eyes came bustling in with a cloth-covered tray in her hands. "You'd be the new marshal," she said. "I'm Agnes Swenson, from the café. Mayor Mitchell asked me to bring some supper over to you."

"Yes, ma'am," Seymour said as he got politely to his feet. "I appreciate it. How much do I owe you?"

Agnes Swenson set the tray on the desk. "Not a blessed thing, Marshal. The town pays for all your meals while you're wearing that badge."

"Well, I . . . I'm much obliged."

Agnes whisked the cloth off the platter of food. Seymour saw fried chicken, mashed potatoes swimming with gravy, greens, and a large biscuit. The tray also had a glass of buttermilk on it, cool enough so that drops of condensation had formed on the outside of the glass.

At the sight and smell of the food, Seymour's stomach rebelled for a second, then settled down. Under the watchful, approving eyes of Agnes Swenson, he sat down and began to eat. With every bite he felt a little better. He washed the food down with swallows of the buttermilk.

"You know, you don't really look like a coward," Agnes commented. "You just look like a nice young man."

Seymour wasn't sure whether to feel insulted or amused. He settled for amused. "You'd better hope I *am* the most cowardly man in the West, as Mr. Heathcote dubbed me," he said. "The town council seems to be counting on it."

"Well, all I know is, you should be careful. Being the marshal is a mighty dangerous job in this town." Her voice caught a little as she went on. "I should know. They talked my husband Axel into pinning on that badge a while back."

Seymour laid down his knife and fork and frowned. According to everything he'd been told, the previous marshal of Sweet Apple had been killed in short order. That meant . . .

"I'm sorry, Mrs. Swenson."

Agnes used a corner of her apron to dab a tear away.

"Just you take care of yourself, Marshal Standish. Don't try to stand up to those bullies and killers. It's enough that the town has somebody to call the marshal again. You don't have to actually *do* anything."

Was that what they really wanted? Just a figurehead, so that the community leaders could claim they had brought law and order to Sweet Apple whether that was actually the case or not? Maybe he was supposed to just sit here in the office and ignore his duties, so that Mitchell and Heathcote and the other politicians could put on a big show and pretend to care about the citizens, all the while allowing the forces of lawlessness to run roughshod over them. A hollow feeling grew inside Seymour's chest as he realized that might be exactly what they wanted.

Well, if ineffectual was what they wanted, he could deliver that, he told himself.

He had been doing it all his life, after all.

Later, after Agnes Swenson was gone, Mitchell and Heathcote returned with everything they had promised. Seymour went into the back room and emerged a few minutes later dressed in black whipcord trousers, a white shirt, and a black leather vest. He wore high-topped boots and a black hat that seemed ridiculously large. Around his hips was buckled a gunbelt and holster of hand-tooled leather. He slipped the pistol into the holster and found that it fit fairly well.

"Don't forget your badge, Marshal," Heathcote said. He had taken the star off Seymour's coat. He held it out to him now.

Seymour took it and pinned it to the vest. "How do I look?"

"Like an actual lawman," Mitchell said.

"Except for the, uh, spectacles," Heathcote said.

Seymour smiled. "Well, they'll have to stay; otherwise I can't see well enough to do my job. Shouldn't I go and make my evening rounds, or something? Isn't that what a marshal does?"

"Oh, don't worry about that tonight," Mitchell said. "There'll be time enough to start that later."

"You're sure?"

"Yes, of course. Just stay here in the office tonight. Let the people get used to the idea of having a marshal again."

It seemed to Seymour that the citizens of Sweet Apple would get used to the idea quicker if he were out and about among them, but Mitchell and Heathcote were both adamant that he didn't have to make rounds tonight.

It would be all right with them, he thought, if he didn't make rounds at all. Ever.

They left, and with a sigh he took his hat off, put it on the desk, and sat down in the swivel chair. To have something to do, he opened the file drawer and started looking through the wanted posters that were jumbled inside there.

He had been at it for half an hour or so when the door suddenly opened. He looked up, feeling a surge of alarm. But instead of some gunfighter who had come to shoot him, he saw Maggie O'Ryan.

Perhaps she was no less dangerous, though, because she stormed into the marshal's office, slapped her hands down on the desk, glared at him, and demanded, "Seymour Standish, have you lost your mind?"

Chapter 18

"M-Miss O'Ryan!" he gulped. "What are you doing here?"

Maggie straightened and crossed her arms over her bosom as she glared at him. "I heard people talking about it, but I didn't believe it," she said. "I had to come see for myself. Now I almost wish that I hadn't!"

"Come to see what?" Seymour forced himself to ask, even though he was afraid that he already knew the answer to that question.

"The biggest fool north of the Rio Grande! Seymour—may I call you Seymour?"

He nodded dumbly.

"Seymour, have you lost your mind? Why in heaven's name would you want to take the job of marshal in Sweet Apple? You're going to get yourself killed!"

Finally, he was able to shake his head. "Mayor Mitchell and Mr. Heathcote and the other members of the town council assure me that won't happen."

"J. Emerson Heathcote is a pompous windbag and the

mayor and the other councilmen aren't much better! How could they promise you that? How could you believe them?"

Seymour leaned forward, getting over his surprise at her visit and warming to his subject. "It makes perfect sense, Maggie. I can call you Maggie?"

She jerked her head in a nod.

Somewhat surprised at his own daring, Seymour went on. "I've encountered three of the most notorious gunmen in the area—Cole Halliday, Jack Keller, and Ned Akin— and lived to tell the tale. Despite everything, none of them were willing to kill me. To do so would be bad for their reputations."

Maggie frowned. "You're willing to stake your life on the fact that three men didn't want to waste a bullet on you?"

"Exactly! I'm untouchable for that very reason."

Her frown deepened. "How do you know that all the gunmen in the area are going to feel that way? What if you come up against one of them who's too drunk to worry about what will happen to his reputation if he shoots you?"

"Well . . . I think the mayor and the council intend for me to avoid such confrontations as much as possible."

"But it's the marshal's job to deal with trouble—" Maggie stopped short as understanding dawned on her pretty face. "Oh, my God. They want you to just sit in the office and pretend to be a lawman."

"I wouldn't have put it quite so bluntly," Seymour said, although the thought had crossed his mind in almost the same words that Maggie had just used.

"That way, the next time there's an election, they can all say that they brought law and order back to Sweet Apple, even though in reality nothing has changed. Seymour, they're risking your life for their own political gain!"

"I don't see it that way," Seymour replied, even though,

again, he'd had the same thought. "I'm getting something out of it, too, you know."

"What, marshal's wages? That can't be much."

"I wrote up three new accounts today for Standish Dry Goods. Mayor Mitchell, Mr. Lesser, and Mr. Manning are all going to purchase merchandise from the company that my uncle and I own."

"So it's just a business deal to you." Maggie sounded disappointed. "You don't really care if you help the people of this town or not."

"You just said you didn't want me to!"

"I don't want you to get yourself killed, that's all!" Maggie held up her hands. "You saved my life, Seymour. I'm grateful to you. I don't want to see you hurt. But the whole arrangement seems so unfair to the town. I . . . I don't know what I want."

Seymour pushed his chair back and stood up. "You think that I was wrong to take the job?"

"Yes, of course."

"Because I might get hurt *and* because I'm not capable of doing it properly?"

"Well . . . look at you! You're no gunman. You're not a fighter of any sort. I doubt that you could subdue a child, let alone a full-grown, angry, drunken man."

Seymour felt his face growing warm as he recalled the two youngsters who had tormented him so when he first arrived in Sweet Apple. Maggie was probably right. Those boys had been unafraid of him for a good reason. He was no threat even to the likes of them.

True or not, her words went through his wounded pride like a knife. He picked up the revolver from the desk and slipped it into the holster on his hip.

Maggie blinked. "Seymour, what are you doing?"

He took a deep breath and said, "I need to make my evening rounds. The mayor and Mr. Heathcote told me it would be all right to skip them tonight, but I have a feeling they'll say the same thing tomorrow. And every other day, as long as I wear this badge."

Maggie shook her head. "Seymour, don't go out there. A marshal's badge is a big target, especially in this town. Some of the men may not be able to resist taking a shot at it, no matter what you think."

A thin smile curved his lips. "Well, then, we should be able to find out in a hurry what sort of lawman I'm going to be, shouldn't we?" He came out from behind the desk and started toward the door.

Maggie tried to get in his way. "This isn't what the council wanted—"

"Perhaps not," Seymour said as he brushed past her. "But I've always tried to conduct myself in an honorable fashion, and that means doing the job I'm being paid to do."

"But you're *not* being paid to enforce the law! You're being paid to pretend—"

He swung around toward her. "To pretend to be a real marshal. That's what you were going to say, isn't it? Well, a real marshal may not be what the council thought they were hiring, but that's what they're getting."

He wasn't sure where the bold words came from. The idea of going out there into the streets of this wild settlement with a gun on his hip and a badge on his chest made him tremble inside. But his knees were surprisingly steady. Once already today, he had gotten his gun and gone out to face a bad man. He was less nervous now than he was then.

Maybe a person could actually grow accustomed to the idea of looking death in the eye. Seymour didn't know.

But if he was going to be the marshal of Sweet Apple, he was going to have to find out.

He opened the door and stepped out onto the boardwalk.

"Seymour!" Maggie O'Ryan said behind him.

Steeling himself not to look back, Seymour walked out into the street. Full darkness had fallen, but fires burned here and there inside barrels and light from the buildings slanted through their windows. The street was bright enough so that Seymour could see several men on horseback and a couple of wagons rolling along. The riders reined in to stare at him as he strode across the street. He told himself he would have to get some spurs, so they would go *ka-chink! ka-chink!* when he walked. He headed toward the Black Bull, which was as loud and rowdy as it always was at this time of night.

That would be as good a place as any to start his rounds.

When he pushed open the batwings a moment later, tobacco smoke, laughter, and the smell of stale beer washed over him. No one in the place noticed him at first, but as he stood there with the badge shining on his vest, more and more people looked in his direction, and when they saw him they fell silent. That silence reached the piano player after a minute or two. He stopped tickling the ivories and twisted around on his stool to see what was going on.

From his position at the end of the bar, Pierre Delacroix said in a tone of disbelief, "Seymour? *Mon ami?* I had heard, but I did not believe . . ."

As Delacroix's amazed words trailed away, Seymour raised his voice and said, "Please go right on with what you were doing, folks. I'm your new marshal, and I'm just making my rounds."

J. Emerson Heathcote stood up from a table in the back

of the room. Seymour noted that it was the same table where he himself had spent most of the day, passed out drunk. Heathcote's face was even redder than usual, indicating that he had been putting away some whiskey himself.

"Seymour!" Heathcote said. "You weren't supposed to—"

He stopped short, and Seymour knew he'd been about to say, *You weren't supposed to act like a real marshal.* Seymour smiled grimly as he said, "I know you and the mayor told me I could assume my duties tomorrow, Mr. Heathcote, but I didn't see any reason not to get started tonight."

"Yes. Yes, of course," Heathcote stumbled. "That's fine, just fine."

Delacroix said, "Everything is under control here, Seymour . . . I mean, Marshal. Your presence is not needed at the moment."

Seymour gave the saloon keeper a curt nod. "All right. If there's any trouble, send someone to find me."

Delacroix nodded, but didn't look like he really meant it. It would take time, Seymour thought, but the people of Sweet Apple would come to realize that he intended to carry out the duties of town marshal as they should be performed.

They would realize that . . . if he lived long enough.

He gave everyone in the room a slow, deliberate look, then nodded as if to agree that everything was under control. He backed through the batwings and onto the boardwalk. His heart was pounding like a trip-hammer and fear fluttered in his belly like a caged bird, but he thought he had been successful in keeping that emotion concealed while he was in the saloon.

As he turned away from the Black Bull, he felt beads of cold sweat on his face. The breeze, still hot from the scorching day just past, quickly dried them.

Seymour made his way along the street, stopping in at the businesses that were still open to introduce himself and have a few words with the owners. He consistently got shocked reactions. Everyone had heard about him becoming the marshal, but no one seemed to have really believed it until they saw with their own eyes the badge pinned to his vest.

He rattled the doorknobs of the businesses that were already closed to make sure they were securely locked. He was aware that people were watching him; he could feel their eyes on him. The sensation made his skin crawl, but he tried to ignore the feeling.

But ignoring his instincts might not be a good idea, he realized as he walked past the mouth of an alley and somebody called softly from the shadows, "Hey, Marshal!"

As Seymour stopped and turned toward the voice, about to say, "Yes?" warning bells went off in his head. Just because the gunmen who frequented Sweet Apple might be loath to kill him in open combat because of the potential damage to their reputations, that didn't mean that some of them might not be averse to shooting him from ambush. If he was dead and no one knew who did the killing, that would eliminate the problem.

That thought flashed through his mind in the second that it took him to stop and turn, and somehow he kept turning, twisting aside and throwing himself to the ground. An earth-shaking roar assaulted his ears. The stygian darkness in the alley was ripped wide open by twin geysers of orange flame. Someone screamed.

Seymour landed hard enough to make him breathless. He gasped as he slapped at the holster and found it empty. The revolver Rebecca had given him had slipped out as he threw himself down. He pawed at the dirt in the alley mouth, searching for it.

He couldn't hear anything except the ringing in his ears from the terrible blast. The vague realization that someone hidden in the shadows had fired both barrels of a shotgun at him seeped into his brain. He touched the ivory grips of the revolver, scooped it up, and wrapped both hands around it. His right thumb found the hammer and drew it back. He held the gun as tight as he could and pressed the trigger.

The shot slammed out and echoed back from the walls of the buildings on either side of the alley, deafening him even more. He cocked the pistol and fired it a second time, then a third, squeezing off the shots awkwardly but with a semblance of speed. Then he rolled to his left, lurched to his feet, and dived onto the boardwalk. He scrambled over next to the front wall of the building and put his back against it.

No one came around the corner from the alley. Seymour kept the gun pointed in that direction as his hearing gradually came back. He became aware of shouting in the distance. It came closer as he pushed himself to his feet, still keeping the revolver trained on the mouth of the alley where the bushwhacker had lurked.

"Seymour! Seymour, for God's sake, are you all right?"

He recognized Heathcote's voice. Turning his head a little, Seymour saw the newspaperman approaching at a run, followed by several other men.

"Stay back!" he ordered. "Someone took a shot at me from that alley!"

Heathcote lurched to a halt, as did the other men. "Were you hit?" Heathcote asked.

"I . . . I don't think so." Seymour shook all over, unable to control the reaction any longer. He clamped his hands harder on the gun and tried to steady it, without much success.

But the danger seemed to be over. There had been no more shots from the alley, and he doubted if anyone would try again to kill him with a growing crowd nearby. Quite a few people had joined the group, including Pierre Delacroix, several of the town councilmen, and even Maggie O'Ryan. Seymour's heart leaped when he saw her. Her face was pale and her lips were pressed together tightly with either worry or disapproval or both. But he saw relief in her eyes, too . . . relief that he was all right.

And that made him feel good, despite the fear that still filled him.

"One of the horses tied here at the hitch rail's got a few buckshot wounds in its rump," one of the men said. "The bushwhacker missed the marshal but got this poor hoss."

That had been the scream he'd heard, Seymour thought. Rather than a human scream, it had been a shrill whinny of pain from the horse.

Somebody lit a lantern and handed it to Heathcote, who shone the light down the alley. "Nobody there now," the newspaperman announced. "You must've run him off, Seymour . . . I mean, Marshal. But look there!"

The tone of surprise in Heathcote's voice made Seymour look where he was pointing. Seymour didn't see anything in the lantern light except some sort of dark, wet splash in the dirt of the alley . . .

"Oh, dear Lord," Seymour said in a hollow voice. "Is that blood?"

"It sure is!" Heathcote was excited. "You winged the son of a bitch, Seymour!"

So he had actually wounded the bushwhacker with at least one of those blind shots, Seymour thought. It seemed impossible. He was no gunman. He hadn't even tried to aim, but rather had just fired in the general direction of the alley as fast as he could.

And one of the bullets from his gun had found its target, ripping through flesh and shedding blood. There was the proof right there on the ground, spilled from the veins of the man who had tried to kill him . . . Odd how the blood was such a dark red in the lantern light that it seemed almost black . . . the blood . . .

Seymour's eyes rolled up in their sockets, and with a soft groan, he fainted dead away.

Chapter 19

Matt Bodine and Sam Two Wolves had been on the trail for four days since leaving the Dutchman's trading post up on the Cap Rock. They had forded the Pecos at Horsehead Crossing, then stopped in the settlement of Fort Stockton, which had grown up around the army post of the same name. It figured that Mallory's gang wouldn't have attacked the place, what with the soldiers being so close by, and that proved to be the case. Matt and Sam asked some seemingly casual questions in a few saloons, and found that no one had seen Deuce Mallory in these parts.

Despite that, the blood brothers were confident that they were still on Mallory's trail. The outlaw was bound for Sweet Apple and then Mexico, and he wasn't letting anything slow him down.

From Fort Stockton, Matt and Sam cut more directly west toward the Davis Mountains. Beyond the mountains lay the border. The desolate Big Bend country stretched to the southeast. Matt was glad Mallory wasn't heading into that hellhole. He and Sam had been to the Big Bend before. It was some of the most rugged, dangerous country in

Texas, and its sweep was vast. Anybody who didn't want to be found could hide out there for months, if not years.

The Davis Mountains, on the other hand, were downright pretty, probably the prettiest part of West Texas. Rugged without being stark or harsh, the green, rolling peaks were covered with trees except at their very tops. Between them were beautiful wooded canyons that followed the twisting courses of cold, sparkling, crystal-clear creeks.

As they rode down one of those canyons, Matt commented, "You know, Montana is home and nothing beats home, but this country down here comes awful close."

"If you don't mind the Apaches raiding across the border from Mexico every now and then," Sam said.

Matt grinned. "Everything worthwhile has its price."

"I can't argue with that." Sam reined in suddenly and pointed down the canyon. "Look there."

Matt looked and saw smoke curling into the air. "Must be somebody's rancho up yonder. You want to stop or ride around it?"

"I could use a home-cooked meal." Sam shook his head. "That supper you fixed last night . . ."

"Hey! What's wrong with my cookin'?"

"There was sand in the biscuits. *And* in the bacon."

"You know how hard it is to keep sand out of everything in West Texas? Besides, a little sand's good for your digestion. Roughage, I think they call it."

"It's rough, all right," Sam said.

They continued their bantering as they rode along the canyon. After a few more twists and turns, they came within sight of the source of the smoke. A good-sized log house backed up against a rocky bluff. The smoke came from a stone chimney at one end of the Texas-style dwelling, built in two halves separated by a covered area in between known as a dogtrot. Nearby was a peeled-pole corral.

And next to the corral was what was left of a barn that had been mostly burned down.

Matt and Sam both reined in and frowned. "There's been some trouble here—" Sam began.

He was interrupted by the crack of a rifle shot and the wind-rip of a bullet passing close between him and Matt.

The blood brothers went out of their saddles, kicking their feet free of the stirrups and diving in different directions, Matt to the left and Sam to the right. They lit running and dashed behind some trees as the rifle continued to blast shots in their direction. Slugs kicked up dirt and rocks from the ground and spooked the horses. The animals turned and galloped back up the canyon. The pack animals followed them.

"Damn it!" Matt said. "There went our rifles!"

"And our extra ammunition," Sam called from his position behind a pine tree about thirty feet away.

"I guess we'd better let whoever's takin' those potshots at us know that we aren't lookin' for trouble." Matt leaned out from behind his tree a little, cupped his hands around his mouth, and shouted, "Hey, you there in the cabin! Hold your fire! We're friends!"

His answer was a shot that plucked the hat from his head and sent it spinning through the air. Matt jerked back behind the tree trunk and turned the air blue with cussin' for a minute.

"Well, *that* didn't work," Sam said with a wry grin. "Any other ideas?"

Matt studied the layout for a moment, then said, "Yeah. One of us works his way around, gets on top of that bluff, and drops a stick of dynamite down the chimney."

"We don't have a stick of dynamite," Sam pointed out. Then his dark eyes narrowed in thought. "But I see something that might work just about as well."

"What the hell are you talkin' about?"

"Look up on the bluff, in that tree just to the left of the cabin."

Matt looked, and a grin broke out on his rugged face. "Yeah, I reckon that'd do the trick, all right. Now the question is, which one of us goes after it?"

"Well, it was my idea—" Sam began.

"So you think you should be the one to carry it out." Matt nodded. "I completely agree. I'll stay here and cover you."

"Actually, I was going to say that since I came up with the idea, I should be the one to stay here and let you get all the glory."

"Oh, I couldn't do that," Matt said with a shake of his head. "You deserve the chance to shine for a change, Sam. You shouldn't be so modest."

Sam glared at his blood brother for a moment, then sighed and said, "Oh, all right." He holstered his gun. "I always was a faster and better runner than you anyway."

Matt just grinned and shook his head. "Not gonna work."

Sam grimaced, took a deep breath, and then burst from cover as Matt thrust the barrel of his Colt around the tree trunk and started blazing away at the cabin. Sam streaked toward the ridgeline, angling away from the cabin as he ran. His arms pumped at his sides and his hat flew off. Matt didn't know if the wind had blown the hat off or if a bullet had plucked it from Sam's head. Matt kept up his covering fire, emptying the revolver at the cabin.

He aimed a little high, though. He didn't know who was in there or why they were shooting at him and Sam, but he didn't like to kill anybody without being sure there was a

good reason. Normally, taking shots at them would be
reason enough, but even though Matt couldn't explain it,
in this case he felt like he ought to be absolutely certain
before he shot to kill.

Sam disappeared into some trees that grew along the
base of the bluff. A moment later, Matt spotted him climbing the slope about a hundred yards to the right of the
cabin. The bluff rose almost straight up for about twenty
feet, but rocks protruded here and there, as did the roots of
some scrubby bushes growing out of the bluff. Those
things gave Sam enough footholds and toeholds so that he
was able to climb to the top without much trouble.

Matt's revolver was empty. He had enough cartridges in
the loops of his shell belt to reload it once, but that was all.
He thumbed in the fresh rounds and snapped the cylinder
closed. He held his fire, though, figuring it was best to
wait until his shots might make a difference.

He watched as Sam made his way along the bluff. Whoever was in the cabin with that rifle couldn't see Sam now,
and wouldn't have been able to see him climb the bluff.
But the rifleman had to have seen which way Sam was
headed, and could probably figure out what he was doing.
Matt figured it was worth one more attempt to talk some
sense into the trigger-happy varmint.

"Hey!" he shouted. "Hey, you in the cabin! We're not
lookin' for any trouble! Hold your fire and—"

Whatever Matt was going to suggest next was drowned
out in a fresh fusillade of shots from inside the cabin.
Splinters and chunks of bark flew from the tree as the rifleman poured lead at it. Matt cursed again and tried to
make himself as skinny as possible, so that all of his body
was shielded by the tree trunk. He was getting a mite annoyed with that fella, whoever he was.

When the firing died away again, probably so that the rifleman could reload, Matt risked a quick look around the tree. He saw Sam crouched atop the bluff, watching. Matt gave him a curt nod, signaling him to go ahead with their plan. Sam returned the nod. He stood up and took off his shirt, revealing his powerful, brawny musculature.

Holding the shirt in his hands, Sam crept toward the gray, oblong object hanging from the branch of a scrubby tree on top of the bluff. He struck quickly, wrapping the buckskin shirt around the thing as he grabbed it and yanked it loose from the tree. Then he turned and ran toward the edge of the bluff. Matt thought he could hear the angry buzzing even from this distance.

When Sam reached the edge, he sailed off it, flying through the air and landing with a solid thump on the roof of the cabin where the smoke was coming from the chimney. Matt watched anxiously as Sam rolled over, keeping the shirt wrapped around the hornets' nest as he did so. Sam surged to his feet, lunged over to the chimney, and dropped the nest down the opening. Then he fell backward on the roof and waved the shirt around, trying to drive away the hornets that had escaped from the released nest.

Most of the furious insects would have still been in the nest, which must have busted open as soon as it hit the bottom of the fireplace inside the cabin. The shooting stopped, to be replaced immediately by high-pitched yells of pain and rage.

The door leading into the dogtrot from the side of the cabin where the rifleman was located suddenly burst open and a man raced out, waving his arms frantically around his head. He had long white hair and a white beard. What appeared to be a black cloud followed him, swarming around him. He sprinted toward the nearby creek and dived in, throwing water up around him in a great silvery splash. The old-timer stayed under the surface of the creek for so long that Matt began to worry that he had hit his head, knocked himself out, and drowned. Finally, though, the old man came up gulping for air.

By that time, the furious hornets were gone, and Matt Bodine stood on the creek bank instead, the gun in his hand pointed toward the old-timer.

The man sputtered and pawed his sodden white hair out of his eyes. "You got me, you damn-blasted owlhoot!" he said. "Go ahead and shoot me, why don't you? See if I care!"

"If you didn't care whether you live or die, you wouldn't have been tryin' to ventilate my brother and me," Matt pointed out. "And by the way, I'm not an owlhoot. Neither of us are."

Welts were starting to come up on the old man's hands and face where the hornets had stung him. He ducked his head under again. Matt knew the water in these mountain creeks was cold all year round. The cold would help numb the stings so that they didn't hurt as much, so he waited patiently for the old-timer to come up again.

By the time he did so, Sam had climbed down from the roof of the cabin and trotted over to join Matt. "You all right?" Matt asked him.

"I got stung a few times," Sam replied, "but I'll live. Who's the old geezer?"

Matt looked at the white-haired man, who had surfaced and was sputtering and gasping again. "Don't know. He hasn't told me who he is or why he was shootin' at us."

"Because you're outlaws!" the old-timer yelled. "Prob'ly part o' that damned Mallory gang!"

That caught the blood brothers' interest. "Mallory's been through here?" Matt asked.

"Who the hell do you think burned down my barn?"

"We don't have any idea," Sam said, "or at least we didn't have until you made that comment, sir."

The old man blinked and frowned. "Sir?" he repeated. "What sort o' trickery are you tryin' to pull, Injun? You *are* a Injun, ain't you?"

"I'm half Cheyenne," Sam replied with pride in his voice. "My father was Medicine Horse, a great chief."

"Cheyenne?" The old-timer grunted. "This here's Comanch' and Apache country. What'n blazes are you doin' down here, boy?"

"We're lookin' for Deuce Mallory and his gang," Matt told him.

The man raked his fingers through his long white hair. "I knowed you two was outlaws. I just knowed it."

"Damn it, we're not outlaws!" Matt was starting to lose patience. "Are you addled or something? We're on Mallory's trail because we want to bring him to justice."

The old man looked back and forth between Matt and Sam. "The two o' you . . . agin upwards o' thirty hardcases and killers? 'Tain't likely, I'm thinkin'!"

"What's your name, sir?" Sam asked.

"Name o' Alby. Alby McCormick."

"Well, why don't you come out of that creek, Mr. McCormick?" Sam suggested. "You must be getting a little cold by now."

"My feet and legs is about plumb froze off," McCormick admitted. He climbed out of the water. Matt and Sam continued to cover him as he did so, even though he appeared to be unarmed. He had left his rifle in the cabin when he ran out with the hornets swarming around him.

When he was dripping on the bank, McCormick went on. "That was a damned dirty trick, throwin' that nest down the chimney like that."

"I wanted to use a stick of dynamite," Matt said, "but we didn't have any."

"Them buzzin' little bastards must'a stung me a hunnerd times or more. You'll be lucky if I don't die."

"I'm not sure their stingers could even penetrate the hide of a leathery old pelican like you."

"Old pelican, is it?" McCormick fumed. "You young whippersnapper! I've whipped better men than you with one hand tied behind my back! I'll do it again, too, if you just give me half a chance, you dadblasted, ringtailed rannyhan! Lemme get my dewclaws on a gun again and I'll dust your britches with lead, you—"

"All right," Sam snapped. "That's enough. Both of you."

"He started it," Matt said.

Sam gestured with his gun. "Come along, Mr. McCormick. We'll go back to your cabin. You should probably get some dry clothes on."

The old-timer frowned. "Might still be some hornets in there."

"I'll fix a torch and smoke them out."

"Yeah, that might work," McCormick said with a nod.

Despite the old man's bluster, Matt figured he was pretty much harmless as long as he was disarmed. Still, Matt kept his gun out as the three of them went over to the cabin. Matt and McCormick watched as Sam wrapped some dry grass around a branch and then set it on fire as a makeshift torch. Sam waved it around inside the cabin so that the smoke would drive out any hornets who still happened to be in there. When it was safe, he motioned for Matt and McCormick to come in.

"You sure you fellas ain't owlhoots?" the old man asked.

"Positive," Matt said. "I'm Matt Bodine, and my blood brother here is Sam Two Wolves."

McCormick's eyes widened. "Matt Bodine the gunfighter?" he asked with a note of awe in his voice.

"I never claimed to be a gunfighter, but I've been in my share of shootin' scrapes," Matt replied with a shrug.

"And Sam Two Wolves," McCormick said. "I've heard o' you, too. Can't believe I was takin' potshots at a couple o' gunnies like you two."

"If you ran afoul of Mallory and his gang and lived to talk about it, I don't suppose we can blame you for being a little trigger-happy," Sam said. "They're as cold-blooded a bunch of killers as we've ever run across."

"You can sure as hell say that again." The old-timer waved a gnarled hand toward the fireplace. "There's coffee in the pot. You boys help yourselves while I put on some dry duds."

A short time later, the three of them were seated at McCormick's rough-hewn table with cups of strong black Arbuckle's in front of them. Sam said, "Why don't you tell us what happened?"

"I was mindin' my own business, as usual, when a couple o' fellas rode up. I run some stock up in the high pastures, not enough so's you'd call me a real cattleman or anythin' like that, just enough to get along. Do a mite o' huntin' and trappin', too, and they's plenty o' fish in the creeks hereabouts. Any man who goes hungry in the Davis Mountains must have a real hankerin' to starve, that's all I got to say about that."

"What about the two men?" Sam prodded.

"Oh, yeah, them. They claimed they wanted to buy some

supplies, but I figure they was just lookin' the place over, tryin' to see if there was anythin' worth stealin'. Reckon they decided there wasn't, 'cause one of 'em up an' took a shot at me without no warnin'. But he didn't take me by surprise, no, sir, 'cause I'm natural suspiciouslike."

"We got that idea when you started shooting at us with no warning," Matt said.

McCormick ignored the comment and went on. "I can still move right spry when I want to. I got inside the cabin here and started puttin' up a fight, and I reckon they figured it'd be more trouble to root me out that it was worth. Anyway, they set my barn on fire and then rode on. I seen 'em join up with about thirty other men, on down the canyon a ways."

"How do you know it was Deuce Mallory's gang?" Sam asked.

"One of the fellas called the other one Deuce, and I seen wanted posters on him once when I was in Fort Davis. I got a good memory for faces, yes, sir, I do."

"Did they say anything else while they were here?" Matt asked.

"Not much. After I traded a few shots with them skunks, I heard 'em talkin' amongst themselves. Mallory said he didn't want to waste no time on me, since he was in a hurry to go eat an apple. I ain't got no earthly idea what he meant by that."

Matt and Sam looked at each other. "We do," Sam said.

"The gang's headed for Sweet Apple," Matt added.

"Sweet Apple?" McCormick repeated. "That hellhole of a town down on the border?"

"That's right. He plans to raid the settlement and then cross the border into Mexico."

"I've heard tell that Sweet Apple's a real rip-roarin'

place. Ol' Mallory might be bitin' off more'n he can chew if he plans to hit that town. O' course, if'n he takes the folks by surprise, he can prob'ly get away with it."

"That's why we're going to try to get there first," Sam said. "We'd like to warn the citizens and the local authorities."

"Local authorities?" McCormick shook his grizzled head. "From what I hear, there ain't no law in Sweet Apple. No marshal, no deputy, no nothin'."

"When did Mallory's gang come through here, Mr. Mc-Cormick?"

"Two days ago, it was. You boys'll have to ride like hell to get in front of him and warn the folks in Sweet Apple. I don't hardly reckon it can be done."

Matt and Sam exchanged grim looks. The old-timer wasn't telling them anything that they didn't already know.

Unless something happened to delay Deuce Mallory and his gang, the outlaws would strike the town before Matt and Sam could get there.

Hell would be paying another call, this time in Sweet Apple.

Chapter 20

The village of Arroyo Seco lay some fifteen miles below the border in Mexico, in the foothills of a small mountain range. It was a farming community, a single street of mud-daubed adobe buildings with a public well at one end and a small church at the other. There were hundreds, if not thousands, of other villages just like it, stretching from one end of the country to the other.

Today, however, one thing made Arroyo Seco different from all the other villages.

Today Diego Alcazarrio was coming.

A small boy noticed the dust first. Earlier, he had spotted a rattlesnake lying next to an abandoned building, coiled in the shadow of a half-collapsed wall. The boy ran to get his father, who, like most of the other men in Arroyo Seco, was a farmer and worked the terraced fields on the slopes of the foothills above the village. The boy's father came back with him, carrying the hoe he used on the crops. Now it would be put to a more deadly use if the snake was still there.

It was. The hour was early and the air at this elevation

was cool enough so that the snake was a little sluggish. As the humans approached, the wedge-shaped head lifted slightly from the thick coils. The obsidian eyes were of little use to the serpent, but the scent glands in its nose told it that a potential threat was drawing near. The rattles at the end of its tail gave a faint, lazy buzz.

The boy pointed it out and his father told him to stay back. Carefully, the farmer approached the snake and lifted his hoe to strike. He wished the hoe had a longer handle. He wished he owned a gun so that he could use it to shoot the snake and look like a hero in the eyes of his son. But the hoe was all he had so it would have to do.

Several other children and a few adults had gathered to watch him kill the snake. The farmer swallowed, took a deep breath, and brought the hoe down as the snake's rattle began to buzz louder.

He missed.

The hoe struck the snake behind the head, but it was only a glancing blow, just enough to annoy the snake. The rattler struck with blinding speed, stretching out nearly its full length. Only sheer terror made the farmer move swiftly enough to avoid being bitten. He let out a yell and went backward, tripping over his own feet and falling. He dropped the hoe and scrambled backward, putting even more distance between himself and the angry rattler as the snake once again drew itself up into a tight coil. The snake's head was up now. Its tongue flickered in and out of its mouth, sensing the air, and its rattles blurred back and forth furiously.

The boy paid no attention to his father's humiliating failure to kill the snake. He was watching the dust he had noticed a few moments earlier, drawing steadily closer to the village. The cloud boiled up from the hooves of galloping horses. The boy heard the rolling rumble and might have thought it to be distant thunder—had not the sky been clear.

When he had first seen the snake, something inside him turned cold with atavistic fear, though his simple, uneducated mind had no concept of such a thing. Now, as he watched the riders come toward Arroyo Seco, he felt even colder inside, as if these strangers were even more dangerous than the big rattlesnake.

In a people who lived so close to the earth, instinct seldom lied. It certainly didn't in this case.

The riders swept into the village, scattering some of the crowd that had gathered. They brought their horses to a halt. Dust swirled around them for a moment, and as it began to clear away the boy stared at the strangers. The men's mounts were big, fine animals wearing expensive saddles and silver-studded trappings. The men's tight trousers and brightly embroidered charro jackets and huge sombreros spoke of wealth, too, as did the well-cared-for guns they wore. From time to time, the Rurales visited Arroyo Seco and the boy had stared at their rifles and uniforms, too, but these men were much more impressive than the Rurales.

The big, barrel-chested man who had ridden at the head of the group looked at the farmer sprawled on the ground, several yards away from the angrily buzzing rattlesnake. He laughed and said, "Having trouble, amigo?"

With a speed that made the boy gasp in awe, the ivory-handled gun on the big man's hip seemed to leap from its holster into the man's hand. The man fired without seeming to aim. As the gun roared, the rattler's head exploded in a burst of gore. The snake's body writhed and whipped madly for several seconds before its nerves and muscles realized that the head was gone and finally relaxed in death. A few final twitches ran through the thick, scaly corpse.

The big man laughed again and said, "Never set out to kill something, amigo, unless you are sure you can accomplish that death." He swung the gun toward the farmer, and for a second the boy thought that the stranger was going to shoot his father, too. Strangely, the prospect didn't bother him that much. He almost wanted to see it happen. His father, after all, was only a poor farmer, and there were millions of them in the world. The big man on the fine horse was more like a god, and a god's will could not, should not, be denied.

But then the man laughed yet again and holstered the weapon. He looked at the boy and asked, "Is there a cantina in this village?"

Wordlessly, the boy lifted an arm and pointed along the dusty street.

"Gracias, muchacho," the big man said. He whirled his horse around and galloped toward the cantina. The others followed.

The boy watched them go. Then he walked over and picked up the hoe that his father had dropped in sheer terror. The boy went to the snake, ignoring the words his father spoke to him, and used the hoe to chop off the rattles. He dropped the hoe and held the rattles in the palm of his hand. A little blood oozed from the place where he had cut them from the snake's body.

The boy's hand closed around the rattles. He would keep them from now on, he told himself, so that he would never forget this day with all its fear and awe.

Down the street, Diego Alcazarrio swaggered into the cantina and called out for tequila for him and his men. The little man who ran the place hurried to bring the bottles and glasses to the hard-faced men who filed in and sat at the tables scattered around the room. It was cool inside the cantina because of the early hour and its thick walls that kept the heat out, but the proprietor began to sweat as he served his new customers.

He recognized Alcazarrio. The man was known throughout the region as a revolutionary who wanted to overthrow Porfirio Díaz, El Presidente. Díaz probably deserved to be overthrown, at least as far as the common people of Mexico were concerned, but while men such as Alcazarrio and those who followed him might call themselves revolutionaries, everyone knew they were actually *bandidos,* out to get everything they could for themselves. They demanded tribute from the peons. They rode into villages and took whatever they wanted—mostly supplies, but sometimes the few coins and other valuables that might be found as well. And sometimes women, the wives and daughters of the villagers. It was difficult to know how to feel about men such as Diego Alcazarrio and those who rode with him. They hated Díaz and the government, and the people hated Díaz and the government. But at the same time, those like Alcazarrio were thieves, rapists, and killers, and the people were afraid of them.

The way Alcazarrio saw it, that was good. The more fear he inspired, the better he liked it. He had thought about killing that farmer, just as an example of what should happen to the weak, but in the end he had decided it would be unwise to do so. If you saw an ant crawling along the ground by itself, you might step on it out of sheer disgust for the creature's lack of size. But stomping right in the middle of an ant bed . . . ah, that was a different thing.

Alcazarrio splashed tequila in a glass and tossed back

the fiery liquor. He refilled the glass and drank again. A familiar, pleasant warmth began to spread through him. His second-in-command, Florio Cruz, sat at the table with him and also drank. Unlike the burly, bearded Alcazarrio, the hatchet-faced Cruz was lean and clean-shaven except for a thread of mustache. He said, "You are sure this is the day the American was to meet us, Diego?"

"You question me?" Alcazarrio asked with a frown.

Cruz shook his head. "Not at all, compadre. I simply hope that we did not ride all this way for no reason."

"I spied a few comely señoritas as we rode into town," Alcazarrio leered. "No matter whether the gringo shows up or not, our visit will not have been for nothing."

Cruz shrugged. He enjoyed women, but actually cared little for them, Alcazarrio knew. Money and power were the things Cruz really lusted for, which made him an excellent lieutenant. As long as he never grew so hungry for power that he would risk trying to take over this band of revolutionaries . . .

Alcazarrio had left a couple of men outside to serve as lookouts. One of them hurried into the cantina after a few minutes and came straight to the table where Alcazarrio and Cruz sat. "A rider comes, Diego," he reported.

"One rider?"

The man nodded. "*Sí,* only one."

Alcazarrio grinned and said, "It must be the American. Only a gringo would be so foolish as to come down here alone." He refilled his tequila glass again and slugged down the stuff, then pushed himself to his feet. Like the bear he resembled, he shambled toward the open door of the cantina, followed by Florio Cruz.

The rider approached Arroyo Seco from the east, so the sun was behind him. All Alcazarrio could tell about the man was that he was slender and probably tall; it was difficult to determine that for sure when a man was in the saddle. The rider had to come closer, almost all the way up to the cantina, before Alcazarrio could make out the thin features.

The American wore whipcord trousers, a white shirt, and a cream-colored Stetson. He reined in and gave the revolutionary leader a curt nod.

"Señor Alcazarrio. We haven't met, but I recognize you from Dolores's description. I'm—"

"I know who you are, Señor." Alcazarrio understood and spoke English fairly well and answered in that language. "You wear no uniform, but you are Major Trevor."

The man grimaced. "No ranks, please. We're a hell of a long way from Fort Sam Houston."

"And you have no wish to be reminded of how you are betraying your fellow *soldados,* eh, Señor Trevor?" Alcazarrio asked with a grin.

Anger smoldered in the American's eyes, but he controlled it. "I have what you wanted," he snapped. "The itinerary for those guns."

"And I have what you want, Señor . . . money." Alcazarrio jerked a thumb over his shoulder toward the cantina. "Come in and have a drink, and we will talk business, eh?"

A muscle in Major Trevor's bony jaw jumped a little, as if in reaction to the obvious distaste he felt toward the man he was dealing with. But he nodded and swung down from the saddle.

Alcazarrio snapped his fingers at one of the village youngsters who had followed the revolutionaries to the cantina. "Hold the gringo's horse," he said to the boy. "Do not let anything happen to it."

The boy said, *"Sí, jefe,"* and sprang to obey. He took the

reins from Trevor, who hesitated for a second before giving them up.

Alcazarrio threw an arm around Trevor's shoulder, taking pleasure in the way the American stiffened in resentment at the familiarity. As long as they each had something the other wanted, they had to tolerate each other. When their deal was concluded, it might be different.

Alcazarrio led Trevor into the cool, shadowy interior of the cantina and sat him down at the table where the half-empty bottle of tequila still stood. He said to the owner, "Another glass, pronto!"

When the three men were seated and Trevor had a glass of his own, Cruz poured the drinks. Alcazarrio lifted his glass and said, "To the success of our arrangement!"

Neither of the other men echoed that toast, but they both drank when Alcazarrio did. When Cruz reached for the bottle again, Trevor shook his head.

"It's too early in the day. One drink is enough for me."

Alcazarrio laughed. "Too early in the day," he repeated. "This is something I have never understood. One time is as good as another, so far as I can see. You would not say that it is too early in the day to enjoy a fine meal or to make love to a pretty señorita, would you, Señor Trevor?"

"Let's get on with it," Trevor suggested instead of answering Alcazarrio's question.

The Mexican's brawny shoulders rose and fell in a shrug. "Of course. Whatever you want, Señor. Tell me about the rifles."

"Five hundred of them," Trevor said as he leaned forward. "Brand-new repeaters being shipped by rail from San Antonio to Fort Bliss in El Paso." He reached inside his jacket and brought out several folded papers. "I have a map of the route and the schedule right here."

He slid the papers across the table toward Alcazarrio.

The revolutionary leader's hamlike paw came down on the documents and drew them to him. He unfolded them and studied them. Though he was not a highly educated man, he knew how to read and write and could even make out most of the English words. And his cunning was second to none.

That was why, working through an intermediary in San Antonio, a beautiful young woman named Dolores who happened to be a cousin of his, he had been able to locate and negotiate with an officer in the American army who was willing to sell out his compadres for the right price. Dolores had arranged the meeting, and now Major Hugh Trevor was here in Arroyo Seco, bringing with him the information that Alcazarrio needed.

The promise of repeating rifles would cause the ranks of his army to swell. They would become a force to be reckoned with, even for that brutal pig of a dictator, Díaz. And with each new success, the number of Alcazarrio's followers would grow even larger, he knew. People made the mistake of thinking him to be a mere bandit. A bandit he was, to be sure, but there was nothing "mere" about him or his plans. He really did intend to overthrow Díaz, and once he had established himself as El Presidente, he would turn his attention elsewhere, beyond Mexico.

For example, it had always bothered him that the damned Texans had ripped away that which was not rightfully theirs. It was past time for Mexico to regain control of the territory north of the Rio Grande, and under Alcazarrio's leadership, that was exactly what would happen.

Or so the future played out inside his head anyway. But the first step, he knew well, was to get his hands on those guns.

"They're not being shipped on a military train," Trevor

was explaining. "The army's trying to keep the whole thing quiet, in fact. They'll be in crates inside a baggage car that's part of a regular train."

"What about guards?" Cruz asked. He liked to think of himself as a strategist, although in truth it was Alcazarrio who came up with all the plans for the group.

Trevor's thin lips curved in a smile. "The army's not foolish enough to rely totally on secrecy. There'll be a dozen armed guards inside the baggage car with the rifles."

"Only a dozen?" Alcazarrio waved a hand as if he were shooing away a gnat. That was all the American resistance would amount to—an annoyance. He frowned as he studied the map some more, trying to figure out the best place to attack the train and steal the guns.

"That's all you need from me," Trevor said. "I'll take my money now. Dolores said you would pay two thousand dollars in gold coins."

"You wish your payment, eh?" Alcazarrio said without looking up from the map. He flipped a hand toward Cruz. "Florio has it."

Trevor turned toward Alcazarrio's *segundo*. Cruz stood up and said, "It is on my horse." He started toward the door of the cantina.

His route took him behind Trevor. Without warning, Cruz suddenly looped his left arm around the American's neck, jerked his chin up, and used his right hand to draw a razor-sharp bowie knife across Trevor's throat. Trevor died without making a sound, blood fountaining out from his slashed arteries. Alcazarrio lifted the papers so that the crimson flood wouldn't splash on them.

Cruz let go of Trevor. The dead man fell forward so that his head landed in the pool of gore that was already forming. Cruz wiped the blade on Trevor's jacket and replaced the knife in its sheath on his hip. He turned to Alcazarrio and asked, "Do you know yet where we will strike?"

Alcazarrio turned in his chair so that he could smooth out the papers on a part of the table that wasn't covered with blood. He pointed at the map and grunted, "Here. The train will stop here for water."

The tip of his blunt, strong finger rested on a spot not far across the border. According to the map, a small settlement was located there.

It was called Sweet Apple.

On a hilltop overlooking the village of Arroyo Seco, a figure crouched behind a rock and trained field glasses on the welter of mud-daubed buildings. The man tensed as a couple of men in sombreros carried something out of the building where all the horses were tied up in front. The watcher put his field glasses on the two men, and his breath hissed between his teeth as he saw that the thing they were carrying was a body. One man had the corpse's legs, the other grasped it under the arms. As the man on the hill watched, the two revolutionaries took the body around to the rear of the building and tossed it into a ditch as if it were nothing more than a sack of trash.

And that was about all it amounted to now, the watcher thought bitterly. He had warned Major Trevor that the damned greasers weren't to be trusted, but as usual, Trevor thought that he knew better than anybody else.

The watcher didn't really give a damn about Trevor. But he *did* care about the money that the major had been promised. Part of the money was supposed to belong to the man on the hill when everything was over and done with.

Distant strains of guitar music drifted up from the village. The *bandidos* who called themselves revolutionaries were celebrating. They had double-crossed the stupid gringo, taken the information he'd brought to them, and given him only death as a reward.

But when the time came, the Mexicans would have a surprise waiting for them, the watcher vowed. He lowered the field glasses and slipped down the far side of the hill to where his horse waited.

A moment later, he was spurring northward toward the border.

Chapter 21

Deuce Mallory always kept an eye on his back trail, and once it became obvious to him that no posse was coming after them, the outlaws slowed down as they headed for the Rio Grande. Mallory was eager to carry out the raid on Sweet Apple and then cross the border into Mexico, where he planned to enjoy a long vacation from robbing and killing, but at the same time there was no reason to get into a rush either. Those poor bastards back in Buckskin were probably still licking their wounds from the damage the Mallory gang had done.

Along the way they had stopped at a few isolated ranches, killing the settlers and taking anything that might be of use. At one place in the mountains they'd run into a cantankerous old-timer who had amused Mallory so much he'd decided to let the geezer live. They'd settled for burning down his barn instead of killing him.

The men were getting a little antsy, though, Mallory sensed. They were ready for action, ready for another big raid. They had too much violence and brutality inside them, and they had to get it out from time to time or they'd be liable to turn on each other. As the leader, Mallory had to gauge things like that and decide when it was time to strike.

That time was coming soon.

For now, though, he was content for the gang to remain another day or two at this camp in a wooded canyon southwest of the Davis Mountains, about halfway between Fort Davis and the Rio Grande. They had been there for a day already, letting their horses rest after the long ride from the Texas Panhandle. Mallory listened to the men laughing and talking and caught the undercurrent of tension in their voices. They had been without women for a while, they were low on booze, and they were edgy.

That was the way he wanted them. Let the steam build up a little more. Then when they hit Sweet Apple, they wouldn't even think about holding back. It would be an orgy of death and destruction, looting and killing and raping.

Just the way Mallory liked it.

He was playing a desultory, small-stakes, three-handed game of poker with Steve Larrabee and Gus Brody when Carl Henderson approached. Mallory figured that Henderson wanted to be dealt into the game, but then he realized that the man had a worried look on his face.

"What's wrong, Carl?" Mallory asked.

"The lookouts spotted somebody comin', Deuce," Henderson replied. "Just one man, but he's hunched over in the saddle like somethin's wrong with him."

Mallory had given orders that a couple of men were to be posted at both ends of this canyon at all times. The last thing he wanted was for the gang to get penned up in here.

He was sitting cross-legged on the ground beside the blanket on which the cards and money were scattered. Like a snake, Mallory uncoiled from that position. Instinctively, his hand moved closer to the gun on his hip.

"Which end of the canyon?" he asked.

"South," Henderson answered with a jerk of his head in that direction.

Mallory motioned to Larrabee and Brody. "Come on. Let's see what this is about."

The four men strode toward the south end of the canyon. Their purposeful manner and the grim looks on their faces attracted the attention of some of the other outlaws. They left behind what they were doing and followed Mallory and his lieutenants, so that there was a sizable group gathering at the south end of the hideout canyon.

One of the lookouts waved to Mallory and said, "You can see him from up here, Deuce."

Mallory climbed to the top of the leaning rock slab where the man was posted with a rifle and a pair of field glasses. He didn't need the glasses to see the approaching rider, who was now about three hundred yards from the mouth of the canyon. As Henderson had said, the man was slumped forward in the saddle and appeared to be holding on tightly to the horn to keep from falling.

Mallory had observed enough badly wounded men in his lifetime—many of whom he had shot himself—to recognize what he was seeing now. "Anybody else out there?" he asked the sentry as he swept his eyes over the brown, semidesert landscape that stretched from the canyon on down to the Rio Grande. He didn't see any signs of movement, but he wanted that estimation confirmed.

"Nobody, Deuce," the lookout agreed. "And I've been watchin' mighty close all afternoon. Whoever that hombre is, he's alone."

The rider kept coming straight for the canyon. Mallory watched him for a moment more, then gave a curt nod.

"It's not a trick," he said, trusting his instincts. "I'm going to see who that fellow is."

With that, he slid down the rock slab to its base, landed lightly on his booted feet, and strode out from the jumbled boulders at the canyon mouth toward the rider. Larrabee, Brody, and Henderson exchanged worried glances and then hurried after their leader.

Mallory thought there was something familiar about the man on horseback. As he came closer, he was sure of it. He had seen the hombre somewhere before. The man's face was gray and lined with pain under a brown Stetson. He wore a buckskin jacket and denim trousers. The jacket hung open, and Mallory caught a glimpse of a dark stain on the gray woolen shirt underneath.

The man had been wounded, all right. Seriously, from the looks of the blood.

The horse shied as Mallory approached. That roused the rider from his semistupor. He raised his head and looked directly at Mallory, who felt a shock of recognition go through him. "Nick?" he said. "Nick Carlisle?"

"Edward," the man called Carlisle croaked. He had to be one of the few men left alive in the world who called Mallory by his given name. "I was . . . hoping I'd . . . find you."

Then he swayed, and was about to fall out of the saddle when Mallory sprang forward to reach up and steady him. "Give me a hand here!" Mallory called over his shoulder. "This man is an old friend!"

Several of the other outlaws ran to help. They lowered Carlisle from the horse's back and carried him up the canyon to their camp. Mallory barked orders. Carlisle was lowered carefully onto a thick pallet made of blankets.

Mallory dropped to a knee beside him and pulled back the jacket and bloodstained shirt to reveal an ugly black bullet hole in Carlisle's torso. A check of the man's back revealed no exit wound. The slug was still inside him.

Carlisle coughed and blood flecked his lips and chin. "I knew you were . . . on your way . . . to Sweet Apple," he said. "Hoped I would . . . run into you."

Larrabee hunkered on the other side of the wounded man and asked, "Who is this hombre, Boss? How's he know about our plans?"

Mallory felt a surge of anger. He didn't like being questioned, even by a trusted subordinate like Steve Larrabee. "I already told you he's an old friend," Mallory snapped. "Nick Carlisle and I were in college together back East, before the bastards who ran the place kicked me out. As for how he knows where we're headed, he and I have kept in touch over the years."

That was true. Through an elaborate set of blind addresses designed to keep their connection a secret since neither man wanted it revealed, Mallory and Carlisle had exchanged letters on a fairly regular basis every few months. In the last letter he had sent to Carlisle, posted in Pueblo, Colorado, Mallory had mentioned his intention to visit Mexico by way of Sweet Apple. That plan had already been in his head although he had yet to share it with the rest of the gang at that time. He had mentioned making a few stops along the way, knowing that Carlisle would understand what he meant by that—raiding, looting, and killing.

"Nick's in the army," Mallory went on. He grinned. "But don't take that the wrong way. He's as crooked as any of us are and has been for as long as I've known him. Isn't that right, Nick?"

"G-guns," Carlisle said, not answering Mallory's rhetorical question. He fumbled at Mallory's sleeve. "Shipment of . . . repeating rifles."

Mallory's grin disappeared. He leaned closer to the dying man with a look of intense interest on his face. "Tell me about it, Nick."

"G-going from . . . San Antonio to . . . El Paso . . . train stops for water . . . in Sweet Apple."

"A shipment of army rifles?" Larrabee said. "That's what he's talkin' about?"

"That'd be worth a fortune," Brody put in.

"Shut up," Mallory told them. "Let the man talk."

Carlisle's fingers pawed feebly at Mallory's arm. "Part-ner of mine . . . Major Trevor . . . set it up with . . . with some Mexicans . . . revolutionaries . . . D-Diego . . . Alcazarrio . . . steal the rifles . . . but Alcazarrio . . . double-crossed him . . . killed him . . . I saw what . . . what happened . . . damn greasers . . . can't let 'em . . . get away with it. . . ."

As Carlisle's voice trailed off, Mallory asked, "Did they shoot you, too, Nick?"

Carlisle managed a weak shake of his head. "I decided to . . . ride up here . . . see if I could find you, Edward . . . but I ran into . . . some Apaches . . . had to fight my way loose from them . . . brought a bullet with me . . ."

"Yeah, I noticed that." Mallory didn't pull any punches. He had known Carlisle too long for that. "You're dying, Nick."

"Y-yeah . . . I know. . . ."

"You want me and my boys to steal those rifles so that this Diego Alcazarrio doesn't get them, is that right?"

"Figure he'll . . . hit the train . . . when it's stopped at . . . Sweet Apple . . . won't be expecting . . . you to hit him."

Mallory nodded. "That's right. We'll take the bastard by surprise." Mallory's voice took on a more urgent tone. "But when will the train be at Sweet Apple, Nick? I have to know when the train will get there."

"In my pocket . . . train schedule . . . details about the shipment . . ." Carlisle laughed, then was wracked by another cough that sent more blood flowing from his mouth. "You can make . . . a big clean-up . . . Edward . . . just kill . . . Alcazarrio . . . for me."

"Sure, Nick, sure," Mallory promised. He lifted one side of the wounded man's jacket and reached inside it to search for the papers Carlisle had mentioned. He found them in an inside pocket, a little bloodstained around the edges but still legible. A quick scan of them told Mallory everything he needed to know. The train carrying the shipment of army rifles in one of its baggage cars wasn't due to arrive in Sweet Apple for another week.

He had delayed this long, Mallory thought. For the sort of payoff he could get for five hundred brand-new repeating rifles, he could wait another week to strike, and the rest of the outlaws would be willing to do that, too, once they heard what was at stake.

Plus there was the matter of avenging the double cross that Diego Alcazarrio had pulled on Carlisle and his partner, a Major Trevor. Nick had been promising for years to use his military connections to let Mallory in on something big; that was the main reason Mallory had stayed in touch with the man and kept him up to date on his plans, just so that something like this could be worked out someday.

Now the stars had finally lined up right . . . except for the fact that Carlisle wasn't going to be alive to enjoy the fruits of his efforts, of course. But that didn't matter all that much to Mallory. Sentiment only went so far. He was willing to carry out Carlisle's wish for revenge on the treacherous Mexicans, but in the end the man's death really meant one less share of the profits to be divvied up.

"Don't worry, Nick, we'll get those guns," Mallory said,

but then he noticed that Carlisle's eyes had turned glassy. His old friend was dead.

Larrabee asked, "What the hell's goin' on here, Deuce?"

Mallory smiled. "I'll explain everything, Steve, but the short answer is that we're going to wait a little longer before we hit Sweet Apple. But when we do, it's going to make us even richer than we'd thought. . . ."

Rebecca Jimmerson carried the telegram into Cornelius Standish's private office and laid it on his desk. The message was in a sealed envelope, as Standish had instructed. He didn't want anyone except Rebecca to get wind of his plans for Seymour. She was the only one he trusted—and he didn't have complete confidence in her.

As he glared at the yellow envelope, he asked, "Is that from Texas?"

"I don't know," she replied. "It was sealed when the messenger brought it."

Standish picked up the envelope and tore it open with eager fingers. Rebecca knew what he hoped to find in there: the news that his nephew Seymour had been killed in Sweet Apple.

But as Standish read the message, an angry frown appeared on his face. One hand crumpled the telegram while the other clenched into a fist and thumped down on the desk. "Damn it!" he burst out.

"Something wrong?" Rebecca asked.

"You always were a perceptive little bitch," Standish snarled at her.

Rebecca kept a tight lid on her own anger. One of these days he would regret how he treated her, she told herself.

But even as the thought went through her head, she

knew how unlikely it was to ever come true. She liked the comforts and luxuries that money provided too much to ever risk losing the position she had.

Besides, she was afraid of Cornelius Standish, most likely with good reason.

"I know you hired private detectives to keep an eye on Seymour," she said. "Is that wire from one of them?"

Standish nodded. "Yes. He's in San Antonio. He says that Seymour has become something of a celebrity in a very short time. Some newspaperman dubbed him the most cowardly man in the West."

Rebecca's smile had a touch of sadness to it. *Poor Seymour,* she thought. The description certainly suited him.

"But here's the worst thing," Standish went on. "Those idiots in Sweet Apple have made him the town marshal!"

Rebecca's perfectly plucked eyebrows arched in surprise. "The town marshal!" she repeated in amazement. "Seymour?"

"That's right. It's ludicrous! It's insane!"

"Of course it is." Rebecca was puzzled about something. "But I don't understand why you're upset about that. You . . . you wanted Seymour to . . . run into trouble, didn't you?"

"I wanted one of those Western gunmen to blow holes in him," Standish snapped in as blunt a fashion as possible. "But according to the detective in San Antonio, the Texas newspapers say that so far he's been successful in facing down several gunfighters. He saved a woman's life and even fought off an ambusher! What the hell is wrong with those Texans? They can't even kill one quivering little mouse of a man like Seymour?" He slammed a fist down on the desk again. "Bah! I should have known that if I wanted something done about this problem, I'd have to take more direct action myself. You simply can't rely on anyone to do what they're supposed to these days."

Rebecca found herself wondering if the woman Seymour had saved was young and pretty. Not that it mattered to her, of course. She'd had her moment of pity and weakness when she took that gun to him before he left Trenton. Since then she had hardened herself to the possibility that she would never see Seymour Standish again. That was just the way things had to be.

But from what Seymour's uncle was saying, not only was Seymour surviving in Texas, he was thriving. Flourishing even. Was it possible that there was really a man under that meek exterior after all?

The question was more intriguing to Rebecca than she would have expected it to be.

"Send for Wilford Grant," Standish said, breaking into Rebecca's thoughts. "I want to see him."

Rebecca frowned. She didn't like Wilford Grant. Standish had hired him on a couple of occasions in the past, when some of the employees of Standish Dry Goods, Inc., had started talking about forming a union. A few broken legs and busted heads had persuaded the employees to abandon that foolish notion. Wilford Grant and a few of his equally brutal friends had provided the incentive.

Rebecca knew that Grant could usually be found in the bar of the Metropole Hotel, several blocks away. She said, "I'll find a boy to take a message to him."

"Right away," Standish snapped.

Several boys hung around the lobby of the office building, seeking work as messengers. Rebecca quickly wrote out a note to Grant, summoning him for an audience with Cornelius Standish, then gave one of the boys a dime to deliver it. She went back to her desk and the work that waited for her, but a feeling of worry nagged at her. She could still hardly believe the things Standish had told her about Seymour. She wished she could see them for herself, with her own eyes.

A half hour later, Wilford Grant sauntered in, accompanied by one of his henchmen, a cadaverous Italian named Morelli. Grant was a little below medium height, but more than broad enough to make up for it. His shoulders were massive, and his arms hung down like an ape's. He wore a brown tweed suit and had a brown derby shoved back on a thatch of coarse black hair. What appeared to be several days' worth of beard stubble fuzzed his thick jaw. He always looked that way, more like an animal than a man, Rebecca thought. But he had plenty of human cunning.

"Go right in," Rebecca told the two men. "He's waiting for you."

"You sure you don't want us to visit with you for a while?" Grant asked with a leer. He always looked at Rebecca with open lust in his eyes, and today was no different.

"No, Mr. Standish is waiting for you," she said again.

Grant shrugged and went to the door of the inner office. He opened it and went through. Morelli followed him and left the door open.

"You got some work for me and Spike, Mr. Standish?" Grant asked in his rumbling voice.

"Indeed I do," Standish replied. "How would the two of you feel about taking a trip west?"

"If the money's right, we'll go anywhere you want. And *do* anything you want."

Even though Rebecca couldn't see Standish, she could imagine the evil smile on his thin lips as he said, "That's just what I wanted to hear. You'll be going to Texas. My nephew Seymour is there, and there's a message I want you to give him." Standish paused, then added, "Morelli, close that door."

The Italian shut the door, so that Rebecca could hear only the low rumble of voice from the inner office without being able to make out any of the words.

But it didn't matter. She knew exactly what Cornelius Standish was explaining to Wilford Grant and Spike Morelli.

He was telling them to go to Texas and kill Seymour.

Chapter 22

Seymour crouched. His eyes narrowed in a determined squint, and his hand hovered over the butt of the gun on his hip. His upper lip drew back in a snarl calculated to strike fear into the heart of the man he was facing.

"You'll rue the day you ever rode into Sweet Apple, you . . . you miscreant. You see this badge? This is my town. I'm Marshal Seymour Standish. *Now slap leather!*"

He grabbed the pistol and jerked it out of the holster. He had figured out that he didn't have to cock it in order to fire it. All that was required was that he point it at the target and pull the trigger. He did so, still snarling.

The hammer fell on an empty chamber with a metallic *click!* that resounded in the office.

That wasn't too bad, Seymour decided as he lowered the weapon. He had gotten the gun out fairly quickly, or at least it seemed so to him. And he hadn't dropped it this time. That was a plus.

The words he had spoken were ridiculous, though. He wished he had read more dime novels so that he would know how a Western lawman was supposed to talk. Somehow he couldn't imagine a real frontier marshal calling someone a miscreant.

Seymour holstered the gun and got ready to try his draw again. He had been practicing for half an hour and his arm was beginning to ache, but it was important that he become more proficient with a firearm. So far he had been lucky. In the week that he had been the marshal of Sweet Apple, no more gunfighters had braced him, and there had been only the one bushwhacking attempt. The professional shootists didn't want to have anything to do with him because of the potential damage to their reputations if they killed him. And since he had been fortunate enough to not only survive the ambush but also to wound the man who had hidden in that alley, anyone else who wanted him dead must have been thinking twice about risking another attempt.

Seymour knew he was lucky to be alive. But what was the old saying? Fortune favors the bold? Well, if he could grow bolder, perhaps fortune would favor him even more. It was worth a try.

He was thinking about his name—Seymour Standish didn't really sound like the name of a Texas lawman— when the office door opened. Seymour swung around to see who was there, and as he did, he realized that he should have loaded his gun. Carrying it around empty probably wasn't too wise.

But his visitor was only Miss Maggie O'Ryan. Although he shouldn't think of her as "only," he told himself. Ever since he had first met her, he'd been drawn to her. She was smart, beautiful, courageous . . . everything, in short, that made her much too fine a woman for the likes of him. But he couldn't help the way he felt.

"Good evening, Miss O'Ryan," he greeted her. He noticed that she looked worried. "What can I do for you?"

"I've just been to visit one of my students," Maggie said. "He wasn't in school today, so I thought I'd go by and see if he was ill."

Seymour nodded. "Very conscientious and commendable of you."

Maggie's face was grim as she went on. "He wasn't in school because yesterday his father beat him so badly that the poor boy couldn't walk today."

Seymour's eyebrows went up. "How terrible! I hope you're going to report this to the proper auth—" He stopped short, then said, "Oh. That's what you're doing, isn't it? *I'm* the proper authorities."

"You may not have noticed, Seymour, but people in Sweet Apple are starting to respect you instead of laughing at you. You've done a good job as marshal."

Seymour wasn't sure what pleased him more—the compliment or the fact that she had called him by his first name. He said, "It's only been a week, and I haven't really done that much."

"You've stopped three saloon fights, and you jailed two men who were drunk and firing their guns in the air. Someone could have been hurt in all of those incidents."

He shrugged. "I'm a salesman by trade, you know. Not a very good one maybe, but I do know how to talk to people. I was fortunate to persuade those men to settle their differences without violence, and as for the two men I arrested . . . well, they were really too inebriated to put up much of an argument."

"You just let them sleep it off and then released them in the morning. You could have fined them or made them stay in jail longer."

Seymour shook his head. "There didn't seem to be any

point in that. They were already so hungover they were suffering a considerable punishment."

"Even so, people can see that you're a reasonable man, and they like that. You're winning them over, Seymour." Maggie looked down at the floor and added, "You've won me over. I . . . I wasn't sure how good a lawman you'd be. But now I think you're doing a fine job."

Seymour's heart swelled. If Maggie admired him as a lawman, then how did she feel about him as a man? He wondered how she would feel about having dinner with him some evening at the café.

At the moment, she was more concerned with her unfortunate student. She looked up and went on. "That's why I think you should go see Mr. Dietrich. If you told him to stop mistreating Randolph, he might listen to you."

Seymour couldn't stop a dubious frown from appearing on his face. He said, "I don't know about that, Maggie." If she was going to call him Seymour, surely it would be all right if he called her Maggie. She didn't object to the familiarity as he went on. "After all, a parent has the right to discipline a child however he sees fit."

"Within reason! Whipping a child until he can't walk isn't reasonable!"

"I agree with you, but the law doesn't really make any distinction about such things."

"How do you know about the law? You were a dry-goods salesman before you pinned on that badge."

Seymour winced a little. He liked Maggie O'Ryan, liked her a great deal, but she could be plain-spoken, even blunt on occasion. Like now.

"I found a law book in the desk," he explained. "I suppose one of the previous holders of this job left it behind.

I've been reading it at night. Studying it. Enforcing the laws is my job now, you know."

She crossed her arms and gave him an intent look. "Well, I'm making an official complaint against Gunther Dietrich, and as the marshal, you're required to investigate."

"I am?"

"You are."

Seymour wasn't sure that was right, but he supposed it wouldn't do any harm to go have a talk with this Dietrich fellow. As he'd told Maggie, he was usually able to use his salesman's skills to persuade people to do what he wanted. Well, sometimes anyway.

He reached for his hat. "Where can I find Mr. Dietrich?"

"I'll show you," Maggie said.

"I don't know if it's a good idea for you to come along."

"Randolph is my student. I'm going."

Seymour could tell that he would be wasting his time by arguing. He put his hat on and nodded. "All right. But if there's any trouble, let me handle it. That's my job."

"Of course."

Fear hopped around inside him like a spooked rabbit as he and Maggie walked along the street. He wondered how big Gunther Dietrich was. He asked, "What does Mr. Dietrich do for a living?"

"He works at the wagon yard."

Seymour nodded. It sounded like Dietrich might be a pretty burly fellow. All the more reason to resolve this peacefully.

The Dietrich family lived in a small adobe house not far from the wagon yard. It was just Randolph and his father, Maggie explained. The boy's mother had passed away several years earlier. That was probably one reason Maggie was so concerned about him, Seymour thought.

Her maternal instinct made her want to take care of him since he no longer had a mother of his own.

Lantern light shone through the windows of the house. Keeping a tight rein on his nervousness, Seymour marched up to the door, followed by Maggie, and rapped sharply on the panel.

When the door opened, the huge shape of the man inside seemed to blot out the light from the lantern. His bullet-shaped head was devoid of hair except for a pair of bushy eyebrows.

"Yeah?" Gunther Dietrich growled. "What do you want?"

Seymour had trouble finding his voice. He swallowed a couple of times. Maggie must have grown impatient, because she leaned past him and said, "This is Marshal Standish, Mr. Dietrich. I've told him about what happened to Randolph."

Dietrich sneered. "So you went runnin' to the law, did you?"

Angered by the way the man looked at Maggie, Seymour finally spoke up. "Mr. Dietrich, it's been reported to me that you're mistreating your son. I've come to ask you to cease such behavior."

"What?"

"Stop whipping Randolph," Maggie said.

Dietrich shook his head. "He's my boy. I'll do whatever I see fit to do. I got the right."

"Not necessarily," Seymour said, thinking back over some of the things he had read in that battered old law book he'd found in the marshal's desk. "There are certain provisions in the law that allow the authorities to remove a child from circumstances that endanger him." More anger welled up inside him, momentarily overcoming the nervousness and fear. "I would think that being beaten past the point of being able to walk would certainly qualify."

Dietrich frowned and shook his head. "What are you sayin'?"

"The marshal is going to take Randolph away from you if you don't start treating him better," Maggie said.

Dietrich's eyebrows jerked around like caterpillars on a hot rock. "Take my boy away from me?" he rumbled. "You'll go to hell first!"

He stepped forward and swung a fist like a sledgehammer at Seymour's head.

The attack didn't take Seymour completely by surprise. He had been able to tell from the first moment of the confrontation how belligerent Dietrich was and knew things might come to this. With his heart pounding, he ducked under the sweeping, roundhouse blow and shouted, "Maggie! Get back!"

Maggie let out a cry of alarm as she stumbled backward. Seymour hoped she had the sense to stay out of this struggle. He leaped to the side as Dietrich swung again, this time an uppercut that would have taken Seymour's head off if it had connected. He put his hand on his gun and shouted, "Mr. Dietrich, stop it! Stop it or I'll have to arrest you!"

Dietrich growled something that Seymour guessed were curses in German. He lunged at Seymour with his arms widespread, obviously intending to wrap up the smaller man in a bone-crushing bear hug.

Seymour twisted away at the last second. He knew that he would stand no chance against the monstrous Dietrich in a fistfight. He had to resort to his gun.

Which, of course, was still unloaded since putting the

bullets back in it had totally slipped his mind after Maggie interrupted his practice in the marshal's office.

Still, the revolver was less likely to break on Dietrich's skull than his hands were. As Dietrich stumbled past him, Seymour yanked the gun from its holster and swung it as hard as he could at Dietrich's head.

Barrel met skull with a resounding *clunk!* Dietrich didn't go down, though, as Seymour had hoped he would. Instead he let out a bellow of pain and annoyance and brought around an arm like the trunk of a young tree in a sweeping blow that crashed across Seymour's chest and knocked him off his feet. Seymour went down hard in the doorway of the house, but managed to hang on to the gun. Maggie screamed his name.

Seymour barely had time to be pleased by that before Dietrich wheeled around and launched a kick at him. Panic erupted inside him at the thought of the big man stomping him to death. He rolled aside frantically, again causing Dietrich to miss. This time Dietrich was thrown off balance. As he tried to catch himself, Seymour lashed out and kicked him in the knee. Dietrich howled and toppled over backward.

Dietrich landed so hard on his back that all the breath was knocked out of his body. He lay there gasping for air like a fish out of water. Seymour scrambled over to him and hit him with the gun again. This time Dietrich's eyes rolled up in their sockets, he let out a groan, and then he lay still as he passed out.

Maggie rushed to Seymour as he pushed himself to his feet. She clutched his arms and asked, "Are you all right? Did he hurt you?"

Seymour took a deep breath and shook his head. "N-no, I'm fine. Just . . . just a bit winded."

And still scared. His heart was pounding like a trip-hammer, its usual reaction whenever he was afraid. But he felt a surge of fierce satisfaction as he looked at Dietrich's motionless form stretched on the ground in front of the house. Seymour could barely believe that he had managed to subdue such a brute. Again, luck had been on his side.

Not only that, but Seymour was beginning to realize that a healthy dose of fear was not necessarily a bad thing. It made a man move faster and fight harder.

"P-Pa?"

The voice from inside the house made both Seymour and Maggie turn. A small blond boy hobbled forward, obviously in pain. Maggie rushed over to him and knelt to hug him.

"It's all right, Randolph," she told him as she patted his back. "Your father won't hurt you anymore."

The boy looked past Seymour at the unconscious form of his father. "Pa!" He tried to pull loose from Maggie's arms.

Seymour put a hand on her shoulder. "Let him go," he said. "He's worried about his father."

She looked up at him, frowning in confusion. "But . . . but the man mistreated him!"

"He's still the boy's father," Seymour pointed out.

Maggie let go of Randolph, who limped over to drop to his knees beside Dietrich. The boy said, "Pa, are you gonna be all right?"

Dietrich let out a groan and began stirring. Seymour took cartridges from the loops on his belt and began reloading his gun. As he did so, he said, "I'm sorry I had to hit him like that, son. He didn't give me any choice. I think that in the future he'll treat you a little better. At least I hope so. If he doesn't, you let me know."

Randolph looked up at him. "Are . . . are you gonna arrest him, Marshal?"

"Not this time, and if he treats you right from now on, I don't think I'll have to." Seymour snapped the gun's loading gate closed and holstered the weapon. "Can you tell him that when he's good and awake?"

"Y-yeah. I guess so."

Seymour patted his shoulder. "Good." He looked toward the street, feeling eyes watching him, and was surprised to see that a group of townspeople had gathered. He said, "Can a couple of you men come help Mr. Dietrich back into his house?"

Two of the townies hurried forward to do as Seymour asked. Maggie asked, "Are you sure you shouldn't arrest him?"

"I think he's learned his lesson." Seymour hoped his confidence wasn't misplaced. And while he had that confidence, he went on. "Would you do me the honor of having dinner with me tomorrow night, Miss O'Ryan?" Since he was asking such a momentous question, it seemed proper to speak more formally.

Maggie blinked in surprise, but after a second she said, "I . . . I think I'd like that, Marshal Standish."

Seymour smiled. To do that took considerable restraint, because what he wanted to do was let out a whoop of glee and leap into the air. He nodded and said, "I'll call for you at six o'clock?"

"That . . . that will be fine. And thank you for helping me this evening."

He gave his hat brim a tug. "That's my job." He offered her his arm. "Now, with your permission, I'll walk you home."

Maggie hesitated, but again, only for a second. Then she linked her arm with his and smiled. "Thank you, Marshal."

As they walked off, Seymour glanced at the crowd again. He thought he saw several admiring gazes from the townspeople. Maybe they really *were* coming to respect him, as Maggie had said.

What he didn't notice was J. Emerson Heathcote, editor and publisher of the Sweet Apple *Gazette,* scribbling furiously on a pad of paper with a stub of a pencil. Heathcote's pudgy face bore the look of a man who had just stumbled over a buried trove of treasure. . . .

Chapter 23

"Was this town here the last time we were down this way?" Sam Two Wolves asked as he and Matt Bodine rode slowly down the main street of the settlement they had come to a few days after their encounter in the Davis Mountains with cantankerous old Alby McCormick.

Matt shook his head. "I don't think so." He pointed to an elevated water tank next to the double line of gleaming steel rails. "And there's the reason why. The railroad hadn't come through yet. The locomotives needed a water stop here, so *viola,* there it is."

"Why'd you call me Viola?"

Matt frowned. "I didn't call you Viola. It's a French word. Means, well, there it is, I reckon."

Sam shook his head. "No, Viola is a woman's name. Or a musical instrument sort of like a violin. You're thinking of v-o-i-l-a, pronounced *vah-lah.* Surely that's the French word you meant."

"Maybe so. But don't call me Shirley."

They glared at each other for a second, then grinned. Sam reined in and called over to a skinny man lounging in the doorway of a general store, "Hey, friend, what's the name of this place?"

"They call it Marfa," the man replied. "Don't ask me why, 'cause I ain't got no idea." Judging by his garb, he was a cowboy, like most of the other men Matt and Sam had seen in the settlement. Now that the Apache threat had been ended for the most part in West Texas, cattlemen were moving in and establishing ranches that sprawled over vast areas.

It was late in the day. The sun had already started to sink below the horizon, and Matt and Sam were grateful that they had come to a town. They wouldn't have to spend another night on the trail. They could wash the dust out of their throats, get a decent meal, sleep in real beds, and maybe even take a bath. Then, after replenishing their supplies, they could start the last leg of their journey. Sweet Apple wasn't more than two days' ride from here, they estimated.

Matt edged his horse closer to the store's porch and asked the cowhand, "Been any trouble around here lately?"

"What sort o' trouble?"

"Outlaws," Matt replied.

The cowboy shook his head. "Ain't heard about anything like that. Been plumb peaceful in these parts 'cept on payday. Then the boys from the spreads hereabouts come into town and blow off a little steam."

"You know where Sweet Apple is?" Sam asked.

"Sure. On up the railroad 'bout thirty or forty miles."

Matt leaned forward in the saddle. "You haven't heard about any ruckuses up there?"

"Nope." The cowboy frowned. "How come you boys're so interested in trouble? Lookin' to make some?"

Matt held up both hands, palms out. "Not hardly. We're

just like what you said it's been around here, mister . . . plumb peaceful."

"Uh-huh." The cowboy didn't look or sound convinced. He shifted the wad of chewing tobacco in his cheek, turned, and went into the store.

Matt and Sam hitched their horses into motion again and headed on down the street toward a large adobe building with a sign on it proclaiming it to be a hotel. In a low voice, Sam said, "It stands to reason that if Mallory and his gang had raided Sweet Apple already, someone here would have heard about it."

"Yeah," Matt agreed. "You reckon that means they haven't hit the place yet?"

"That's the only thing that makes sense."

"But why not? We know that's where they were headed, and they were far enough ahead of us that they should've gotten to Sweet Apple a couple of days ago."

"Something happened to delay them," Sam mused. "Or Mallory changed his plans for some reason and isn't even going there anymore."

"If that's what happened, then how in blazes are we gonna find them? They could be anywhere west of the Trinity by now."

Sam could only shrug. He didn't have an answer for his blood brother's question.

They came to a livery stable before they reached the hotel, and stopped there to make arrangements for their saddle mounts and packhorses to be taken care of for the night. Then they moved on to rent a pair of rooms. The hotel clerk looked a little askance at Sam, and might have been about to say something about his Indian blood, but the sight of the double eagles that Matt dropped on the desk changed his mind.

They had brought their saddlebags with them from the livery stable. As they were about to go upstairs to their rooms, something caught Sam's eye. He picked up a folded newspaper from one of the chairs in the lobby and asked the clerk, "Mind if I borrow this?"

The man shrugged. "You can have it as far as I'm concerned, Mr. Two Wolves. Someone who's staying here must have left it there."

"Thanks," Sam said with a nod and started up the stairs after Matt.

"Interested in catching up on the news?" Matt asked when he saw the paper in Sam's hand. "Might be something about Mallory and his gang in there."

"That's not why I picked it up," Sam said. He followed Matt into one of the rooms they had rented and unfolded the newspaper. "I saw something about Sweet Apple." He pointed to one of the headlines and read, "'Scaredest Man in the West Becomes Fighting Marshal.'"

"Let me see that," Matt said as he reached for the paper. "I didn't know Sweet Apple had a marshal. The place has got such a bad reputation I'm surprised anybody would even take the job."

Both of them scanned the densely printed columns of type. The newspaper was the Sweet Apple *Gazette,* edited and published by one J. Emerson Heathcote according to the masthead. It was dated the day before, so the blood brothers knew that someone on an eastbound train must have picked it up in Sweet Apple, probably read it on the train, then discarded it here in the hotel.

In flowery prose under the byline of J. Emerson Heathcote himself, the story told how Seymour Standish, late of Trenton, New Jersey, had arrived in Sweet Apple a little over a week earlier and quickly established a dubious reputation as

Seymour the Lily-Livered, the Most Cowardly Man in the West. But through a bizarre set of circumstances, Standish had taken on the job of town marshal, in addition to being a traveling salesman for Standish Dry Goods, Inc., also of Trenton, New Jersey, the job that had brought him to Texas in the first place. To the enormous surprise of everyone—no doubt including Standish himself—he had actually done a good job as marshal, heading off some saloon brawls, surviving an ambush attempt, and knocking out a local bully.

"This is damn near the craziest thing I've ever heard," Matt declared. "Whose idea was it to make a rabbity traveling salesman the marshal of Sweet Apple?"

"It makes sense in a bizarre way," Sam said. "What's more important to most gunfighters than anything else?"

Matt nodded. "Their reputation. I see what you're gettin' at. Folks'd laugh at a man who went out of his way to kill some cowardly little worm."

"From the sound of this newspaper story, though, Marshal Standish is getting a reputation of his own." Sam shook his head. "If he's not careful, that'll get him killed."

Matt folded the paper and slapped it against his leg. "Well, there's nothin' in here about Mallory's gang attacking the town, so I reckon that answers our question about whether or not they've raided Sweet Apple yet."

"Unless Mallory hit the town today," Sam pointed out. "That's yesterday's paper."

"Yeah. Maybe those folks over in Sweet Apple are just a hell of a lot luckier than they know. We'll head over there first thing in the morning, and if Mallory hasn't gotten there yet, we can warn this Marshal Standish."

"You mean we'll tell the Most Cowardly Man in the West that a gang of thirty or forty vicious outlaws is on its way to kill him and loot the town he's supposed to protect?"

A grim chuckle came from Matt. "I reckon that'll be a good test of just how much Seymour Standish has grown in the job."

A train whistle blew as Matt and Sam led their horses out of the livery stable the next morning. The blood brothers had had a good night's sleep in the hotel and a hearty breakfast in the place's dining room. Now they were about ready to hit the trail again, but at the sound of the shrill whistle, Sam said, "We're idiots."

"Speak for yourself," Matt said. "But, uh, how come you think we're idiots?"

"We were going to spend the next two days in the saddle when we could take the train and be in Sweet Apple before the day is over."

"We didn't know that," Matt pointed out. "We hadn't checked the schedule at the train station."

"Only because we were too dumb to think of it!"

"Well, let's go down there and take a look now. If that's a westbound pullin' in, it sure would be quicker to catch a ride on it."

By the time they reached the depot, the train had rolled in and steamed to a stop with the locomotive positioned to take on water from the elevated tank. It was indeed a westbound. Matt held the horses while Sam hurried into the station to buy tickets and arrange to have their horses loaded onto one of the cars. Luckily, there was room for both of them and the four animals.

With the reins in his hand, Matt stood beside the steps leading down from the station's platform. The rails were only a few yards away. The puffing and hissing of steam made the horses a mite skittish. Matt spoke to them in a quiet voice to calm them down.

While he was doing that, his eyes noted a couple of women on the platform. Young ladies actually, probably around twenty years old. Both wore traveling outfits. One was a blonde; the other had coppery red hair under her neat little hat. They had climbed down from one of the passenger cars and were strolling around the platform. Stretching their legs before boarding the train again, Matt thought, although it wasn't really proper to think of legs where young women were concerned. Those were limbs they walked around on. And mighty pretty limbs, too, Matt was willing to bet.

Pretty or not, Matt had other things on his mind besides women, so his attention drifted away from them. A few minutes later, Sam came out of the station. He held up the tickets to show that he had gotten them. Matt nodded . . .

Then his head snapped around as a loud, angry voice came from the other end of the platform. "Come on, darlin', ain't no need for you to act like that! My pard an' me just want you and your friend to come have a drink with us."

Matt saw two men confronting the pair of attractive young women he had noticed earlier. The men were large, unshaven, and roughly dressed. Each carried a big gun on his hip. Matt's eyes narrowed as the two women tried to step around the men, only to have the hombres move to block them.

"Just leave us alone," one of the women said. The blonde, Matt noted.

"Or you'll be sorry, you saddle tramps!" the redhead added in an angry tone that indicated her temper matched her hair.

One of the men stepped closer to her, glowering at her. "No call for you to talk to us like that," he said.

Matt looked around, saw a post nearby, and wrapped the horses' reins around it, pulling them tight. Sam had almost reached the end of the platform. He looked surprised when Matt bounded up the steps to meet him.

"What are you—" Sam began.

Matt nodded toward the two men and two women. Sam turned, saw their tense, angry attitudes, and understanding dawned on his face.

"We're going to take cards in that game, aren't we?" he asked.

"Unless those two varmints fold pretty quicklike, we are," Matt replied in a hard voice. He strode toward the other end of the platform.

The conductor appeared next to one of the passenger cars and hollered, "'Boooooard!"

The blonde said, "We have to get on the train." She tried again to get around the men blocking her and her friend.

One of them reached out and grabbed her roughly by the arm. "Not until you've had that drink with us, gal," he said with an ugly grin.

As Matt and Sam passed the conductor, Matt looked over at the blue-uniformed man and snapped, "Hold that train."

The conductor started to say, "Young fella, I can't—"

"He said to hold the train," Sam put in, his voice just as flinty as his blood brother's had been. "We have tickets, and so do those two young ladies."

The conductor swallowed, no doubt recognizing the dangerous looks on the faces of the two big, muscular young men. "All right, but make it fast," he said to their backs. They were already past him by the time he spoke.

"Let go of her!" the redhead said as she reached for the

man who had hold of her friend. The other man grabbed her arm and yanked her toward him.

That was a mistake. She hauled off and punched him in the face.

The man let out a yelp of pain and surprise and jerked back. Blood dribbled from his nose, where the redhead's hard little fist had connected solidly. "You damn hellcat!" he yelled. "I'll paddle your behind!"

"No, you won't," Matt said from behind him. "Step away from those ladies, both of you."

"Right now," Sam added.

The men swung around, fury on their beard-stubbled faces. "You two boys run along," one of them said with a sneer. "This ain't none o' your business."

"We're making it our business," Matt said. "Leave those ladies alone, or you'll answer to my brother and me."

The redhead snapped, "You don't have to do this. We can take care of ourselves."

The two hardcases ignored her, and so did Matt and Sam. The other man said, "Brother? He looks like a stinkin' half-breed to me."

"You say that like it's a bad thing," Sam said. "I prefer to think of it as having the best of two different heritages."

"Well, I think you stink, Injun!"

Sam glanced over at Matt and commented, "His inventory of insults seems to be rather limited."

"Yeah," Matt said. "I reckon that's because he's a half-breed, too—half-pig, half-skunk."

The man's face contorted with hate and rage. "I'll kill you, you bastard!" he howled as he clawed at the revolver on his hip.

Matt didn't want bullets to start flying here on the station platform. There were too many innocent people around for that, including the two young women. So, moving with the same sort of blinding speed he would have used if he'd been making a draw of his own, he stepped forward and slammed a fist into the man's face before the hombre could clear leather.

All of Matt's considerable muscle power went into the blow. It landed cleanly on the man's jaw and sent him flying backward. He crashed into the blonde and knocked her down as she let out a startled cry.

The other man lunged at Matt, swinging a fist at his head. Sam intercepted him and grabbed his arm. Pivoting smoothly, Sam hauled on the man's arm, stuck his hip out, and executed a neatly done wrestling throw. The man yelled in surprise as he found himself flying through the air upside down. He landed on the platform on his back with a jarring impact that took his breath away and left him half-stunned.

With the fight knocked out of both of the lecherous hardcases, Matt and Sam turned to the two young women. The blonde was picking herself up off the platform. Sam moved to help her, but she pulled away, saying in a cool voice, "That's not necessary."

"None of that display was," the redhead added. "We could have handled those two ourselves."

"Yeah, you looked like you were doing a fine job of it," Matt shot back, stung a little by their ingratitude.

"We were getting around to it," the redhead said. Her hand moved near the stylish little bag she carried, and a pistol appeared in it as if by magic. Matt blinked in surprise, and when he looked over at the blonde he saw that she was holding a gun as well.

"If they'd pushed us much farther, we would have ventilated the varmints," she said.

"But our fathers taught us not to kill anybody we don't have to," the redhead added.

Matt and Sam both stared. The two young women might be dressed like Easterners, but clearly they were both frontier gals. They held the guns like they knew how to use 'em and wouldn't hesitate to do so.

"Uh, gentlemen," the conductor said nervously from behind Matt and Sam, "we're falling behind schedule. Can the train leave now?"

Matt turned and nodded. "I reckon." He glanced over his shoulder at the women. "Were you ladies ready to go?"

"More than ready," the blonde said. "I wish we hadn't even gotten out here to stretch our legs."

She didn't say "limbs," Matt noted. Another indication that they weren't the prissy Eastern girls they appeared to be at first glance.

As they put their guns away, Matt thought about offering his arm to the redhead, but he figured she'd just refuse it. She had defiance and independence written all over her pretty face. He and Sam moved aside and let the two women go ahead of them toward the steps leading up to the vestibule at the front of the passenger car where they had been riding.

Behind them, the two hardcases groaned and started trying to struggle to their feet. They lurched upright, snarled, and reached for their guns.

Instinct warned Matt and Sam at the same moment, or maybe it was the whisper of gun metal on holster leather. They whirled, their hands streaking for the Colts. The two hardcases had called the tune, and now they'd have to dance to it. Gunplay could no longer be avoided.

So Matt and Sam intended to win this fight they had been forced into.

The two hardcases had their guns drawn before Matt and

Sam cleared leather. But it was the guns of the blood brothers that spoke first. Matt's twin Colts roared at the same time, sending two bullets crashing into the chest of the hombre on the left. Sam's revolver blasted a fraction of a heartbeat later. The man on the right doubled over as the slug from Sam's gun ripped into him. Each of the hardcases managed to get a shot off, but the bullets thudded harmlessly into the thick planks of the station platform. The two men hit those planks themselves a second later, collapsing in death.

"Good Lord!" the conductor gasped as he stared wide-eyed at Matt and Sam. "I never saw shooting like that before."

Matt walked along the platform to check on the two men, even though he was sure they were dead. Sam turned to the two young women, who stood at the top of the steps, looking as stunned as the conductor was. "I'm sorry you had to see that, ladies," Sam said. "Those fellows didn't give us much choice, though."

"I never saw anybody so slick on the draw," the redhead said. "Who are you, mister?"

"My name is Sam Two Wolves." Sam inclined his head toward Matt. "That's my blood brother, Matt Bodine."

The conductor's eyes widened even more, although that didn't seem possible. "Bodine and Two Wolves! The notorious gunfighters?"

"I don't know how notorious we are," Sam said in a mild tone, "and we never sought a reputation as gunfighters—"

"They're both dead," Matt said, interrupting as he strolled back along the platform. He had holstered his left-hand Colt and was replacing the spent cartridge in the right-hand gun. "I looked through the lobby, and I think I saw a fella with a tin star on his shirt runnin' up the street. Reckon you'll have to hold that train a little longer, Mr. Conductor."

Chapter 24

The nervous conductor fidgeted and fumed as the train was delayed a little more than half an hour while the marshal of Marfa questioned Matt and Sam and the two young women. The lawman's eyes narrowed in suspicion when he found out who Matt and Sam were. Their reputation had preceded them, even in this new, isolated little settlement in far West Texas.

But the marshal recognized the names of the young women, too, when the redhead introduced herself as Jessica Colton and the blonde said that she was Sandra Paxton.

"Your pa wouldn't be Shad Colton, now would he?" the lawman asked Jessica.

"That's right, Marshal."

He looked over at Sandra. "So that would make your pa—"

"Esau Paxton, that's right," she said. "Jessie and I have been at school back East. We're on our way home."

"And our folks are expecting us," Jessica put in with a toss of her head. "So we'd like to get this train moving again as soon as possible."

"Yes, ma'am, I understand, Miss Colton," the marshal said. "But I got a couple o' dead men layin' here, and from what I'm hearin', you and Miss Paxton were involved in them gettin' that way."

"It's not the ladies' fault at all, Marshal," Sam said. "Those men accosted them, and Matt and I put a stop to it. The fight was over. They were the ones who insisted on bringing guns into it."

"So you killed 'em both?"

"Wasn't time for anything fancy," Matt drawled. "They had their guns out first."

"That's the way it happened, Marshal," the conductor said. "I saw the whole thing."

"So did we," Sandra said. "Mr. Bodine and Mr. Two Wolves had no choice but to protect themselves."

Jessica said, "Hell, we would've shot those two polecats ourselves if we'd had a chance."

Matt managed not to chuckle, but he couldn't stop the grin that stretched across his face. All he could do was look down at the station platform in a feeble attempt to hide the amused expression. Jessie Colton sure had a fierce nature about her.

The marshal asked a few more questions, then said, "Well, I reckon it's pretty cut-and-dried what happened here. We'll have to have an inquest, but the verdict's gonna be that you boys ventilated these two skunks in self-defense. They've been hangin' around town for a couple of weeks, gettin' drunk and causin' trouble, so nobody's gonna be too upset that they're dead."

"So we can be on our way?" Sam asked.

The lawman rubbed his jaw and grimaced. "Well, you really ought to stay here and testify at the inquest. . . ."

"We can't do that," Matt said. "We have to get to Sweet Apple."

"We've given you our statements," Sam said. "Write them up and read them into the record when you have the inquest. That ought to be sufficient."

"It'll have to do," Matt said. "We're gettin' on that train."

"Hang on a minute," the marshal urged. "I'll get the ticket clerk from inside the depot. He can write up what you said, and you boys can sign the statements. You can wait that long, can't you?"

Matt and Sam looked at each other and shrugged. "I'll write the statements," Sam offered. "You can see about getting the horses loaded on the train, Matt."

"Sounds good to me."

Jessie Colton sighed. "So we're going to have to wait even longer?"

"It won't take but a little while, Miss Colton," the marshal assured her. "If your pa asks about it, tell him we got things handled just as fast as we could."

The lawman seemed worried about offending Shad Colton. Matt and Sam didn't know why, since neither of them had ever heard of the man before. Obviously, Colton was some sort of big skookum he-wolf in these parts. Sandra's father, Esau Paxton, seemed to be regarded pretty much the same way.

It didn't take long for the remaining two chores to be taken care of. Sam wrote out the statements while Matt got the horses loaded. Then Matt and Sam both signed the statements and gave them to the marshal.

"This ought to take care of it," the lawman said with a grateful nod. "If there are any more questions, you boys said that you're headed for Sweet Apple?"

"That's right," Sam said with a nod. "But I don't know how long we'll be there."

"Depends on what we find," Matt added without explaining just what they were looking for.

He and Sam climbed onto the train, and the conductor was able to take up the temporary steps at last and wave to the engineer to get the train moving. The whistle shrilled and steam hissed as the locomotive lurched forward. With only a slight jolt the rest of the cars followed.

As Matt and Sam started along the aisle of the car they had boarded, they found Jessica Colton and Sandra Paxton sitting on one of the bench seats, facing forward. An empty rearward-facing seat was across from the two young women. Matt and Sam glanced at each other, then took that seat.

"I think we can protect ourselves now," Jessica said with a tart tone to her voice. "There shouldn't be any more trouble between here and Sweet Apple."

"I hope not," Matt said. "We're peaceable sorts, Sam and me."

"One killing before breakfast is enough for you, is that it?" Sandra asked.

"You said it yourself, those men didn't give us any choice," Sam pointed out. "We don't go around looking for gunfights, no matter what you may have heard about us."

"Oh, so you're so famous we're supposed to have heard of you?" Jessica said.

"That star-packer back there sure had," Matt said.

"Yes, and he seemed to think you were a pair of troublemakers," she replied.

"Look, we were just trying to help you—"

Sam and Sandra both held up their hands and said, "Stop," at the same time.

"There's no point in arguing all the way to Sweet Apple," Sandra explained. "It really won't take all that long to get there, so why don't we try to pass the time pleasantly?"

"Sounds like a good idea to me," Sam said. "Why don't we start by you ladies telling us some more about yourselves?"

Jessica looked like she thought that wasn't a very good idea, but Sandra said, "Our fathers sent us back East to school, as we mentioned before."

"They thought we needed somebody to teach us to be proper young ladies," Jessica said. She followed that statement with a disdainful snort. "As if that's important out here in Texas. We already knew how to ride and rope and shoot."

"There are other things to life besides those," Sandra said.

Jessica's look made it clear she didn't agree with that, but she didn't say anything.

Sandra turned back to Sam. "You sound like an educated man, Mr. Two Wolves."

"I went to school in the East, too," he said. For the next few minutes they talked about the education each of them had received. From the corner of his eye, Matt watched Sam and could tell that his blood brother was a mite taken with Sandra Paxton.

He couldn't say the same for himself where Jessica Colton was concerned. That hombre who had grabbed her back in Marfa was right about one thing—she was a hellcat. A *redheaded* hellcat at that. Matt pitied the gent who ever got involved with her.

Over the next half hour, more information about the young women came out as Sam and Sandra talked, and Matt found himself interested in spite of himself. It seemed that their fathers, Shadrach Colton and Esau Paxton, were cousins and had come to West Texas with their wives a little more than twenty years earlier to start a ranch near where the settlement of Sweet Apple had eventually sprung up. Jessica and Sandra had both been born out here, only a few days apart, in fact. They had been raised together and were best friends as well as second cousins.

The CP Ranch—for Colton and Paxton, of course—had flourished despite the sometimes harsh weather, the threat of Indians, and the Mexican rustlers from below the border who sometimes raided across the Rio Grande just like the Apaches did. Somewhere along the way, though, something had happened to drive a wedge between the cousins, and a final split had occurred while Sandy and Jessie, as they were known, were off at school. The Colton and Paxton families had always had separate homes anyway, so the spread was divided and each house served as the headquarters for a new ranch.

"Do you know what happened to cause the trouble between them?" Sam asked. "Not that it's any of my business, of course . . . but I *am* curious."

Sandy shook her head. "No. Whatever it was, our fathers always kept it to themselves. But we haven't let it affect us, have we, Jessie?" She smiled over at the redhead. "We're still best friends."

"I just hope that doesn't change once we get back," Jessie said with a slight, worried frown.

Sandy shook her head. "Nothing's going to come between us. We've been through too much together. Why, once we helped fight off an Indian attack when we were only eleven years old. One of the men who was defending a rifle port was wounded, so Jessie grabbed up his gun and told me to load for her."

Jessie smiled at the memory and said, "My shoulder was bruised for a month from the recoil of that rifle. But I dusted the britches of several of those damned Apaches." She glanced at Sam. "No offense intended, Mr. Two Wolves."

Sam grinned. "None taken. Matt and I have had some run-ins with the Apaches in the past. I don't like 'em either."

"I hope you ladies do manage to stay friends," Matt said. "Might not be easy if your families are feudin', though."

"Maybe it hasn't gotten that bad," Jessie said.

"I hope not," Sandy added. In what was evidently an attempt to change the subject, she asked Sam, "Why are you and Mr. Bodine going to Sweet Apple? Not that *that* is any of *my* business."

Matt and Sam looked at each other for a second. "We're looking for some fellows," Sam said without offering any further explanation. Matt knew his blood brother was thinking the same thing he was. Since it was possible that the Mallory gang might not even attack Sweet Apple, it didn't make sense to panic folks just yet. They would talk to the marshal there first and try to get a better idea of what the situation actually was.

"Oh," Sandy said. Matt got the feeling that she was a mite offended by Sam's reticence. He didn't particularly care. Once they reached Sweet Apple and these girls were reunited with their families, he and Sam might not ever see them again.

The engineer highballed it, trying to make up for the time lost in Marfa, but there were several flag stops between there and Sweet Apple. So it was nearly midday when the train finally rolled up to the Sweet Apple station. Matt and Sam looked the town over with great interest. No buildings were on fire, the street wasn't littered with the bodies of men and horses, and folks strolled here and there seemingly without a care in the world.

Deuce Mallory hadn't been here yet. That was for damned sure.

As the train shuddered to a halt, the conductor came along the aisle calling, "Sweet Apple! Sweet Apple! We'll be here fifteen minutes!"

Matt and Sam got to their feet, as did Sandy and Jessie. "Can we help you with your bags?" Sam asked the young women.

"No, our folks will be here," Jessie answered, "and probably some of the ranch hands. So we don't need your help."

"But thank you anyway," Sandy added.

That was fine with Matt. He wanted to find the marshal and deliver the warning about Mallory's gang. He jerked his head at Sam and said, "Come on. Let's get the horses."

Sam tugged on the brim of his hat, smiled at the women, and said, "So long, ladies. It was an honor and a pleasure to make your acquaintance."

"Thank you for everything, Mr. Two Wolves," Sandy said. "And you, too, of course, Mr. Bodine."

"I still say we could've handled those rannies by ourselves," Jessie muttered. She headed for the car's vestibule without looking back.

Matt and Sam went the other way and dropped down from the rear platform without the aid of steps. As they walked along the station platform toward the livestock cars where their horses had made the trip, Sam looked back over his shoulder. So did Matt, allowing his curiosity to get the better of him for a moment.

Two separate groups of people were waiting for Jessie and Sandy. A brawny, red-haired, red-faced hombre threw his arms around Jessie and hugged her, while a petite brunette and a flock of redheaded kids gathered around her and got their hugs in turn. The man had to be Shad Colton, the brunette his wife, and the youngsters Jessie's younger brothers and sisters.

A few yards away on the platform, a thin-faced man with a fringe of gray hair around his ears and a hat thumbed back on a mostly bald head waited for Sandy, along with a plump, pretty woman about the same age who had only a few streaks of silver in her blond hair. Two blond boys in their teens—twins, from the look of them—were there, too. Sandy's brothers, Matt guessed.

Even though not that much distance separated the two groups on the platform, it was like a range of mountains was between them. Nobody from one bunch even glanced in the direction of the other bunch. It was a damned shame when families who had been close had a falling-out like that, Matt thought briefly.

Then he forgot about the Coltons and the Paxtons and their troubles and turned his attention to reclaiming the saddle mounts and packhorses so that he and Sam could go and hunt up the famous—or infamous, if you wanted to look at it that way—Marshal Seymour Standish.

A few minutes later, leading the animals, they walked down Sweet Apple's main street. A bystander pointed out the marshal's office to them. Of course, there was no guarantee that Standish was at the office, but they didn't have any better place to start looking for him, Matt thought as he and Sam approached the squat adobe building.

They tied the horses at the hitch rack out front and stepped onto the porch. Without knocking, Matt opened the door and walked into the marshal's office with Sam right behind him.

They both stopped short at the sight of a man standing there pointing a gun at them.

Chapter 25

It took all of Matt's self-control not to slap leather. Even as fast on the draw as he was, he doubted if he could get his gun out and fire before the man in the marshal's office squeezed the trigger. Instead, he said, "Hold it! Don't shoot, mister. We're not lookin' for trouble."

The man with the gun looked even more surprised than Matt and Sam were. He lowered the weapon hastily and said, "I'm sorry. Don't worry, it's not even loaded."

Matt and Sam started to breathe again. What they had thought might be a very close call wasn't really a threat after all.

The man was undoubtedly Marshal Seymour Standish. He had a badge pinned to his black leather vest. A slender man of medium height, he looked smaller than he really was next to the brawny pair of blood brothers. Spectacles perched on his thin nose. Remembering the reference in the newspaper story to "The Most Cowardly Man in the West," Matt thought Standish fit that description better than he did that of a fighting marshal. How could anybody be both?

Standish holstered his gun and asked, "What can I do for you gentlemen?"

Matt gestured at the revolver on Standish's hip. "That gun's not loaded?"

"No. I was just practicing my draw when you came in."

"Hadn't you better load it? What if there was some trouble you had to handle? You *are* the marshal, aren't you?"

"That's right, I am. And I suppose I *should* put the bullets back in the gun."

"It shoots better that way," Matt said.

As Standish took some cartridges from an open box on the desk and began sliding them into the empty chambers of the gun's cylinder, he said, "You haven't told me why you're here. Have you come to report a crime?"

"You could say that," Sam replied with a nod. "It just hasn't occurred yet."

Standish frowned. "You're reporting a crime that hasn't occurred? That's a bit unusual, isn't it?"

Matt said, "Call it delivering a warning then. There's a gang of outlaws on the way here to raid the town. They plan to clean it out of everything valuable, kill anybody who gets in their way, burn down half the buildings, and kidnap the prettiest women they can find before they run off across the border into Mexico."

Standish's eyes widened more and more in amazement as Matt talked. He almost dropped the gun he was holding. Some of the bullets did slip out of his fingers and clatter to the desk. But he managed to raise the revolver, point it at Matt, and Sam again, and order, "D-drop your guns!"

"Hang on," Matt said. "Why are you pointin' that thing at us?"

"You s-said you were delivering a warning. Doesn't

that mean you're members of this outlaw gang you were talking about?"

"Hell, no! We've been chasin' those damn owlhoots for more'n a week, ever since they raided another settlement up on the Panhandle."

"We came down here to stop them," Sam said. "We want to help you, Marshal."

Standish looked like he wasn't sure whether he believed that. He asked, "Who are you?"

"I'm Matt Bodine. This is Sam Two Wolves."

Matt could tell that their names meant nothing to Standish. That wasn't really a surprise. According to the story they'd read in the *Gazette,* Standish had come to Texas from somewhere back East—New Jersey, that was it, Matt recalled . . . wherever the hell *that* was—and had been a traveling salesman before accepting the marshal's job. It stood to reason that he might not have heard of Bodine and Two Wolves.

"Are you lawmen of some sort?" Standish asked. "Texas Rangers perhaps, or U.S. marshals?"

"No, we're just a couple of hombres who hate outlaws," Matt explained.

"We were in that other town when Mallory's gang raided it," Sam added. "We saw firsthand what they're capable of, and we want to keep them from doing it again down here."

"Mallory?"

"Deuce Mallory. He's the leader of the gang," Sam explained. "Have you heard of him?"

Standish shook his head.

"Well, if you had," Matt said, "you'd know what a low-down snake he is. And Sam and me, we sort of make a habit of stompin' snakes whenever we get the chance." Matt gestured at the revolver still clutched in the marshal's hand. "So why don't you put away that smokepole, and we can sit down and talk about what we need to do to get ready for Mallory."

"Get ready?" Standish repeated with a frown. "You mean—"

"I mean you and the folks here in Sweet Apple are gonna have to defend the town. Otherwise, Mallory and his men will overwhelm it and take over. And trust me, you don't want that."

Standish shook his head. "No. No, I don't." He holstered the gun, then sunk into the chair behind the desk. He put his head in his hands and practically moaned, "Oh, Lord, what's going to happen next? I'm not cut out for this!"

Matt and Sam looked at each other and frowned. They had run across a lot of star-packers in their adventurous career, but never one who acted quite like this.

Matt didn't really know what to say. "Uh, Marshal Standish," he ventured. "Seymour . . . You mind if I call you Seymour?"

Without lowering the hands that covered his face, the marshal shook his head.

"Seymour, we may not have much time," Matt went on. "You need to, uh, pull yourself together. There's a lot to do."

Seymour looked up. "What? What can we do? If there's an army of outlaws about to descend on Sweet Apple, as you say, then the situation is hopeless. We need to get word to the Rangers, or perhaps the U.S. army, and hope that help will arrive here in time."

"Sure, send for the Rangers," Sam said. "It can't hurt anything. But you can't count on them getting here before Mallory does."

"That's why you've got to be ready," Matt said. "We'll help you."

"But . . . but there are only three of us. And even men as competent as you two appear to be, Mr. Bodine, can't stand up to that sort of odds."

"You're gonna have to talk to men that you trust here in town," Matt said. "Tell them to keep the news under their hats for now, because you don't want to panic folks. But if you could round up a couple dozen men who are willing to fight, who'd be ready when the outlaws get here so they don't take us by surprise, and it might make all the difference in the world."

"I . . . I don't see how it's possible. It seems so far-fetched . . ."

"Sweet Apple's got a reputation as a tough town," Sam pointed out. "There are bound to be plenty of men around here who are willing to fight."

Seymour frowned in thought. "Well, maybe . . ."

"You don't have much choice," Matt said. "You either fight . . . or roll over and die."

"You don't want to do that," Sam added.

"No," Seymour said. "No, I don't." He took a deep breath. "Very well. I . . . I can start talking to some of the townspeople . . . men I know . . . I suppose I could deputize them. . . ."

"Just make sure you talk to fellas you can trust."

"You have to understand," Seymour said. "I haven't been the marshal here for very long. And to be honest, I'm more a figure of mockery than anything else. I don't really *know* who I can trust."

Sam said, "Make your best guesses. You don't want word of this leaking out just yet."

"For one thing," Matt said, "it's possible Mallory and his gang might not even show up here. They should've been here before now. We thought we'd get here to find the town half-destroyed."

Seymour turned even paler than he already was. "Good Lord," he muttered. "Is there such savagery lurking around every corner out here in the West?"

"Usually." Matt went around the desk and clapped a hand on the marshal's shoulder. "But now that you realize that, Seymour, you've got a better chance of living to see the sun rise tomorrow."

The blood brothers spent a while telling Seymour about the Mallory gang's raid on Buckskin. Hearing all the details made the marshal blanch even more, but Matt and Sam thought it was important that Seymour understand exactly what he might be up against.

They wanted to know exactly what sort of man they'd be working with, too, so Sam said, "Tell us about what's happened in Sweet Apple since you've been here, Seymour. We read a story in the *Gazette,* but I'm sure there's more to it than that."

Seymour made a face. "Mr. Heathcote thinks that I'm good copy, as he calls it. When I first arrived he built me up to be a cowardly buffoon—which I am, I suppose—but he was also one of the men who came to me and asked me to take the marshal's job."

"A man's only as cowardly as he believes himself to be," Matt drawled.

"And as for being a buffoon," Sam said, "I can already tell that that's not the truth. You're an intelligent man, Seymour."

"I suppose so," Seymour said with a sigh. "It's true that I always enjoyed school. I've thought before that I should have found some sort of academic career. I was never cut out to be a salesman either. But my father was the owner of the company, and he expected me to follow in his footsteps. . . ."

"Sam and I both know what it's like when a fella wants to please his pa. But when you come right to it, every man has to figure out his own trail, not just follow somebody else's, no matter how much you admire him."

"Yes . . . Yes, I suppose you're right. But that doesn't help us now, does it?"

"Nope," Matt agreed. "Right now you're here, and those outlaws are maybe on their way, and that's what you've got to deal with."

Looking more decisive than he had so far, Seymour stood up and reached for his hat. "Let's go," he said. "I have an idea about where to start recruiting defenders for the town."

The three men left the marshal's office and walked along the street toward the Black Bull Saloon. Along the way, Matt felt someone watching him and turned his head to look at the boardwalk. A couple of men were loitering there in front of a hardware store. Something about them was vaguely familiar, and after a second he recalled that he had seen both of them on the train from Marfa. They must have gotten off in Sweet Apple, too. Both men looked out of place. They wore Eastern suits, including derbies. One was short, broad, muscular, and very hairy. The other man was tall and thin, with cold, reptilian eyes and swarthy skin. Matt felt an instinctive dislike for both of them, but the men turned and headed the other way down the street, so he put them out of his mind for now.

He and Sam had more pressing problems. A whole outlaw gang full of them, in fact.

Seymour pushed the batwings aside and led the way into the Black Bull. No one in the place paid much attention to him, which told Matt that folks were getting used to Seymour being their marshal, as odd as that was on the face of it.

Seymour approached one of the men standing at the bar, nursing a mug of beer, and said, "Mr. Halliday, I'd like to talk to you, if you don't mind."

Halliday was a hard-looking man with mean little eyes. Matt and Sam had encountered his type many times before. A two-bit gunman who was no doubt dangerous— but not as dangerous as he thought he was.

Halliday greeted Seymour with a sneer. "Well, if it ain't our famous lily-livered marshal. What do you want, Seymour? Want me to shoot that hat full o' holes like I did your last one?"

Matt stepped to one side and Sam to the other so that they flanked Seymour. "The marshal said he wants to talk to you, mister," Matt snapped.

"I'd listen, if I was you," Sam said.

Halliday's eyes flicked back and forth between them. "Who the hell are you two?" he demanded. "Seymour the Lily-Livered's new deputies?"

Matt and Sam looked at each other and shrugged. "How about it, Marshal?" Matt asked. "Are we officially deputized?"

"I . . . I suppose that would be best. Consider yourselves deputy marshals of Sweet Apple."

Halliday hadn't lost his sneer. "That still don't tell me who you are."

"Name's Matt Bodine."

"And I'm Sam Two Wolves."

Recognition flared in Halliday's eyes. He knew those names, all right. He knew that Bodine and Two Wolves belonged to the same brotherhood of the gun that he did . . . only at a much higher level. "What do you want with me?" he snarled. "It's two against one." He wasn't counting Seymour.

Matt shook his head. "We're not lookin' for trouble, Halliday."

"The marshal wants to talk to you," Sam said. "That's all."

Slowly, Halliday lifted his left hand and rubbed his jaw. "Well . . . I reckon that's all right."

Seymour nodded and said, "Thank you, Mr. Halliday. Now, if you'll be so kind as to wait just a moment . . ." He went over to one of the tables, where several men had watched the confrontation with looks of surprise and puzzlement on their faces. "Mr. Keller, Mr. Akin, would you join us?" Seymour turned back toward the bar. "And Mr. Delacroix, you, too?"

A man in an expensive suit who stood at the bar asked in a Cajun accent, "What are you up to, Seymour?"

"I'm putting together a small . . . discussion group, let's call it. I'd like to talk to the four of you in my office."

"Are you arrestin' us?" one of the men at the table asked.

Seymour shook his head. "Not at all. As I said, I'd just like to talk to you."

The man called Delacroix smiled. "Why not? I am glad to oblige the friend of the charming Miss O'Ryan."

Matt didn't know what that was about, but he saw the way Seymour's ears suddenly turned red. Whoever Miss O'Ryan was, Matt figured that the marshal was smitten with her.

The seven men left the saloon and walked toward Seymour's office. Along the way, Matt looked around for the two Eastern dudes he had noticed earlier, but he didn't see them.

"All right," Halliday growled when they reached the

office and the door was closed behind them. "What is it you and these hired guns o' yours want, Seymour?"

Looking at Halliday, Keller, and Akin, Seymour said, "I've had trouble with all three of you men, but I bear you no ill will. I understand that you're all proficient with firearms—"

"Try us any time you want and find out for yourself, Seymour," Keller said.

Seymour held up his hands. "No, no, that's not what this is about. You're tough men. I know that." He looked at the saloon keeper. "You, too, Mr. Delacroix, otherwise you wouldn't have been able to be a success in your profession. I need some tough men to give me a hand."

They all stared at him, clearly not understanding what he was getting at. Delacroix said, "You wish to deputize *us, mon ami?*"

"Well . . . unofficially, yes."

A bark of harsh laughter came from Halliday. "I'm no damn lawman."

"I did say it would be unofficial."

"Why should we want to help you?" Akin demanded.

Seymour's answer was blunt, and Matt was glad he'd finally stopped beating around the bush. "Because there's an entire gang of outlaws on their way to Sweet Apple, and if we're not ready for their arrival, they might just wipe out the entire town."

Chapter 26

The three gunmen and the saloon keeper just stared at Seymour for a long moment, as if he had spoken to them in some foreign language they didn't understand. Finally, Delacroix asked, "How do you know this, Seymour?"

"They told me," Seymour replied with a nod toward Matt and Sam.

"You know who Bodine and Two Wolves are?" Halliday asked. "Gunfighters, that's who they are. Just a couple o' driftin' hellions, on the lookout for trouble."

"That's not quite true," Matt said.

Halliday bristled. "You callin' me a liar, Bodine?"

"I'm sayin' that you're misinformed about Sam and me," Matt said in a cold voice. "And you'd better listen to the marshal here, because he's right about what might happen. Deuce Mallory and his gang nearly destroyed a whole town up in the Panhandle a couple of weeks ago. We were there and saw it with our own eyes."

"How do you know this man Mallory and his cronies are headed here?" Delacroix asked.

"We went after them," Sam explained. "We didn't ever

catch up to them, but we did get our hands on one of Mallory's men who'd been left behind because he was wounded. He's the one who told us that Mallory and the rest of the gang planned to attack Sweet Apple and then duck across the border into Mexico."

"But if this is true," Delacroix said, "why have the outlaws not attacked the town already? You admitted that they were ahead of you and you did not catch up to them."

Matt shrugged. "Yeah, they should've been here before now. We don't know the answer to that."

"Maybe they ain't comin'," Akin said. "Maybe they decided to raid someplace else."

"That's a possibility," Seymour admitted. "But the possibility still exists that they'll come *here,* and so we have to be prepared for them."

"Prepared how, *mon ami*?" Delacroix asked.

Seymour looked around at them. "We have to get ready to fight."

Again a moment of silence passed as the men mulled over what Seymour had said. Then Halliday asked, "Why us? It ain't like we're your friends, Seymour."

"No . . . but you live here. When Mallory and his men attack, you'll be in as much danger as anyone else in Sweet Apple. The difference is that men such as yourselves are capable of fighting back."

"Damn right we can fight!" Keller said. "I ain't afraid of no owlhoots!"

"How many men does Mallory have?" Delacroix wanted to know.

"We're not sure," Matt said. "Somewhere between twenty and thirty is a good guess. But there could be as many as forty of the varmints, and they might've picked up even more along the way as they came down here."

"The seven of us cannot stop them."

"You probably know other men you can trust," Seymour said. "Men who can handle themselves in a fight. Help me spread the word . . . but only to men who are willing to keep that knowledge to themselves. We don't want everyone in the town panicking over something that might not even happen."

The hardcases thought it over. "I never helped the law before," Keller muttered.

"Somethin' about it rubs me the wrong way," Akin added.

Halliday silenced them with a slash of his hand. "Sweet Apple's *our* town, damn it. And Seymour may be lily-livered, but he ain't stupid. I've heard of Deuce Mallory. They say he kills folks like we'd step on a bug. There ain't no human feelin' in him. I don't want to see what him and two dozen snakes just like him would do to this town."

"Neither do I," Delacroix agreed. "Two of my bartenders are rugged, courageous men, Seymour, and they can keep their mouths shut. I can recruit them to our cause."

Halliday rubbed his jaw. "I know some ol' boys who like a good scrap, too. I reckon they'd agree to give us a hand and keep their traps shut."

Akin and Keller shrugged and went along with the others, each offering to find some more defenders among the settlement's more disreputable elements.

"I'll speak to the members of the town council, too," Seymour said, "but for the moment I can't thank you gentlemen enough. With your help, we will prevail if those outlaws make the mistake of attacking Sweet Apple."

"How much time do we have to get ready?" Halliday asked.

Seymour looked at Matt and Sam. "We honestly don't know," Matt said. "Mallory could strike at any time. Might be a good idea to post a lookout at the highest point in town to give us some warnin' if a large group of riders approaches."

"That would be the roof of the Black Bull," Delacroix said. "I'll send a man up there as soon as I get back to the saloon."

Seymour nodded in approval of that plan. "The rest of you spread out through town and find more men we can trust."

They started toward the door, but Halliday paused and looked back with a frown. "Are you sure you're the same hombre I hoo-rawed down at the train station the day you got here, Seymour?"

"I don't know." Seymour smiled. "Sometimes I feel like a different man. A new man."

"Yeah, well, a bullet don't care about things like that, so when the time comes . . . keep your head down."

Since Matt and Sam didn't really know anyone in Sweet Apple, they left it up to Seymour and the men he had already recruited to put together the rest of the force that would defend the town in case the Mallory gang raided it. That afternoon, they saw a wagon roll out of the settlement carrying Jessie Colton and the rest of the Colton clan. Her father Shad was at the reins, handling the team of fine black horses. Half-a-dozen hard-faced cowboys rode behind the wagon, punchers from the Colton spread, no doubt.

A short time later, the Paxton family departed in much the same manner, traveling in a big, sturdy wagon, accompanied by several gun-hung waddies. Matt and Sam noted that the families seemed to have made a point of leaving Sweet Apple at different times.

"Do you think we should have warned them about Mallory?" Sam asked.

Matt thought it over and then shook his head. "From the way the girls were talking, their ranches are a good long way out of town. They shouldn't be in any danger."

"Mallory and his men might raid the ranches."

"Mallory's not a rustler," Matt said. "Wide-looping cattle is too much work for a varmint like him. He's just interested in loot that he can grab without going to a lot of trouble, like in a bank." Matt paused. "And killing. He's interested in killing."

"We ought to take a ride out to those spreads and warn them," Sam insisted.

"Maybe we will in a day or two, after we've got things more squared away here."

Sam went along with that idea. The biggest threat was still definitely directed at Sweet Apple.

By that evening, Seymour was able to tell Matt and Sam that a force of twenty-two men, including the three of them, had been assembled to defend the town in case of attack. Of course, other men would fight, too, if it came to that, but these twenty-two knew in advance of the possible danger and would be ready at all times to oppose it. The only outward sign of that, however, was the presence of three men on guard duty—one on the roof of the Black Bull, another in the bell tower of the mission on the edge of town, and the third perched on the roof of the hotel. If any of them detected any signs of an attack, they would fire three shots in the air to alert the rest of the defenders.

The nearest telegraph office was at Fort Davis, which was several days' ride away, but a rider had been sent there to wire the Texas Rangers for help. Any assistance from the Rangers was probably at least a week off, though, and

Matt and Sam both had their doubts the outlaws would delay their attack that long.

Although most of them didn't yet know the danger they were in, the citizens of Sweet Apple were pretty much on their own.

That evening, after having supper with Matt and Sam, Seymour set out to make his rounds by himself, as he usually did. For the time being, he didn't want to vary his routine. Matt and Sam had alerted him to the possibility that Mallory might have spies in Sweet Apple. Strangers came and went all the time in the settlement. The defenders didn't want to tip their hand and allow Mallory to discover that he would meet heavy resistance when he raided the town. It would be different, Matt said, if such a possibility would deter the outlaws from attacking. On the contrary, though, such a discovery would probably just make them launch their strike sooner, before the citizens had time to get any more organized.

Listening to the blood brothers talk, Seymour realized just how much he had to learn about strategy if he was ever going to be a good fighting man. Not that such a thing had ever been one of his ambitions until now . . .

He had just checked the door at the saddle shop when he felt his heart give a little jump as he recognized a figure ahead of him on the boardwalk. Maggie O'Ryan was coming toward him. She paused suddenly, as if she had just noticed him, too, and wasn't sure whether to keep coming or not. They were still rather shy around each other, despite the fact that they had had supper together twice. Seymour wasn't officially courting her, at least not yet, but they were steadily edging in that direction.

Maggie lifted her chin and started walking toward him again. Seymour swallowed and resumed his own journey along the boardwalk. When they got closer to each other, he nodded and said, "Good evening, Maggie."

"Hello, Seymour," she replied. "How are you?"

"Fine, fine," he said, hating the small talk that seemed to be one of the requirements of a new relationship like this. What he really wanted to do was to take her in his arms and kiss her. But he couldn't do that, of course. It would be highly improper.

And he hadn't yet learned to say to hell with propriety.

He felt worry course through him when he thought about the fact that Maggie would be in danger, too, if the Mallory gang attacked the settlement. Maybe he ought to warn her—

He caught himself before he said anything about it. The outlaws might have bypassed Sweet Apple and already be in Mexico by now. Until that could be determined one way or the other, he didn't want to cause Maggie any unnecessary worry.

Instead he asked, "How has attendance been at school the past few days?"

She smiled. "Surprisingly good. Oliver Delacroix has even been there every day. It's like the parents in Sweet Apple have finally realized how important it is for their children to get an education. My hope is that the town is beginning to settle down at last. After all, we have a real marshal now."

His natural self-deprecation made him start to say that he didn't know about that, but he stopped himself and said, "And a real school as well. Civilization's getting quite a foothold here."

He was about to ask her to have dinner with him again sometime, when a couple of figures suddenly loomed up behind Maggie on the boardwalk. One of them, a short, broad man, bumped heavily against her shoulder as he started past. She cried out softly as the collision made her stumble a step to one side.

A sneer contorted the unshaven face of the man who had run into her as he said, "Watch where you're goin', girlie." His companion, a tall, skinny man, gave an ugly laugh.

Anger flared up inside Seymour. "Stop right there, you two men!" he said.

They came to a halt and glared at Seymour. "What in blazes do you want, mister?" the burly one demanded.

"I want you to apologize to the lady," Seymour snapped. "You were the one who ran into her."

"That ain't the way I saw it." The man turned and ran his eyes insolently over Maggie. "Anyway, I don't apologize to greaser whores."

Maggie gasped in outrage and shock. Seymour's anger turned into fury as he reached for his gun and said, "By God, sir, you're under arrest—"

"Seymour, look out!" Maggie screamed.

But the warning came too late. Both of the strangers had reached under the coats of their Eastern suits with surprising speed and pulled out pistols. Shots roared and flame spouted from the weapons as they opened fire.

Matt and Sam had told Seymour to make his rounds by himself, as he usually did, but that didn't mean they were leaving the safety of the town to the inexperienced young lawman. They started making a circuit of Sweet Apple for themselves, keeping to the shadows and looking for any indication that Deuce Mallory might be trying something sneakier this time, like infiltrating some of his men into the settlement before attacking with the rest of his gang.

"Something's happened," Sam mused as he and Matt made their way behind the livery stable. "Mallory wouldn't change his tactics like this without a good reason."

"I reckon I agree with you," Matt said. "Shocked the hell out of me that he hadn't already hit this place when we got here."

"You think he's not even coming?"

Matt didn't answer for a long moment as he pondered the question. Then he said, "You know how it feels when somebody's got a gun pointed at you?"

Sam snorted. "You know damn well I do."

"Well, that's the way I feel . . . like I've got a big ol' target painted on my chest and somebody's drawin' a bead on it. That tells me Mallory's still out there, and that he plans to raid this place sooner or later."

Sam thought it over and then nodded. "My instincts tell me the same thing. It's just a matter of time."

They moved on, circling the livery stable. Everything about the settlement was peaceful and quiet this evening except for the usual night noises, which in Sweet Apple included tinny piano music and brassy laughter from the saloons.

The blood brothers paused in the thick shadows at the mouth of an alley. Sam said quietly, "Look over there, across the street."

Matt looked and saw Seymour Standish talking to a young woman who was short and a little stocky but still very pretty with long dark hair. Light from the window of a nearby building shone on the two of them.

"That must be Miss O'Ryan," Sam said. Seymour had mentioned her a couple of times. Matt and Sam gathered from what he'd said that Maggie O'Ryan was the local schoolteacher. They also knew that Seymour liked her.

"Betcha he kisses her," Matt said with a grin as he nudged an elbow into Sam's side.

"Seymour? I don't think so. I know we haven't known him that long, but even though he may not actually be the most cowardly man in the West, I think he's still plenty scared of Miss O'Ryan."

"What is there to be scared of? She's just a pretty girl. That's what a fella does when there's a girl he likes. He kisses her."

"Not everyone has your confidence, Matt," Sam pointed out.

"Yeah, well, they ought to. You can't go through your whole life worryin' about every little thing—"

He stopped short as two figures came out of the shadows on the boardwalk across the street. One of them ran into Maggie O'Ryan and nearly knocked her down.

"Did you see that?" Sam said as angry voices rose. "We'd better go over there and see if we can give him a hand."

But there was no time to do that. Seymour yelled something about the men being under arrest and grabbed for his gun. But the two strangers were faster.

Not faster than Matt Bodine, though. As the men had moved into the light, he'd recognized them as the sinister-looking varmints he had spotted earlier. He had no idea who they were, but he had seen enough gun-traps engineered to recognize what was going on here. The two men had bumped Maggie solely for the purpose of angering Seymour and giving them an excuse to kill him.

Matt's twin Colts flickered from their holsters. Even though the range and the light were a little tricky and Seymour and Maggie were awfully close to the two would-be killers, Matt fired from the hip. There wasn't time for anything else.

Both of the strangers got shots off, but the bullets screamed off harmlessly into the night as Matt's slugs slammed into the men. Seymour had gotten his revolver out late and fired, too, adding to the sudden deafening racket of gunfire in the street. The two strangers staggered back. The tall, skinny one twisted around several times and then pitched forward on his face. The short, broad one fell to his knees and swayed there for a moment before toppling to the side and rolling off the boardwalk like a log.

Neither of them moved again.

Matt slid his guns smoothly back into leather and said to Sam, "Come on."

They broke into a run as they crossed the street. Seymour still held his gun in his right hand, but his left arm was around Maggie O'Ryan as she pressed her face against his chest and shuddered in fear. "It . . . it's all right," he was telling her as Matt and Sam trotted up. "Those men won't hurt you. You're not hurt, are you, Maggie?"

She stopped trembling long enough to shake her head. "I . . . I'm fine, Seymour. None of those shots hit me."

"Me neither," he said. He sounded like he couldn't believe that. His eyes were wide with amazement as he looked over at Matt and Sam.

"What happened here, Seymour?" Matt asked, knowing that Sam would follow his lead.

"Those . . . those men," Seymour said with a vague wave of his gun toward the bullet-riddled corpses. "One of them bumped into Miss O'Ryan here, and they were very rude, and I was going to arrest them for . . . for disturbing the peace, but then they drew their guns and . . . and my God, I never heard so many shots in my life. . . ."

"Yeah, you were blazin' away at 'em when we came up, Seymour. That was good shootin'."

Seymour looked at the gun in his hand, then at the dead men, then back at the gun. "I . . . did that?"

"Those varmints are ventilated good an' proper, and you and the lady are all right, so I reckon you must have."

"But . . . who are they? Why would they try to kill me?"

"I reckon they must've been rude to Miss O'Ryan to prod you into drawin' on 'em."

"It was a trap designed to get rid of you, Seymour," Sam added.

Seymour sounded utterly baffled as he said, "Why would anyone go to that much trouble?"

Matt slapped him on the back. "Because you're the fightin' marshal of Sweet Apple, that's why. Things have changed since you got here, Seymour. You've grown up. Might as well get used to it."

Seymour's eyes blinked behind his spectacles. "Yes, I . . . I suppose I have," he said.

Then he jammed his empty gun back in its holster, put both arms around Maggie, and brought his mouth down on hers in a kiss. She was obviously startled at first, but then she relaxed in his embrace and started returning the kiss.

Matt nudged Sam again and said from the corner of his mouth, "Told you."

Chapter 27

As the blood brothers dragged the corpses down the street to the undertaking parlor, Sam said, "I can't believe you went through that whole charade just to get Seymour feeling bold enough to kiss Miss O'Ryan."

Matt chuckled. "That wasn't the only reason. If he's gonna be able to deal with Mallory and all the other trouble he'll be facin' as the marshal of Sweet Apple, he's got to believe in himself."

"Yes, but now he's liable to be overconfident and get in over his head. He may try to tackle trouble that he can't handle. After all, he believes he just gunned down two men who were trying to kill him."

"We'll eat that apple when it falls off the tree," Matt said. "Right now, he believes he can stand up to whatever comes at him. That's half of actually being able to do it right there."

"Maybe so."

They left the bodies of the would-be killers with the undertaker, who had already turned in for the night and answered Matt's pounding on the front door of his establishment in his nightshirt. From there they went to the Black Bull, talked to Pierre Delacroix for a while, then headed for the hotel and turned in themselves.

As a consequence of the way their drifting usually landed them in trouble, the blood brothers had developed the habit of sleeping lightly. Tonight was no different. Trouble would have roused them instantly from slumber.

But Matt and Sam both slept through the night and woke the next morning refreshed, and with the knowledge that Deuce Mallory and his gang still hadn't shown up.

What the hell was going on? Matt asked himself. Was it possible that Mallory really had decided to leave Sweet Apple alone?

After having breakfast in the hotel dining room and washing the food down with several cups of strong black coffee, Matt and Sam walked over to the marshal's office. They found Seymour behind his desk, looking at some papers spread out in front of him.

"One of the desk drawers was full of old wanted posters," Seymour explained. "The Texas Rangers and the U.S. marshal's office must have been sending them out on a regular basis for months, even though Sweet Apple didn't have a lawman most of that time. Someone stuck them in the desk for lack of anything better to do with them."

Matt and Sam pulled up chairs, turned them around, and straddled them. "Find anything interesting?" Sam asked.

"Actually, I did." Seymour turned one of the papers around and pushed it across the desk toward the blood brothers. "There are several wanted posters for Deuce Mallory in here, along with some of the men suspected of riding with him. This one goes back a couple of years and was issued because of a bank robbery Mallory pulled off in Wyoming."

An artist had drawn a likeness of Mallory on the reward dodger, no doubt based on the testimony of witnesses who had seen the outlaw. Matt and Sam looked at the portrait of a man with a lean but not unhandsome face. The description printed underneath it said that Mallory was about six feet, two inches tall and had dark red hair.

"We never actually got a look at the varmint up in Buckskin," Matt said. "Let's see those other posters."

They studied the pictures for several minutes. Drawn by different artists in different locations, following an assortment of bloody-handed crimes, all the portraits of Mallory bore enough of a resemblance to each other for Matt and Sam to accept them as accurate representations of the outlaw.

"We'll know him if we see him," Sam said.

"What about the notices on the other members of his gang?" Matt asked. "Let's have a look at them, too."

As best they could, they memorized the features of Mallory's subordinates. The names of some of the men were incomplete or unknown, but Matt and Sam filed away the names of Jacob Pine, Gus Brody, and Steve Larrabee. They seemed to be three of Mallory's top lieutenants.

With apparent casualness, Matt asked, "How's Miss O'Ryan this mornin'?"

Seymour's voice was stiff as he answered, "I wouldn't know. I haven't seen her since I walked her home last night following that unfortunate incident."

"By unfortunate incident, you mean those two Eastern dudes who tried to kill you . . . or that big kiss you laid on the schoolma'am?"

Matt and Sam both grinned as Seymour's ears turned a bright shade of pink. He ignored the question and said, "I spoke to Harry Tallent, the local undertaker, this morning. He went through the belongings of the two dead men."

"Find enough cash to take care of buryin' 'em?" Matt asked.

Seymour nodded. "Yes, and he found a letter as well that identified the, uh, large, hairy one as a man named Wilford Grant. There was nothing to say who the other man was. But that's not the interesting thing. The letter to Grant was sent to an address in Trenton, New Jersey."

Matt and Sam both looked surprised. "You're from Trenton, aren't you, Seymour?" Sam asked.

With an expression on his face that was worried and puzzled at the same time, the marshal nodded. "That's right. I was born and raised there."

Matt said, "But you didn't know that gent?"

"I never saw him before," Seymour said with a shake of his head.

"There's got to be a connection," Sam said. "It's too big a coincidence to think that those fellows came all the way out here from your hometown, then just happened to run into you and try to bait you into a gunfight so they could kill you."

Matt nodded, frowned in thought, and said, "Somebody sent 'em after you."

"But that's impossible!" Seymour said. "I don't have any enemies back in Trenton. I . . . I was well liked by everyone who knew me."

"Not everybody," Sam said.

Seymour gave a stubborn shake of his head. "I refuse to believe that. I've been over it and over it in my mind, and no one in Trenton has any reason to want me dead."

"What about that uncle of yours, the one who sent you out here?" Matt asked.

"Uncle Cornelius?" Seymour was aghast. "I've known

him my entire life. He's my *uncle*, for God's sake, my father's brother."

"Hamlet's uncle had a few dirty tricks up his sleeve," Sam pointed out.

"There you go again, bringing up Shakespeare," Matt said. "You're not the only one who's read the classics, you know."

"I've seen those yellowbacks you carry around in your saddlebags. I'd hardly call Ned Buntline dime novels classics."

"Well, that just shows what you know." Matt turned back to Seymour. "Somebody's got it in for you. That's just plain fact, whether you want to admit it or not, Seymour. And that's on top of the threat from Mallory and his bunch. You'd better keep your eyes wide open all the time."

Seymour nodded glumly. "I'm afraid you're right."

"I know I am. We'll watch your back as much as we can, but we won't always be around here."

A look of alarm came into Seymour's eyes. "You're leaving?"

Sam shook his head. "Not until this business with Mallory is over and done with," he assured Seymour. "But the time will come when we need to move along."

"We're fiddle-footed," Matt explained. "Can't ever stay in one place for too long. Too many things left to see somewhere down the trail."

"I couldn't live like that," Seymour muttered. "I already find myself putting down roots here, and I never expected that."

"I reckon there are worse places to settle down," Matt said with a smile. "Sweet Apple ought to get plumb peaceful before too much longer."

"How do you figure that?"

"Place has got a gunfightin', town-tamin' marshal now," Matt said.

Seymour looked like he didn't know whether to feel proud . . . or sick with worry.

Time dragged, as it always did when men were keyed up to face danger and then it failed to arrive. Matt and Sam spent the day checking with the defenders who were scattered around town, seeing that they were in good positions to fight off an attack and suchlike. As far as the blood brothers could tell, all the men who had been recruited to defend the settlement were doing as they had been asked to and keeping their mouths shut. There was no air of panic to be found in Sweet Apple, only grim readiness among those few who knew about the threat that the town might be facing.

The heat became sweltering during the afternoon. The sky turned brassy. Men and animals sought whatever shade they could find, and anyone who ventured out into the brutal sun started sweating within seconds. But the parched West Texas air dried that sweat up almost as fast as it formed. Sweet Apple dozed in the heat.

The whole town seemed to heave a sigh of relief as the sun finally set. Evening shadows formed. The air was still hot, but at least the fierce glare of the sun was gone until morning. Matt and Sam sat in tipped-back chairs on the hotel porch with their hats pulled low over their faces and watched under the brims as riders moved slowly along the street. Nobody was going to get in a hurry in weather like this.

Suddenly, Matt started to sit up. He forced himself to sit still and not show any reaction to the man he had just noticed riding by. He watched from the corner of his eye as the stranger reined to a halt in front of the Black Bull, tied his horse to the hitch rack, and went into the saloon.

Sam had noticed the tensing of his blood brother's muscles, even though it wouldn't have been apparent to anyone else. "Something wrong?" he asked, pitching his voice low enough so that only Matt would hear it.

Matt sat up and let the legs of his chair come down on the porch with a quiet thump. He thumbed his hat up to its normal position. "Did you see that fella who just rode past? He went down to the Black Bull. That's his grulla tied up in front of the saloon now."

"I saw him," Sam said. "Can't say as I paid that much attention to him."

"Well, keep an eye on his horse. I'm gonna take a walk over to Seymour's office. There's something I want to be sure about."

"What if the hombre you're talking about comes out of the saloon?"

"Follow him," Matt said. "I shouldn't be long, though. I'm either right or wrong."

"Are you trying to be enigmatic?"

Matt smiled. "Nope. Just don't want to look like too big a fool if I'm wrong . . . and don't go sayin' that it's already too late for that."

With a casual wave, Matt started down the street toward the marshal's office. He moved at a leisurely stroll that concealed the tension he felt.

Earlier in the evening, he and Sam had seen Seymour and Maggie O'Ryan walk over to the café to have supper together. Then later, the two of them had returned, arm in arm, to Seymour's office. Knowing Seymour, Matt didn't figure he would be interrupting anything *too* improper, but when he reached the marshal's office he knocked on the door anyway before entering.

Seymour and Maggie were on opposite sides of the room by the time Matt got inside. Seymour stood at the desk while Maggie was over by the gun rack, pretending to admire the Winchesters and shotguns arranged there. But both of them were a little flushed and breathless, so Matt figured there'd been some sparking going on a moment earlier, until he knocked.

"Oh, hello, Matt," Seymour said. "I was about to, uh, escort Miss O'Ryan home and then get started on my evening rounds. Perhaps you'd like to accompany me?"

"No, thanks, Seymour. I need to look through those wanted posters again."

Seymour frowned. "The ones we were looking at this morning?" He reached for one of the desk drawers. "Of course. I have them right here. Is something wrong?"

Matt glanced at Maggie and said, "No, nothing's wrong. I just, uh, like to look at wanted posters."

Maggie put her hands on her hips and gave a sigh of exasperation. "Oh, please," she said. "That lie wouldn't fool one of my students. I know something's going on. Seymour, you've been as nervous as a cat this evening."

"But that's the way I normally am," he suggested.

Maggie shook her head. "When you first came to Sweet Apple, yes. But not now, Seymour. You've changed, probably even more than you realize yourself." She looked back and forth between Seymour and Matt. "There's going to be some sort of trouble, isn't there?"

Seymour stammered a little and looked to Matt for help. Matt shrugged and said, "You're her beau, Seymour. It's up to you how much you want to tell her."

"I . . . I'm what?"

"My beau," Maggie said. "And I'm not the least bit embarrassed to say that." The blush on her face indicated that might not be completely true, but the stubborn look in her eyes and the defiant tilt of her chin told Matt that Miss Maggie O'Ryan had taken a step from which she would not be turning back. She went on. "I'm actually a little offended that you don't trust me enough to tell me what's going on, Seymour."

"That's not it!" he said. "That's not it at all. I just thought it best not to worry you if there was no need—"

"If you're worried, then I need to be worried, too."

Seymour couldn't argue with logic like that. Leastways, he wouldn't if he had any sense, Matt thought. But Seymour's love life was the least of his concerns right now. "I still need to take a look at those reward dodgers," he reminded Seymour.

The marshal said, "Oh, yes," and opened the drawer to take out the stack of papers. He handed them to Matt, who spread them out on the desk and pawed through them until he found the one he was looking for.

Matt separated out the wanted poster and slapped it down on the desk by itself. "That's him," he said. "It's a good likeness."

Seymour looked at the paper and read aloud, "Jacob Pine. You saw him, Matt?"

"Riding down the street bold as brass, no more than five minutes ago."

Maggie asked, "Who's Jacob Pine?"

"He's an outlaw," Seymour explained. "He works for a man named Deuce Mallory." Seymour turned back to Matt. His face showed the strain of the thoughts that were going through his mind. "That means . . ."

Matt nodded. "Mallory must've sent him into town to

have a look around and make sure nobody suspects anything. They could be plannin' the raid for later on tonight."

Maggie gulped and said, "Raid?"

Seymour went to her and drew her into his arms, clearly no longer caring that Matt was there. "Don't worry," he told her. "You'll be safe. I'll see to that."

Maggie pushed back a step. "I'm not worried about myself. I have students here in Sweet Apple. If they're in danger, Seymour, you'd better tell me."

Seymour looked around. "Matt . . . ?"

"Go ahead and tell her," Matt said with a nod. "But you've got to keep this to yourself, Miss O'Ryan, at least until we find out for sure what's going on."

"How are we going to do that?" Seymour asked.

Matt's voice was grim as he replied, "Sam and I are gonna have a little palaver with Jacob Pine."

Chapter 28

"He's still in the saloon," Sam said when Matt returned to the hotel porch a few minutes later. "Now are you going to tell me what this is all about?"

Matt nodded. Quietly, he explained, "When the fella rode past a while ago, I thought he looked familiar. I checked those wanted posters Seymour has of Mallory and his gang, and sure enough, that hombre was one of them. Name of Jacob Pine. One of Mallory's right-hand men."

Sam stiffened just as Matt had when he recognized Pine. "That means . . ."

"Mallory sent Pine in to scout out the place," Matt agreed, knowing that was what Sam was thinking. "The raid has to be soon."

"What are we going to do?"

"I thought we'd get out hands on Pine and have a talk with him, try to find out exactly what Mallory is plannin' to do . . . and when."

Sam stood up. "I remember reading about Pine on that wanted poster. He's a vicious killer like the rest of the gang. What makes you think he'll tell us anything?"

A grim smile touched Matt's wide mouth. "Why, I got a crazy redskin who likes to torture white-eyes that I'll turn loose on him if he doesn't talk."

Sam shook his head. "My professors would be so disappointed in me."

"Come on. We'll wait until he comes out of the Black Bull and then grab him."

They angled across the street toward the saloon and took up positions in the mouth of the alley beside the Black Bull. Time dragged, but both Matt and Sam had the patience to wait in situations like this. After a while, the man they were looking for came out of the saloon and walked over to the hitch rack where his horse was tied. By the time Jacob Pine reached the animal, Matt and Sam were ambling past as if they had no interest in him.

When the blood brothers struck, it was swift and unexpected. Matt clamped an arm around Pine's neck from behind and dragged him away from the horse. With his other hand he jerked the gun from the holster on Pine's hip. At the same time Sam put a hand over Pine's mouth to stifle any outcry that might escape despite Matt's chokehold on the outlaw's throat. Sam held up his bowie knife with his other hand and let Pine see it. Pine got a good look at it since the tip of the deadly blade was only a couple of inches from his right eye.

Pine started to struggle as Matt dragged him toward the alley. Sam tapped the owlhoot on the head with the bowie's handle, stunning him for a moment. That was all Matt needed to finish hauling the prisoner into the shadows. They took him behind the Black Bull, lashed his hands behind his back with his own belt, and propped him against the wall.

Matt had switched his grip so that his hand was now

fastened around Pine's throat, keeping him from crying out. Sam leaned close to the outlaw and waved the knife in front of his face. Enough moonlight penetrated back here so that silvery glints flashed off the blade. Sam's face was set in a savage snarl quite unlike his usual expression.

"Listen, mister," Matt said. "We know who you are. You're gonna answer some questions, and if you don't, I'm gonna let my friend here go to work on you with that knife. First he'll cut off your ears . . ."

Sam tapped each ear in turn with the flat of the blade. Pine shuddered.

"When he gets done with that, he'll slice off your nose," Matt continued. "Then things'll start to get really interestin'—and painful."

Sam leaned closer and bared his teeth in a grimace that made him look half-insane. Maybe more than that.

"I'm gonna let off on your throat," Matt said. "Don't try to yell. Don't even think about it. You got that?"

Pine managed to jerk his head in a tiny nod. His eyes were wide with fear.

Matt released some of the crushing pressure on the outlaw's throat. Pine gasped for air for a couple of seconds, then rasped, "Wh-what do you hombres w-want? If you're plannin' to rob me—"

"We're not thieves," Matt said. "Like I told you, we just want answers."

"I don't know nothin'—"

"You know your name, don't you? You know that you're Jacob Pine."

The startled hiss of breath between the captive's clenched teeth told Matt that he hadn't made a mistake. This man really was one of Mallory's lieutenants. But Pine tried to deny it anyway.

"You got the wrong man, mister, I swear—"

"Don't waste our time," Matt cut in. "Where's Mallory? When does he plan to raid the town?"

"Damn it, I don't know what you're talkin' about!" Pine's voice was practically a wail. Knowing Mallory's reputation, Matt wasn't surprised that Pine didn't want to betray the leader of the gang.

Matt looked at Sam and nodded. Sam grabbed Pine's left ear and pulled it out straight from the outlaw's head. That had to hurt by itself, but then Sam laid the razor-sharp edge of the blade against the tight-drawn skin.

"Stop! Don't do it! I . . . I'll tell you what you want to know!"

Matt smelled the acrid stink of urine and knew that Pine had pissed his pants in terror. That was a little easier than he had thought it might be. He had hoped that they wouldn't have to cut the varmint's ears off for real.

They might have done it, though, what with the life of every man, woman, and child in Sweet Apple being at stake.

"Make it quick," Matt snapped. "Where's Mallory and the rest of the gang?"

"About f-five miles north of here." Pine panted a little in his terror.

"Why hasn't he raided the settlement already? We know that's what he planned to do."

Pine didn't ask how the blood brothers had discovered that. He just said, "D-Deuce found out . . . that the army's bringin' a shipment of guns through here on the train. He's gonna hit the town while the train's stopped here and get the rifles, too."

Matt and Sam exchanged a quick glance. This was the first they had heard about a shipment of military rifles.

That put a different light on things. Deuce Mallory was going after an even bigger prize than usual.

That meant he would be even more ruthless than usual.

"So he's been waitin' for those guns to get here?"

Pine nodded. "Y-yeah."

"When are they due?"

Pine hesitated. Sam reached for his ear again, and the outlaw bleated, "Tomorrow mornin'! They'll be on the westbound train that's supposed to roll in at nine o'clock! But . . . but that ain't all." A note of eagerness came into Pine's voice, as if he thought that spilling something else might improve his chances of getting out of this without losing his ears or nose or any other important body parts. "Deuce ain't the only one who's after the guns."

"What are you talkin' about?" Matt demanded.

"There's a Mexican . . . Diego Alcazarrio . . . calls himself a revolutionary but I reckon he's really just another *bandido* . . . He knows about the rifles, too, and plans to steal them."

A chill went through Matt. Having the threat of Mallory's gang hanging over Sweet Apple was bad enough. Now Pine was telling them that they might have to deal with a small army of Mexican bandits as well.

"Alcazarrio's plannin' to hit the train here?"

Pine shook his head and said, "I . . . I don't know. That's the truth, mister. I got no idea what that greaser's gonna do. But he might. That's worth somethin', ain't it? Ain't it?"

"You know anything else?" Matt asked.

"Not a damned thing. I swear. I'd tell you if I did." Pine swallowed. "How about lettin' me go? My life won't be worth a plugged nickel if Deuce ever finds out I talked. I'll ride west toward El Paso and you'll never see me again. I won't warn Deuce that you're expectin' him. I swear it."

"Mallory sent you into town to have a look around and make sure nobody knows he's comin'?"

"That's right."

"What's he gonna do if you don't come back?"

Pine hesitated. "He'll attack the town anyway. He wants those guns more'n I've ever seen him want anything before." The outlaw licked his lips. "I helped you, didn't I, mister? You can give me a break. It won't hurt nothin'."

"It'd hurt the memory of those people you helped murder in Buckskin," Matt said. Then his fist crashed against Pine's jaw in a short, powerful blow that rocked the outlaw's head back and knocked him out cold.

Sam sheathed the bowie knife, bent at the knees, and let the senseless owlhoot fall forward over his shoulder. He straightened. "We're taking him to Seymour's office and locking him up?"

"That's right," Matt said. "We need to tell Seymour that things are even worse than we thought."

In less than twelve hours, the train carrying those rifles would be rolling into Sweet Apple, with killers converging on the town from the north and possibly from the south.

Matt and Sam had a lot to do between now and then.

Deuce Mallory paced back and forth on the sandy rise, his anger growing with each step. He peered to the south, where the settlement of Sweet Apple was located about half a mile away. Then he glanced to the east, where the sky was growing gray with the approach of dawn.

Mallory swung around toward the rest of the gang. They sat their saddles uneasily, knowing that Mallory was upset and knowing as well that there was no telling what he would do if he lost his temper.

"Jake should have been back a long time ago," Mallory snapped as he stalked over to take the reins of his horse from Steve Larrabee, who had been holding them while Mallory paced and waited for Pine to meet them as planned.

"Maybe he just got drunk and passed out in some whorehouse, Deuce," Larrabee suggested.

Mallory shook his head and then swung up into the saddle. "He knows better than to do something like that. He knew I was expecting his report. He got himself arrested and thrown in jail—or gunned down in a fight." Mallory rubbed his jaw in thought. "Sweet Apple's a rough place. Plenty of hombres there who fancy themselves fast guns. Somebody could've goaded Pine into a showdown, I suppose."

"That'd be the best thing for us in a way," Larrabee said. He frowned. "But what if the law caught him? What if the folks in Sweet Apple know we're comin'?"

Mallory waved a hand. "It doesn't matter. Those rifles will be there in a little while, and I want them. I intend to have them." He sneered. "I'm not afraid of a bunch of settlers. Those hardcases in Sweet Apple aren't nearly as dangerous as they think they are. Not compared to us."

Larrabee looked like he hoped Mallory was right about that.

Mallory turned in his saddle and said, "Gus."

Brody rode up alongside him. "Yeah, Deuce?"

"We're proceeding as planned. Take the boys you picked out and plant that dynamite where I told you to."

Brody nodded. "Sure, Boss. Once it blows, that train won't be able to go anywhere. It'll be stuck there while we clean it out."

"That was the idea," Mallory snapped. "Get going."

Brody wheeled his horse, motioned to several of the

other outlaws, and rode off into the darkness. They would do their work under cover of what little night was left.

Larrabee risked asking, "Are you sure about this, Deuce? We could be ridin' into a trap."

"The trap hasn't been made that can catch me," Mallory said with complete confidence. He gave a curt nod in the direction of Sweet Apple. "Soon that whole town is going to belong to us."

South of Sweet Apple, another group of riders moved through the night toward the settlement. Water still streamed from the coats of their horses after fording the Rio Grande a short time earlier. Diego Alcazarrio rode proudly at the head of the group. If those who thought of him only as a bandit could see him now, he told himself. Riding like a general at the head of an army. A small army, to be sure, but still an army.

Alcazarrio called a halt when he and his men were approximately a mile south of the town. They hid themselves in a dry wash so that anyone who happened to be riding by in the early morning wouldn't see them. All the rebels had to do was wait until the train carrying the guns arrived at Sweet Apple. From here they would be able to hear the train's whistle as it approached. That would be the signal for them to mount up and begin their charge. They would sweep into town, ruthlessly overwhelming any opposition, capture the train station, kill the small force of gringo soldiers guarding the weapons, and take the rifles for themselves. Like any good general, Alcazarrio could see the whole thing in his mind, as vividly as if it had been painted on canvas before him.

He felt impatience nagging at him, but suppressed the

feeling. Soon his *revolucion* would enjoy its greatest success so far. He could afford to wait a little while. He even told himself to savor the moment.

By the time this morning was over, Diego Alcazarrio and his men would be a force to be reckoned with in Mexico. El Presidente Díaz would quiver in fear if he knew what was going to happen today.

Alcazarrio smiled. That image of a humiliated Díaz in his mind helped the time pass faster.

Seymour had been shocked when Matt Bodine and Sam Two Wolves brought in the prisoner and tossed him in one of the cells. He had been even more shocked when the blood brothers explained to him about the army rifles that would be on the train when it rolled into the station the next morning at nine o'clock, too tempting a target for both the gang of outlaws and a band of Mexican revolutionaries to pass up. This was the first Seymour had heard about a shipment of guns or Mexican rebels. As he tried to take it all in, he wanted to ask himself what else could possible go wrong.

He managed not to do that. No sense in tempting fate.

Because no matter how bad things were . . . they could always get worse.

The first thing Seymour did after Matt and Sam explained the situation was to walk down to the adobe cottage where Maggie lived and knock on her door. They had parted somewhat uneasily earlier, after Matt's visit to the marshal's office and the revelations Seymour had been forced to make to Maggie. Now he wanted to give her the whole story. She needed to know.

"Oh, my God," she said when he had finished explaining. "So soon?"

Seymour nodded. "Nine o'clock in the morning. But we'll be ready for them, and that includes you, Maggie."

"Me? What can I do to help fight outlaws and . . . and revolutionaries?"

"You'll have a school full of students," Seymour said. "It's a nice sturdy building, and it's quite a distance from the train station. Matt and Sam and I are going to pass the word that everyone in town should send their children to school in the morning, even the ones who normally don't. Once they're there, *keep them there* until Matt or Sam or I come to you and tell you it's all right to let them go again."

"You're counting on me to protect all the children in town?"

Seymour smiled. "I have confidence in you. And there will be several armed guards there with you, too."

"Oh, Seymour," she said as she came into his arms, causing him to reflect wryly that the situation wasn't all bad. It gave him an excuse to hug her and comfort her.

After leaving Maggie's a short time later, Seymour had joined the effort that Matt and Sam already had under way, going around town and alerting their makeshift defense force of the impending attack. Not only that, but now that they knew the time of the raid, they began to spread the word even more, knocking on doors and waking people up and recruiting more defenders. Most people agreed to send their children to the school first thing in the morning, with only a few insisting on keeping the youngsters with them. Matt, Sam, and Seymour made it clear that it was important to keep things looking as normal as possible in Sweet Apple the next morning.

Seymour had questioned the blood brothers about that very thing. "Isn't it possible that if we fortify the town so that Mallory knows we're ready for him, he'll decide not to attack us?"

Matt shook his head. "The chances of that happenin' are pretty slim. If this was one of his normal raids . . . if it wasn't for those guns coming in on the train . . . he *might* decide it wasn't worth the fight."

"But according to Pine, he wants those rifles so much that he'd risk it no matter how prepared we are," Sam said. "That's why our best hope is to take him by surprise. Let him come in thinking that he's going to ride roughshod over the town . . ."

"And give him a hot-lead welcome that he isn't expectin'," Matt concluded.

That made sense, Seymour supposed. He had to put his trust in Matt and Sam. They knew a lot more about fighting outlaws and killers than he did. They had been at it for years, instead of mere days.

By the time the sky turned orange with dawn and the sun peeked over the horizon, armed men were hidden on the roofs of half the buildings in town. Others waited inside or in alleys. It was still a couple of hours until the train carrying the rifles would arrive, and Seymour knew that time would seem endless. A few men walked or rode or drove wagons along the street, just to make the town look normal in case anyone was observing it from a distance.

Seymour, Matt, and Sam waited in the marshal's office, watching the performance that was being put on. Seymour felt himself sweating despite the fact that the air was cooler in the morning like this. The ticking of the clock on the wall was unnaturally loud.

"Time sure flies when you're havin' fun, don't it?" Matt asked with a grin.

Seymour's spectacles had slipped down a little on his nose. He said, "Remind me again why I decided to *stop* being the most cowardly man in the West. Seymour the Lily-Livered wouldn't ever get into a mess like this. He'd faint dead away from fear first."

Matt and Sam both chuckled, but before either of them could say anything, the sound of a whistle cut through the still morning air. All three men stiffened and glanced at the clock. Straight-up nine. The train carrying the army rifles was on time.

And it was about to roll into Sweet Apple.

Chapter 29

"No need to hurry, Seymour," Matt said a couple of minutes later as they walked down the street toward the train station. "We've got plenty of time."

Matt and Sam flanked the marshal. The blood brothers carried their own Winchesters, while Seymour's hands were wrapped around one of the shotguns from the office. There was nothing unusual about a lawman and his deputies meeting a train. Most frontier star-packers would mosey down to the depot whenever a train came in, just to see who got off. It was part of the job.

The engineer sounded the whistle again as the locomotive *chuffed* past the platform. With a screech and rattle, the train came to a stop as Matt, Sam, and Seymour walked through the station lobby. Steam hissed as they stepped out onto the long platform.

They didn't know which of the freight cars the crates of the rifles and the troopers guarding them were in, so Matt nodded toward the conductor as the blue-uniformed man hopped down from one of the passenger cars. With Matt and Sam right behind him, Seymour went over to the conductor and said, "I'm Marshal Standish. I have a very important question to ask you."

The conductor didn't look too impressed. "What's that, Marshal?" he said.

Seymour dropped his voice to a hushed tone. "Which of the cars is that shipment of army rifles in?"

The conductor's eyes widened in surprise. He tried to recover, but it was too late. Still, he said, "I don't know what you're talking about, Marshal."

"I think you do," Seymour insisted. "There's a shipment of five hundred army rifles on this train, being guarded by a squad of troopers from Fort Sam Houston. The guns are bound for Fort Bliss in El Paso. *Now* do you know what I'm talking about?"

"Damn it, that was supposed to be a secret!" the conductor hissed. "The army swore to me that nobody would know about it."

"It gets worse," Matt drawled. "There's a gang of outlaws who have their eyes on those guns. They're liable to attack at any time, so you'd better warn the officer in charge of those guards."

The conductor jerked his head in a nod and started to swing around. "I reckon I'd better—"

Before he could finish the sentence, a pair of explosions blasted through the morning air. The ground shook from the force of the detonations. The explosions were close by, but not at the station itself. As the conductor ripped out a startled curse, Matt looked around and saw a cloud of dust rising a couple of hundred yards east of the station.

"They blew the tracks to the west, too," Sam said. "The train's stuck here."

Pretty good tactics, Matt thought. If Mallory's gang hadn't dynamited the tracks, an alert engineer might've thrown steam to his engine and got the train rolling again before the outlaws could take it over.

Matt gave the conductor a push. "Go warn the soldiers!" Then he and Sam and Seymour ran back into the station.

The shooting had started by the time they raced through the lobby. The blood brothers expected as much. Mallory wouldn't waste any time after setting off those explosions. As the three men ran out the front of the station, they saw the outlaw horde boiling down the main street of Sweet Apple toward them. Mallory and his men were firing and yelling as they came.

But they were meeting unexpectedly fierce resistance. Shots blasted from the men hidden on the roofs, and those defenders inside the buildings and on the ground unleashed a withering storm of lead, too. Some of the defenders fell from the deadly accurate fire of the outlaws, but more of the raiders pitched from their saddles.

That didn't stop Deuce Mallory and the knot of men who were right behind him, probably the rest of his most trusted lieutenants. They kept galloping toward the train station, firing as they came. Matt and Sam each dropped to a knee, brought their rifles to their shoulders, and opened up on the outlaws. Flame lanced from the muzzles of the Winchesters. A cloud of gun smoke and dust rolled over the street, clogging the morning air.

Some of the soldiers from the train ran around the station and joined the fight. That was enough to turn the tide for good. Bullets shredded Mallory's men. The boss outlaw himself, though, seemed to have some sort of mystical shield about him, continuing the attack untouched despite the swarm of bullets in the air around him. He was close enough now so that Matt and Sam could see his face. They saw disbelief there, disbelief that for once his plans weren't working. Mallory's intended victims were fighting back rather than dying.

But even stronger was the fanatical hatred that distorted the features of Edward "Deuce" Mallory. For years he had devoted his life to evil and had been convinced that nothing could stop him. Now, without warning, everything was going wrong.

Mallory had it coming, Matt thought. Sooner or later, justice caught up to everybody.

So far in the battle, Seymour hadn't fired a shot. But now Mallory was bearing down on him as he stood there between Matt and Sam. Either of them could have downed the crazed outlaw chieftain, but instead Matt shouted, "He's yours, Marshal!"

Seymour lifted the shotgun. He was just acting instead of thinking. Instead of being scared of what might happen. *Just do what's right,* he told himself. *Just do what's right.*

He saw the flash of Mallory's gun, felt the fiery path that the bullet traced along his side. The impact of the slug twisted him half around. But Seymour didn't fall, didn't falter. He lined both barrels of the Greener on Mallory and pulled the triggers.

The shotgun's boom smashed into his ears, which were already half-deafened from the racket of battle. The butt of the weapon slammed heavily into his shoulder, driven back by the recoil. Seymour staggered but caught himself, and when he looked through the cloud of smoke, he saw Deuce Mallory flying backward out of the saddle, a huge, bloody hole chewed into his chest by the double load of buckshot. Mallory was dead before his body thudded to the ground and sprawled limply in the dust.

Matt Bodine was on his feet again, catching hold of Seymour's arm to steady the wounded marshal. Seymour felt a hot wetness on his side. "Am . . . am I hit?" he gasped. His voice sounded strange to his ears as his hearing began to return.

"Looked to me like you just got nicked," Matt said. "I don't reckon it's too bad."

"Is it . . . is it over?"

All of Mallory's men were down. Some were dead, and the others were badly wounded.

But the battle wasn't over, because at that instant more shooting broke out from the other side of the train. "The Mexican rebels!" Sam exclaimed as he and Matt and Seymour turned. "Has to be!"

They ran around the station to the end of the platform and looked through one of the gaps between the cars. Another force of mounted men charged toward Sweet Apple, this time from the south. Matt caught glimpses through the dust of tall, steeple-crowned sombreros.

"It's Alcazarrio and his men!" he called to Sam. "Let's get on top of one of those cars! Seymour, get us some help!"

Seymour nodded and turned to run unsteadily back to the street, where he waved and shouted for the defenders who had wiped out Mallory's gang to hurry to the depot and fight off this second attack.

Meanwhile, Matt and Sam dropped their empty rifles and scrambled up to the top of one of the freight cars, using the grab bars bolted to the car as a ladder. They unleathered their Colts and started firing down into the mass of bandits who had closed in on the train from that side. Bullets sung through the air around them and plucked at their clothes.

Suddenly, the door on the south side of the freight car on which they stood slid open and a deadly chattering filled the air. Matt let out a whoop as he drew a bead on one of the *bandidos,* squeezed off a shot, and saw the man pitch out of the saddle. "They've got a Gatling gun in there!"

Sure enough, the soldiers sent along to guard the shipment of rifles had brought a Gatling gun with them. Matt and Sam had had no idea that was the case, because they and their fellow defenders from Sweet Apple had stopped Mallory and his gang from ever reaching the train.

But now, with Alcazarrio's so-called revolutionaries practically overrunning the train, the Gatling gun made all the difference in the world. As one of the troopers turned the weapon's crank and another fed in the belts of ammunition, a fierce stream of lead hosed out from it and scythed through the Mexican bandits. Men flew from their saddles, some of them almost cut in half by the bullets. Shouting curses in Spanish, many of the ones who hadn't been gunned down turned to flee. Some of them made it and some of them didn't. Matt and Sam accounted for some of the ones who didn't.

Matt was drawing a bead on the big bandit who seemed to be in charge when a bullet clipped him on the thigh and knocked his leg out from under him. As he sagged to the roof of the car, Sam leaped over to him and shouted, "Matt! You're hit!"

"I'm fine," Matt yelled, feeling the exasperation more than the pain, at least right now. "Get that big son of a bitch! I'll bet he's Alcazarrio!"

Sam snapped a shot at the man, but more dust and smoke swirled as he pulled the trigger, and when it cleared, his target was gone. Sam didn't know whether he had hit the man or not.

Once the back of this second attack was broken, it didn't take long for the surviving members of Alcazarrio's band to take off for the tall and uncut. The town's defenders and the troopers threw a few last shots after them to speed them on their way. As Sam helped Matt to his feet, Matt grinned and said, "They won't slow down until the Rio's a long way behind them. They're goin' home empty-handed, too."

The blood brothers climbed back down to the ground, Matt somewhat awkwardly because of his wound. He leaned on Sam as they went to look for Seymour.

They found him sitting in a chair inside the station lobby with Maggie O'Ryan fussing over him, worried to death because of the bloodstain on his shirt. A gray-haired man wearing the uniform of a major ripped Seymour's shirt open to take a look at the wound. "He'll be fine, ma'am," the officer assured Maggie. "That bullet just grazed the marshal. I'll have one of my men patch it up, if you don't have a doctor here."

Ignoring the major's hand on his shoulder, Seymour pushed himself to his feet as he saw Matt and Sam. "Are you all right?" he asked them.

"Yeah," Matt said. "I got a little scratch, too, but it's not any worse than that nick you got, Seymour. And somehow Sam here came through without even that much."

"Clean living," Sam said with a grin.

"Dumb luck is more like it."

"Alcazarrio?" Seymour asked. "Wasn't that his name?"

"We don't know if he got away or not," Matt replied. "But the fight's over. It really is this time. The bandits who lived through it lit a shuck out of here. They'll be licking their wounds for a long time."

Seymour was paler than usual, probably from loss of blood. "And the army rifles?"

"Safe and secure, thanks to you and your friends, Marshal," the officer said. "I'm Major Stilwell, and I'm in your debt, Marshal . . . ?"

"Standish," Seymour said. "Marshal Seymour Standish."
Stilwell frowned. "Not the—"

"That's right," Matt said with a grin. His leg was starting to hurt a little now, but he didn't care. "Marshal Seymour Standish, who just killed Deuce Mallory and broke up maybe the worst gang of owlhoots and killers west of the Mississippi. Just imagine what he could do if he wasn't the most cowardly man in the West."

A booming voice said, "I can assure you, gentlemen, I'll never be writing *that* baseless canard again!" J. Emerson Heathcote, editor and publisher of the Sweet Apple *Gazette,* limped up, using a rifle as a makeshift crutch. He appeared to be wounded in the leg, too. "I owe you an apology, Seymour," he went on. "This whole town does. We were wrong about you, my boy, completely wrong. Why, we might have been overrun by outlaws from both directions if it weren't for you! You're the hero of the battle of Sweet Apple, and that's the way I intend to write about you from now on!"

In an aside to Sam, Matt commented, "And there's nothing like a new hero to sell some newspapers, now is there?" Sam just smiled, grunted, and shook his head.

Seymour turned to Maggie. "The children?" he asked. "Are all the children all right?"

She nodded. "The fighting never came near the school. You were right, Seymour. That was the safest place for them."

"I'm glad." Seymour put his arm around and drew her against him, being careful to hold her close to the side away from his wound. "But these two fellows deserve all the real credit and thanks," he went on as he turned toward Matt and Sam. "They were the ones who made it all possible."

"We weren't holdin' you up when Mallory was practically right on top of you and bullets were flyin' all around," Matt said.

"That was all you, Seymour," Sam added. "Like it or not, you *are* a hero."

Seymour summoned up a smile. "Maybe . . . we *all* are. Now, if you'll excuse me, there's something I've been meaning to do."

"Kiss that pretty little gal you've got your arm around?" Matt asked with a grin.

"Later," Seymour said. "Later . . . for sure . . ."

Then his eyes rolled up and he fainted, not from fear this time, but because of the blood he had shed defending everything that was dear to him.

Chapter 30

"The . . . hero . . . of . . . Sweet Apple!" Cornelius Standish said, barely able to force the words out because of the fury that threatened to choke him. He slammed a fist down on the newspaper in front of him on his desk. It was an Eastern paper, but it had picked up a story from Texas, a story about the fierce battle between outlaws and Mexican bandits on one side, and the army and the citizens of Sweet Apple on the other. According to the paper, those citizens had been led in their valiant defense of the town by their fighting marshal, Seymour Standish.

"Was he badly hurt?" Rebecca Jimmerson asked. She had brought the newspaper to Standish, but hadn't had a chance to read the story thoroughly.

"He's fine! That boy has more pure dumb luck than anybody I've ever seen! Obviously, Grant and Morelli failed. For all I know, they may even be dead by now." Standish snorted. "Seymour probably killed them. According to this he's turned into some sort of . . . of pistoleer!"

Rebecca didn't see how that was possible. The Seymour

she had known had been terrified of his own shadow. How could he have transformed himself into an actual lawman?

And yet it seemed undeniable that was what had happened. The newspaper story made it clear that Seymour had spearheaded the defense of the town and played a major role in routing the bandits. Rebecca picked it up and read it while Standish fumed.

"Well, look at it this way," she finally ventured. "From the sound of this, Seymour intends to remain in Sweet Apple. At least he's out of your hair, Cornelius."

"The hell with that! He still owns half the company. He's still a threat to my plans." Standish leaned back in his chair and chewed on his lower lip for a moment as he frowned in thought. When he spoke again, it was with a cool, deadly calm. "Clearly, my mistake was to trust someone else with such an important job. I'm going to have to supervise it personally."

Rebecca stared at him. "You mean—"

"I mean I'm going to Texas! And once I'm there, I'll make sure that spineless little worm never comes back to ruin things for me again!"

Rebecca's heart started to pound. From what she had read in the paper, Seymour wasn't as spineless as he had been when he left New Jersey. Somehow, he had grown a backbone. But would that be enough to protect him against his own uncle?

Rebecca didn't know . . . but she had a feeling Cornelius Standish would have a surprise waiting for him when he got to Texas.

And so might she, because she knew suddenly that she was going, too.

She had to see the new Seymour Standish with her own eyes.

* * *

Hiding in a cave like animals! It was disgraceful! But yet, the remnants of his "army" had been forced to flee when they encountered a patrol of Rurales not long after crossing the border into Mexico. Alcazarrio had ordered the retreat because he had lost too many men in Sweet Apple and the survivors were too shot up to mount an effective fight against the Rurales. After a running battle, they had finally shaken the pursuit and slunk off into the hills to hide.

Florio Cruz came into the cave, his knife-thin figure silhouetted for a second against the light outside. His wounded left arm hung in a crude sling. Alcazarrio himself was sitting propped up against the wall of the cave. Two bullets had torn through his body, but they had gone all the way through and the wounds were now bound up tightly. Alcazarrio was too tough to be killed by only two bullets. He would recover to fight again, and soon.

Cruz hunkered on his heels. "I have posted sentries as you ordered, Diego. No one will get in . . . or out."

"Some of the men still want to go home, do they?" Alcazarrio said. "The dogs! I am tempted to let them go, so they will not hinder us when we assemble another force of *real* fighting men!"

"It may be harder to find men who want to ride with us now," Cruz pointed out. "Once the story of what happened at Sweet Apple is known far and wide—"

"Sweet Apple!" Alcazarrio spat. "How I hate the name of the place!" His eyes narrowed. "The men will come, but we need some plan to attract them. Something daring and audacious. Something that will strike at the gringos."

Cruz frowned. "I thought our goal was to overthrow that pig of a Díaz."

"It is." Alcazarrio shrugged his broad shoulders, wincing a little at the twinges of pain that caused in his torso. "But everybody hates the gringos. Díaz will still be there after I have my revenge on that damned Sweet Apple, and everyone in it!"

Seymour still moved a little stiffly from the bandages wrapped tightly around his midsection under his clothes. But several days had passed since the battle around the railroad station, and he was determined not to neglect his duties any longer. Matt and Sam had been filling in as his deputies—unofficially, since the town couldn't afford to pay them anything and the blood brothers didn't want a real job anyway—but today Seymour had gotten dressed and was walking down the street with a shotgun tucked under his arm. Sweet Apple had been very quiet and peaceful since all the trouble with Mallory's gang and Alcazarrio's *bandidos,* but Seymour figured that all hell could break loose again at any moment. All hell *would* break loose again sooner or later. That was just the way these frontier towns were.

He took a deep breath, wincing a little as that pulled at his bandages. He didn't care. It felt good being back to work. Not that he hadn't enjoyed lying in bed and being fussed over by Maggie for the past few days. They were closer than ever now, and Seymour found himself filled with the real hope that they might have a future together.

Because he intended to stay in Sweet Apple from now on. He needed to get in touch with Cornelius, he told himself, and let his uncle know that he needed to find a new salesman to handle this territory. Seymour's days of selling dry goods were over.

Matt and Sam were sitting in front of the hotel, their chairs tipped back as they took life easy for a change. Matt's leg was still a little stiff and sore from the bullet crease on his thigh, but the wound was healing well and he knew he'd be able to ride again before too much longer. He wasn't in any hurry to leave, though. His restless nature hadn't reasserted itself just yet.

Sam nudged him in the side and said, "Look who's coming."

Matt grinned as he let the front legs of his chair settle down to the porch. He stood up and leaned on the railing as he said, "Howdy, Seymour. It's good to see you up and about again."

"It's good to *be* up and about again," Seymour replied with a smile of his own. "I take it everything's been quiet?"

Sam nodded. "That's right. We thought there might be some trouble a little while ago when folks from the Double C and Pax came in about the same time, but they went on about their business."

The Double C was the ranch owned by Shad Colton, so named because of his wife Carolyn's initials. Pax, of course, was the Paxton spread. The wagons that had come into town from both ranches carried the Colton and Paxton women, evidently intent on picking up supplies and doing some other shopping. Those wagons had been trailed by an escort of cowboys from each ranch, and those tough rannies had eyed each other suspiciously as they passed in the street. There was certainly no love lost between the two spreads, although Jessie Colton and Sandy Paxton still seemed to be good friends and had greeted each other warmly. They had been back East at school when the rift between their fathers developed, and so far they weren't having any part of it.

Matt didn't know how long that could last, though, with the obvious hostility that the ranchers felt for each other. That attitude was passed on to the men who worked for them, since cowboys had a tendency to ride for the brand above all else.

In this case, the riders from the Double C had gone to the Black Bull while Jessie and her mother were shopping, and the Pax hands had gone to one of the other saloons. As long as the groups kept their distance from each other, there likely wouldn't be any problems.

"I can't thank you two enough for everything you've done," Seymour said now as he stood on the hotel porch with Matt and Sam. "If you hadn't shown up when you did, the town might have been wiped out."

"Nah, you'd have figured out what to do, Seymour," Matt said. "You've got a lawman's instincts."

"I wish I could believe that," Seymour said with a faint, rueful smile.

"Believe it," Sam said. "That's the first step to making it come true."

Seymour nodded slowly. "You know, that's probably right." He squared his shoulders. "Now that I'm back on my feet again, I can't ask you to stay here and help me. I'll be all right."

Matt slapped his injured leg lightly and said, "I don't reckon I'm in shape to ride just yet."

"We don't mind hanging around for a while," Sam added. "Sweet Apple sort of grows on you, despite all the rough edges it has."

"Yes," Seymour said, and from the expression on his

face Matt and Sam knew he was thinking about Maggie O'Ryan. "It certainly does grow on you."

Before they could say anything else, shouts suddenly sounded from down the street. The three men swung around and looked to see that a confrontation was going on in front of the general store. Both ranch wagons were pulled up in front of the high porch that served as a loading dock, and the Colton and Paxton women stood there looking distressed while the cowboys from each of the spreads jawed angrily at each other in the street. The punchers had gotten their drinks and then headed to the store to accompany the women back home, and bad luck had seen both groups arrive there at the same time.

"That's not good," Seymour muttered as the shouts grew louder and fists were clenched. "I'd better get down there and put a stop to that before it turns into a real ruckus."

"A real ruckus," Matt said with a grin. "You're startin' to sound like a Westerner, Seymour."

The marshal gave them a nod and said, "There's nothing I'd rather be." Then he started toward the scene of potential trouble, moving quickly despite the stiffness from his injuries.

Before he could get there, somebody threw a punch, and in the blink of an eye a brawl was going on in the middle of the street between the Double C punchers and the Pax riders, despite the shouts of the women for the men to stop it.

Matt and Sam glanced at each other. "Looks like Seymour may need a hand after all," Sam said.

"Oh, yeah," Matt said. "Let's go!"

And with grins on their faces, the blood brothers plunged right back into trouble again.